The Goddess Effect

PRAISE FOR *THE GODDESS EFFECT*

"*The Goddess Effect* is a fall-on-the-floor funny, fresh, and modern take on one woman's journey to hell and back—and by 'hell and back,' I mean a three-month stay in Los Angeles. Here, the devil smells of Santal 33, has hair that cascades in beachy waves, and wears this season's Rick Owens. Our charming tour guide of Hades on the 405 is Anita Kathlikar, the hilarious love child of Bridget Jones and Lucille Ball who I didn't know I needed but ended up loving more than I can tell you. Sheila Yasmin Marikar is a pitch-perfect comic genius who delivers a sparkling miracle of a book that left me asking: What exactly is my soul's highest purpose and what exactly is the best Instagram filter for this picture of my power greens smoothie and collagen toast?"

—Kevin Kwan, bestselling author of *Crazy Rich Asians* and *Sex and Vanity*

"Fresh, bitingly modern, and laugh-out-loud funny, *The Goddess Effect* is more than a page-turner—it's also razor-sharp commentary on the cult of wellness. I can't wait to read more from this talented debut author."

—Andrea Bartz, bestselling author of *We Were Never Here*

"Sheila Yasmin Marikar's writing is prismatic . . . She had me laughing in one breath, cringing in the next, only to turn on a dime and knock the wind out of me with her honesty. *The Goddess Effect* skillfully sends up our current obsession with image, tech, and wellness, but at its heart is a timeless human truth: there's nothing we won't do to belong."

—Megan Angelo, author of *Followers*

"Sheila Yasmin Marikar's novel is a witty and compelling exploration of growth, identity, and power. *The Goddess Effect* is impossible to put down. Readers everywhere will root for Anita on her journey full of self-discovery and surprises. Told with a rare blend of humor and insight, this delicious story will captivate readers from beginning to end!"
—Saumya Dave, author of *What a Happy Family*

"I finished *The Goddess Effect* in a single sitting. Sheila Yasmin Marikar's assured voice and incisive observations had me laughing out loud one moment and covering my mouth in shock the next. A stellar debut with the perfect number of twists, turns, and Lululemon references."
—Colleen McKeegan, author of *The Wild One*

"Snappy, voyeuristic, and upsettingly relevant, *The Goddess Effect* takes us on a heart-pumping romp through the 'cult' of contemporary wellness. Either ironically or sincerely, if you've ever opted to add CBD to your oat milk latte, moon bathed a crystal, dropped $110 on a pair of yoga pants, cried under the mood lighting of a fauxspirational fitness class, or made any other questionable life decision in pursuit of self-actualization and belonging, you will feel both riveted and attacked by this incisive, page-turning tale."
—Amanda Montell, author of *Cultish: The Language of Fanaticism* and *Wordslut: A Feminist Guide to Taking Back the English Language*

"As a New Yorker who once moved to Los Angeles in search of herself, I know Anita's inner struggle and yearn to prove something (anything?) all too well. Full of laughable bits on the LA Erewhon-fueled lifestyle we all love to hate, this story will make you cringe, laugh, and most of all relate."
—Arianna Margulis, author of *But Like Maybe Don't?*

The Goddess Effect

A NOVEL

Sheila Yasmin Marikar

Little
a

Text copyright © 2022 Sheila Yasmin Marikar
All rights reserved.

Published by Little A, New York

www.apub.com

Amazon, the Amazon logo, and Little A are trademarks of Amazon.com, Inc., or its affiliates.

ISBN-13: 9781542039550 (hardcover)
ISBN-10: 154203955X (hardcover)
ISBN-13: 9781542039574 (paperback)
ISBN-10: 1542039576 (paperback)

Cover design by Caroline Teagle Johnson

Printed in the United States of America

First edition

For Anitas everywhere

1

I was doing fine until my screen stopped working. It went black in the middle of a cooking competition show. The challenge was to create a four-course meal in thirty minutes, and every course had to include kelp. I jabbed the screen in the spot where the power button had been—nothing. The screen to my right showed the flight path. The woman in front of it had slumped against the window and drawn the hood of her sweatshirt tight over her head. The screen to my left showed an Adam Sandler movie. The guy in front of it had noise-canceling headphones on and pretzel crumbs on his chest. He was asleep, too.

I pressed the flight attendant call button. Twice. It didn't make a sound so I didn't know if it had worked. The flight attendant—James, according to his name tag—reset my entertainment system once, twice, and, after the third time, leaned over the Adam Sandler fan, who had started snoring, and said, "You know, you could just stream it on your phone or laptop."

I'd neglected to charge my laptop, and the plug kept slipping out of the outlet below my seat. My plan, before boarding, had been to spend the flight making lists—to-dos, goals, potential story ideas—but I must've known that what I really wanted to do was drink mini bottles of Kendall-Jackson merlot and watch garbage TV. I did not have the willpower to look at my phone without opening Instagram, and that would mean spending twenty-four dollars for Wi-Fi that would cut out every time we flew over a mountain.

"My power outlet doesn't work," I told James. "Can I move to another seat? Anything in Economy Plus?" I was in 38E.

"Sorry, babe. Fare difference. It's against the rules. These refurbished planes, sometimes they work, sometimes . . ." He shrugged. "Email customer service, maybe you can get some miles."

I flopped back. A few minutes later, James reached over and placed a new mini bottle of Kendall-Jackson merlot on my tray, no words, not even a glance in my direction. I mouthed "thank you" the next time I caught his eye. You *should* email customer service, I told myself. You should email customer service and say nice things about James. Write it down now, so you don't forget.

From my backpack, I fished out a Moleskine notebook and rose gold pen, both new, both purchased the previous week at a cutesy stationery shop on the Upper West Side, even though both were cheaper on Amazon, because I felt I "owed it" to the small businesses I'd sporadically frequented over the course of seven years to visit them one last time before I moved. I had smiled meaningfully at the woman who rang me up. She was looking at her phone.

I bent back the cover and ran my hand over the first smooth ivory page. A realization: I could make lists in this Moleskine. Didn't Hemingway do that, or something? Maybe my malfunctioning entertainment system had been a sign. A sign from the universe. A sign that the universe had my back and did not want me to spend precious mental energy wondering what candied kelp tasted like. (Bad, right? It had to be bad.)

I wrote *GOALS* in capital letters and underlined it, to indicate the seriousness of the list. Then:

1. Get job at Gonzo

2. Become next Christiane Amanpour (minus war zones, plus wellness centers/lifestyle drugs/raves, etc.)

3. WELLNESS

That one was in all caps because I knew that wellness was important even though I wasn't entirely sure what it meant. Sweating more? Meditating? Green tea?

4. Try new things

5. Find your tribe

6. Drink less

I paused, took a sip of merlot, and added:

6. Drink less unless drinking helps with finding tribe, trying things, wellness/self-care

Another sip.

7. OWN YOUR POWER

Another sip.

8. Prove to Mom that you know what you're doing

9. Call Mom more

I heard my dad's voice in my head.

10. FACETIME Mom more.

Another sip, and my plastic cup was empty. *Own your power.* Where did that even come from? Right, I remembered, Instagram, through which I had scrolled, like my life depended on it, as the plane lifted off and until the very last bar in the stairway to LTE went gray. Before takeoff, I had looked up Kirtee and taken in her latest post: engagement photos on the Brooklyn Bridge. She wore a glittering blush-pink lehenga from Falguni Shane Peacock, the Mumbai designers who generally made outfits for Beyoncé and Lady Gaga but took on a regular old brown girl every once in a while; he—Neil, my ex—wore a tux. Tom Ford, according to the tag. He looked trimmer. Fitter.

I had zoomed in on Kirtee's midsection—her outfit revealed a good six inches of it—and yep, my suspicions were correct: she had abs. Not bodybuilder-style abs, but gentle striations, a delicate six-pack for her delicate body. A stone sank in my stomach, my flabby, hanging-over-the-waistband-of-my-four-year-old-leggings-from-Target stomach. I felt the urge to crumple my phone like a Budweiser can. An untenable urge—how would I order an Uber?—so I did the next best thing, pulled up @Affirmations, scrolled hard enough to make my thumb hurt.

I closed my notebook and closed my eyes. Get up, I told myself. Walk around. Stretch. You're allowed to do that on planes. You *should* do it, for circulation and whatnot. Blood clots. Snoring Adam Sandler fan's seat was reclined just enough that I could probably lunge into the aisle without waking him. If I held on to the headrest of the seat in front of me, I had just enough room to swing my leg over his lap without brushing my butt against his face. Just like they did on the moon, one small step for man, one giant leap for—

He jerked forward. The tip of his nose bounced off the ass seam of my leggings. Most action I'd had in months. I stumbled over him, into the aisle.

I blushed furiously and said "sorry" seven times. He looked stunned and mildly annoyed, but I gathered, from the color rising through his cheeks, that he also wanted this interaction to end as soon as possible.

I tugged at the sides of my cardigan and strode quickly up the aisle, like someone who knew what they were doing, like someone who didn't go around backing their ass into strangers' faces. James was watching me, trying not to laugh, doing a bad job. "How do you generally compensate the on-board entertainment?" I asked when I reached the galley that separated economy from business. "Venmo? Amex points?"

He scoffed. "The hand job in 17A last week—*that* deserved some Amex points. You . . ." He screwed up his face and did a mental calculation. We looked about the same age. He seemed fun. Like, weekends in Palm Springs with a house full of guys, a buffet of drugs, and a "what happens here, stays here" policy type of fun.

"You, my dear, get this," he said, reaching for another mini Kendall-Jackson and placing it in my palm.

Great job, I thought, *two* complimentary wines, eighteen dollars saved—your mom would be so pleased. (Not that she condoned drinking on planes. Free things—she very much condoned things that were free.) I unscrewed the cap and took a swig from the bottle.

"Going to LA for work?" James asked, plucking the empties from a shelf of water bottles and throwing them in the recycling.

"Sort of," I said, quietly thrilled at his interest. Maybe James knew people who knew people. Maybe James would be the key to me making it in Los Angeles. "I got sick of New York." I'd practiced this line enough that it almost sounded believable. "It's been seven years. Time for a change."

"Oh, so she's *moving*," James trilled. "What was the last straw?"

I knew the moment: Thursday, September 19, three-quarters of the way around the Eighty-Sixth Street reservoir. I had woken up too late that morning to run—I had woken up too late many mornings in a row to run—and dragged myself to the reservoir after work. You'll feel better afterward, I told myself, clear eyes, full heart, etc. But I couldn't get into a groove. It all seemed so pointless. How many times had I run this loop? Five hundred? Five thousand? Was I any better off now than I'd been when I first moved to New York, bright-eyed and determined to become a Big Fucking Deal? No. I was no deal. I was floundering. No amount of laps would change that. I stopped on the west side of the reservoir, hands on hips, swallowing back what I told myself was phlegm but knew was something else.

The crunch of gravel and panting brought me back to reality. I barely understood the word *move* before this dickbag in Under Armour and one of those water bottle belts rammed into my elbow. He turned back, gave me a dirty look, and resumed talking to some similar dickbag on the other end of his earbuds about "going long on a *massive* equity op—a yard, at *least*."

That was the last straw. That seemed like a lot to unload on James.

"I was over my job, over my tiny studio apartment. I felt like all I'd ever be doing is working to pay the rent."

"Mm-hmm."

"LA seems like something worth trying"—I was giving James a version of the speech I gave to my friends, my mom, myself every few hours—"and there's this co-op in Venice that's putting me up for three months while I find a job and figure things out, so what do I have to lose, right?"

"A co-op?" He frowned as he twisted the cap off a bottle of water and took a glug. "Like, an apartment building?"

"It's actually a house," I said. It's actually a commune, I thought, but that word gave me the creeps. "It's called the Gig, maybe you've heard of it? The Style section did a piece about it."

"Oh." He nodded. "I think I saw that. *That's* where you're going to live? Isn't it a commune?"

"It's not, like, drum circles and patchouli and group sex." Judging from the (many) photos I'd swiped through, the Gig looked like Soho House, or at least what I remembered of Soho House from my grand total of two visits to the one in the Meatpacking District. Mismatched furniture, reclaimed wood, pops of color—apart from Scandinavia, pretty much everywhere in the world looked like that.

"It's basically a cool coworking club with bedrooms and a backyard. There's a head unicorn—that's his actual title, it's on his LinkedIn— who stocks the house with food and toilet paper and whatever else from Amazon. There are dinners and events and beautiful people that you get to be friends with from day one. I get my own room with its own bathroom, *and* it's two blocks from the beach, and did I mention that I'm living there for free for three months?" How the last part alone didn't justify my decision, I couldn't understand.

"Honey, you said you've been in New York for seven years?"

I nodded.

"Don't you know not to trust anything that's free?"

"Would that include free mini bottles of wine dispensed by judgy flight attendants named James?"

"Touché, babe." He cheersed me with his water. I liked him. I wondered if he always did this with passengers or if I was special. I asked about him. Getting other people to talk about themselves was one of my specialties, listening, nodding, mm-hmming at the right intervals. He'd grown up in Atlanta, had started flying with Southwest, had been with United for two years, wanted to do more of the international routes. "New York to LA to Sydney is my favorite. Not knocking Venice, but Bondi is *everything*."

"Would you ever move there?" I'd reached the end of bottle number three.

"Are you crazy? No one leaves New York."

2

James sent me back to my seat with a fourth cup of wine—poured from one of the bottles reserved for business class, a Sonoma pinot noir—after another flight attendant bustled into the galley and made a show of rearranging the snack baskets while glaring at us every three seconds. "No one leaves New York." That kept ringing in my head as I settled back into 38E. Adam Sandler fan was awake and jumped out of his seat as I approached, clearly scarred.

Pooja had said something similar. "Why can't you just work for Gonzo from here?" she asked, when I joined her for one of her prework Drybar appointments the week before I moved. She was a junior partner at some schmancy, multiname law firm and the proud owner of a 5.02-carat oval-cut Harry Winston diamond, courtesy of a fair-skinned first-generation Indian American management consultant who stood five inches taller than her. Even in her highest heels, they still looked good in photos together. She got her hair blown out twice a week.

We were in the waiting area. I was sipping the pretty much cold complimentary coffee; Pooja was holding a steaming cup from La Colombe that probably cost eleven dollars. She had a prepaid blowout package that was supposedly about to expire and offered me a session—altruistic, maybe, but I suspected that what she really wanted was someone to feel superior to for an hour. I'd do anything for a free scalp massage.

"Emilia said they had something for me in LA." A stretch, but Pooja didn't need to know that.

"Also, going from broadcast to cable, isn't that a downgrade?"

"No one watches ABN, you can tell by all the mesothelioma ads." I didn't expect Pooja to get it. The week that everyone was talking about Gonzo's Fyre Festival documentary, Pooja texted me, What's this festival of fire? Are you going? "Also, Gonzo's not just cable, they're light-years ahead with internet and social, and you know my issues with ABN—it's the same with all the broadcast networks. They're stuck in the eighties." I once got a chin-length bob because the broadcast coach ABN kept on retainer said long hair made me look like Pocahontas.

"They really screwed you," Pooja said. "I still can't get over that governor. How crazy do you have to be to film a sex tape and then forget about it?"

My moment in the sun had been the six months I spent following the governor of North Dakota as she campaigned for president . . . until TMZ dropped the sex tape she filmed with not one but two of her subordinates. My last exclusive with the governor, the last ABN piece of mine that made air, had been about her new mission, to raise money for research into "latent periodic amnesia," a condition that she and some doctor said affected a hundred thousand Americans every year. I was convinced she'd paid off the doctor but couldn't find enough evidence to please Standards and Practices. After my campaign stint ended, HR shunted me into a producer role at *American of the Week*, which was like *20/20* but for even older people. Getting sent to *American of the Week* was like being put out to pasture. Subtext: get a new job or die of boredom.

"Honestly, it's fine," I told Pooja. "Gonzo's the dream." Gonzo was the news provider for twenty- and thirtysomethings in the know, "digital natives," "digital nomads," aka, people who did not actually use those terms. Since Gonzo had launched, I'd applied for a few of their New York–based jobs, all shots in the dark, and never gotten more than a generic "application received" email. A couple of weeks after that light-bulb-moment reservoir run, Dane Ditch, Gonzo's LA-based founder and CEO, came to New York for a future of media conference. After the 4:00 p.m. panel, another rehash of legacy media vs. internet upstarts, while sycophants swarmed Dane at the cocktail hour, I sidled up to Emilia Kent, his right-hand woman and Gonzo's head of squad. It was my finest hour. A-plus networking. Our conversation lasted as long as it took me to drain a glass of Woodbridge chardonnay—five minutes, at least, possibly as many as eight. She kept beaming and brushing against my arm. Not how I expected a human resources executive to act, but I wasn't about to complain. She could sexually harass me if it meant she'd give me a job. I'd have been honored. She looked like Scarlett Johansson.

"We're expanding in every which way, to every corner of the universe and beyond," she had said, "but LA is where the magic happens. You should come." And then she winked. I swear, she winked. I hung on those five-to-eight minutes. Hung on them despite the fact that she had not responded to the several emails I had sent since then.

"Well, yay, dream job," Pooja said, tapping her mini Ugg boot and glaring at the receptionist, as if that would make her call our names sooner, "but what about a guy? Don't give me that look, Ani, we're past thirty. Our most fertile days are behind us. Dating in LA, with all those actresses and models and influencers." She wrinkled her nose. "I'd be intimidated, and I'm a size zero."

What I thought: Why am I friends with this person? What I said: "It's not like dating here is some kind of dreamworld. Remember the last guy I met on Bumble? That 'vegan for ethical reasons' who lectured me for ordering a cheese plate?" He'd worn a #Feminist T-shirt and said that OnlyFans was a vehicle for female empowerment.

"Yeah, cheese is really bad for you, though." She pouted and gazed out the window at a woman in a Moncler puffer, pushing a stroller down Union Square South. "I wish Amit knew more guys that we could set you up with. I really thought we'd hit the jackpot with Neil. By the way, don't worry, I'm going to make sure he and Kirtee are on, like, the other end of the ballroom. I'll talk to Amit's mom. There's gotta be *someone* we can introduce you to at the wedding, even if they're from India. Some of these FOBs are pretty cool now, although dorky software engineers are also good because they're loyal and . . ."

The world revolved around Pooja, and in her special universe, rules that applied to me pertained not at all to her, so while me moving to LA was a terrible idea, her getting married in LA, before an assemblage of six hundred that would include my ex-boyfriend and his new fiancée, was fabulous. Inevitable. "A show of respect," she once said. Facts: Amit's family—new money, and lots of it—lived in Orange County and was paying for the wedding, so she didn't have much of a choice in where it would take place. Amit's dad had opened the first Vajra Jewelers in Artesia, the Little India of Los Angeles, in 1982. Four decades later, Vajra had hundreds of locations across the country, was basically Zales for brown people, which meant that Amit could get wholesale (or better) pricing on pretty much any diamond Pooja desired. Except what she actually desired: a Harry Winston. "Like, if you were Ally Hilfiger, you wouldn't wear Tommy to your wedding," she had said, when she showed me her ring for the first time. It made her finger droop. I asked if she could type while wearing it.

Part of me was jealous of Pooja, all the money she was marrying into, the fact that she'd never have to work again if she didn't want to. But it all felt so typical. She was doing exactly what was expected of her, marrying an Indian guy with an Ivy League degree. Snore.

"All of his cousins are wifed up," she was saying. "Wait—there might be one left. Oh my gosh." She grabbed my arm. "How fun would that be if we were related?"

The receptionist called her name, and I silently thanked God. I could take Pooja in doses. Portioned-out, known-you-my-whole-life-but-would-not-be-friends-if-we-met-now doses. Didn't everyone have friends like that?

We sat in silence while the stylists scrubbed our scalps and administered massages that, in my opinion, were better than sex. During the actual blowing-out part, I thought about what Pooja said. Was I ready to go toe to toe with *Bachelor* contestants and Instagram models? There had to be some normal guys in LA, right?

After the stylists smoothed shine serum on our flat-ironed ends, Pooja and I made eye contact in the mirror. "How's your mom coping with everything?" she asked.

I sighed. "She's kind of freaking out."

"Understandable."

My dad had died six months before. Heart attack on the tennis court. I didn't like thinking about it. I liked talking about it even less, feeling the pity waft off the other person. I wondered what he would say about me moving to LA. I thought that if he were in my position, he would understand.

"The thing is, they moved here from *India* to find themselves, and I can't move across the country? To a city that has, like, dozens of nonstop flights between here and there every day? Does she expect me to be one New Jersey Transit ride away from her forever?"

"Yup," said Pooja. "My mom would freak if I ever left the tristate area. I told Amit that, on our second date, like, 'I know your family owns half of Orange County, but if you think I'm going to get implants and—'"

"It's not like I see her that much, anyway," I went on. "Even when my dad was there, I'd go home maybe once a month."

"You know it's not about that. It's the proximity. She likes knowing that you're close."

"She'll deal. I took her to Verizon to upgrade her iPhone so we can FaceTime without her video freezing. And she has your mom and all of their temple friends." I reached over for the flat iron, still hot, and re-pressed the layers framing my face. Indian daughters—especially single Indian daughters who were also only children—did not abandon their mothers after their fathers died. They moved in. They prayed. They made and drank chai. But I hadn't caused my dad's heart attack—his third, not a surprise. I wasn't the one who let him get away with not taking Lipitor. I didn't even know he was supposed to be taking it, until it was too late.

"And she knows that she's going to see you soon—just two months between when you leave and *THE. BIG. DAY.*" Pooja squirmed happily in the revolving salon chair. "Did I tell you that Amit's parents are chartering a jet for the New Jersey VIPs? And that my mom convinced yours to come? Ani, do you have any idea how *epic* this is going to be?" She made a little *squee* sound and kicked her feet.

Of course I knew. Of course my mom had asked me, no less than a dozen times, whether pausing her year of mourning to attend the wedding would "look nice." My reply: "Who's keeping track?"

I glanced at the flight path on the monitor in front of the woman by the window. We were over Nevada. We were—I was—over two thousand miles away from Pooja and my mom. Two months. I had two months to get my shit together, to figure out how to thrive in LA. I had plenty of time. Oodles of it. I downed the last of my wine, stuffed the cup in the seat-back pocket, and closed my eyes.

3

The jolt of the plane touching down woke me up, and in my somewhat drunk and disoriented state, I had no witty retort for flight attendant James when he said, "Bye, babe, don't join any cults, mm-kay?" as I clumsily navigated my carry-on. Energy that might have been used to come up with a quip had been drafted into the task of not letting my phone fall into the crack between the aircraft and the jetway, something I worried about every time I got on or off a plane.

I expected everyone at LAX to look like influencers, but they looked like the occupants of pretty much every other airport: rumpled, frustrated, in a hurry. Still, scanning the terminal, I had to stop myself from grinning like a moron—I'd made it. I was here. "I said I'd do it and I did it," like Drake said. I wished I had Drake in my ears at that moment, but my headphones were in some undisclosed location in my backpack, and I didn't have the gall to just play him on speaker, like people who actually gave no fucks did.

On the way to baggage claim, I scrolled through my feeds. Only two new messages, one from my mom, asking if I'd landed, and one from Praveen, a GIF of Lindsay Lohan emerging from a bright blue swimming pool and a question: Is this you yet? I chuckled. Oh, Praveen. If he wanted Lohan, Lohan he would get.

I was mentally staging a postable moment when I saw an auntie in front of Hudson News. Sari, glasses, gray hair braided and bunned at the nape of her neck. "Beti?" she was calling. She looked lost.

"Auntie? Do you need help?"

She clutched my forearm and said something in Hindi. I bit my lip and apologized for not understanding. I looked at the boarding pass in her quivering hand. "Gate 54, that's just over here. I'll walk you, o—I mean, TK?" One of four Hindi phrases I knew, the one for *okay*, that peppered the aisles of New Jersey Subzi Mandis like so many bags of Hot Mix. All those times my mom had dragged me to Iselin had been good for something.

She let me escort her to the gate and let me go once we spotted a family, mom yelling at dad, stroller on its side, toddler chewing the edge of an iPad. Clearly, auntie's absence had been felt. She gave me a head wag and a namaste. The mom—beti, presumably—spotted me and mouthed "thank you."

At baggage claim, I hauled my two banged-up Aways off carousel six. The most sensible way for me to get to the Gig was to take a shuttle bus to a parking lot and then order an UberX. But I'd been thinking: the most *fabulous* way for me to get to the Gig was to order an Uber Lux. An Escalade. A vehicle that would pull up to the curb right in front of me, with a driver who would heave my bags into the trunk without my having to ask, who would come around to open my door and maybe, if I asked nicely, take a photo of me climbing in—the perfect thing to send to Praveen, to post, to prove that I had, indeed, arrived. It would cost $87.30. An UberX would cost $12–$14. Could you put a price on triumph, though? Did an Uber Lux not count as self-care?

The driver crouched down as I dangled off the passenger's side entrance, jutted my hip, pointed my chin, did all the things.

Praveen: Oo she fancy . . . and possibly pregnant? That angle

I flopped back against the cool leather seat. Couldn't please Praveen. My work husband, my gay best friend, my toughest critic. But that's why you like him, I reminded myself. He keeps you on your toes. If anything, you should thank him. What if you'd posted that photo without consulting him first? You kind of *do* look pregnant. God forbid.

The console contained four mini bottles of Kirkland water. I opened one and stared out the window. We veered left, off one highway and onto another, and the Pacific came into view. It was flatter than I expected, less turquoise and more gray, but that didn't stop me from lowering the window and taking fifteen blurry, terrible photos. Stories or Feed? Definitely not the quality of image I generally preferred for Feed, but this, my actual arrival in LA, deserved documentation, inclusion in the public record, and really, unposed blurry photos were kind of a trend now, no one wanted to look like they were trying too hard. What was I even thinking, dangling off the Escalade? Amateur hour.

No. 14 was workable. If I fine-tuned it in VSCO, upped the brightness, added a filter—C9 could make a puddle look like the coast of Positano—it could work. Off-kilter but still aspirational. What to say?

Hopped off the plane at LAX (Dated, does not make sense unless it's actually a picture of you and Miley.)

Westward, ho (Nerdy, ho-y, Oregon Trail–y.)

California, here we come, right back where we started from (But you were born in New Jersey, WTF are you talking about, even?)

My phone buzzed with an incoming FaceTime from my mom. Shit. I hadn't texted her back, and now she probably thought I was dead.

"Haven't heard from you. Is everything okay?" I heard her voice but saw the kitchen ceiling, fluorescent lights, so out of date, so very sad.

She asked about the flight, whether they had fed me, whether my bags made it—the usual stuff. She had driven me to Newark that morning. There wasn't much to discuss. Well, there wasn't much I wanted to discuss. I could confirm my existence to her at regular intervals, nod and mm-hmm as she told me what she was making for dinner, do the absolute bare minimum, but just below the surface—surely, she could sense it—resentment seethed. She didn't know me. She didn't know what I'd been through, the past year, having to deal with the death of my dad, having to deal with *her* falling to pieces at the funeral that I'd been forced to plan, that she could have prevented. Quitting my job, even. She'd gotten a PhD but had never worked a day in her life.

The driver turned off the highway as she was telling me about something some auntie posted on Facebook. "I should go," I said. "I need to get myself together." Truth: I wanted to be able to record the Escalade pulling up at the Gig, if the light hit right.

"Will someone be there to greet you?"

"Given that eight other people live there, yeah, I'm sure."

"Maybe I can stay on the line, until you establish a point of contact."

What was I, an extension cord?

"When you get to your room, find a place for those things I gave you."

"What things?" The granola bar and bruised apple she'd shoved into my palm before we left the house?

She gave me a meaningful look. "You know, the Ganesha, the lamps." Since my dad's death, her adherence to Hindu rituals had kicked up eleven notches. Every day, another festival, another puja, another God to pray to. He hadn't believed in any of that.

I groaned. "I told you, I'm not setting up a shrine in my room."

"You can still find a nice place for those idols. Don't just shove them in a drawer somewhere, is all I'm saying. They're *sacred.*"

I pictured her anxiety coursing across the country, through the cellular towers, wave after wave, cresting and crashing on their only natural destination: me, one of those stanchions under the boardwalk that would never really dry.

"Your trial run, that starts tomorrow?" It never fails: tell your mother you have to go, and she'll come at you with a barrage of questions she conveniently neglected to ask until that moment.

I flattened my mouth into a line and nodded. I'd told my mom that Gonzo had given me a three-month trial run, and that, on top of the "scholarship" I'd received from the Gig—with Indians, it was never bad to allude to academia—meant that I needed to relocate to Los Angeles right away.

"Do one namaskar for Saraswati, goddess of learning. You'll recognize her in the box—she's holding a veena. If this Gig has candles, you can light one, and if they have flowers—surely, they must have *some* type of flower in the yard, you can—"

"Fine, sure." I had zero intention of removing Saraswati and Co. from the plastic case in which she'd packed them, but it was easier to lie and get on with my life.

"Just, take care," she said by way of parting, her usual goodbye. It was a combination of "I love you"—which neither of my parents had ever said out loud; my dad thought it was too American, too smarmy— and "don't die." In the past, I had taken "take care" to mean "I love you," but lately, it sat firmly in the territory of "don't die."

I rolled down the window. "Inhale the good shit, exhale the bullshit." Another social media aphorism that I regularly applied to real life. I inhaled exhaust fumes and exhaled guilt. Maybe not all of it. Was I a terrible daughter? I wondered. I could be worse, right? I could be addicted to meth. That would definitely be worse.

The Escalade slowed down as we approached the compound I'd googled so many times, it felt surreal to see it in real life: 559 Sunset, formerly a low-rise apartment building, broken down, stitched back together, and rechristened the Gig by Adil Mehta, who made his first million in the first dot-com boom. I had emailed Miguel, the Gig's head unicorn, my flight information, and he had responded with hearts, stars, lightning bolts, and a note that an Uber from the airport should cost "like twelve dollars," which was how I knew that this wasn't the type of commune that fetched you from LAX. Probably no commune did. Even the Manson girls hitchhiked. At least I had Uber.

The driver put the Escalade in park and jumped out to unload my bags. I hopped down and blinked at the palm trees, the bougainvillea, the general lack of activity. A quiet street was good, right? You couldn't buy this kind of quiet in New York.

"Here you go," said the driver, setting my three suitcases at my feet. I thanked him. I looked at the front door. Hm. Miguel had said he'd be here. Maybe he was inside. Maybe he was orchestrating a surprise welcome party, and all I had to do was ring the doorbell and fall into a sea of open arms that would embrace me and then deal with my over-stuffed suitcases without me having to ask.

"Would you mind just watching these for a minute?" I asked the driver. "Sorry! Thanks so much!" I ran up to the landing and pressed the video doorbell. It lit up but didn't make that noise that all the video doorbells make. Interesting. I pressed my ear against the door. Heavy bass. Signs of life, signs of *fun*, even. Oh, this was going to be good, if I could figure out how to get in. There was a keypad lock and a large brass doorknob. It wouldn't budge. No biggie. Miguel had probably sent me the door code, and in my preflight excitement, I'd probably failed to register it.

"Ma'am?" the driver called from the street.

"Sorry!" I said. "Forgot my keys. I'm gonna call my, uh, husband—one sec!" I said "sorry" again. I liked to be overly apologetic and thankful toward strangers. In my mind, this counterbalanced how I behaved toward people I actually knew and made me a good person.

I pulled up our message thread. No door code. No cell phone number or social media handle, either. Maybe he responded crazy fast to email. Maybe he was, like, making email sexy again. I started tapping out a message but got stuck on what tone to strike: direct (*hello, I'm here, let me in*) or overly friendly (*hiiiiiii omg so excited, I'm right outside!*) or—

"Ma'am?" the driver called again.

Fuck. Was I at the wrong address? Had the Gig not accepted me after all? Had they found a questionably biased post on one of my social media feeds from long ago and decided that I did not belong? Had I been canceled, and did I not know it? I was doing a mental audit of everything I'd ever done on Twitter and debating whether or not to run back to the Escalade and get on the next flight to New York when the door flung open, revealing a guy who looked like one of those blow-up Gumby things they put in front of car washes. He wore shiny purple short shorts and a matching tank top.

"Ready for your love," he sang, draping his palm, briefly, on my shoulder. Inside, electronic music thrummed at a volume that made me wince.

"Why, thank you," I replied, trying to be coy, but he'd spun away, and I realized, as I took in the Edison bulb chandelier, cracked, cognac leather couch, and various surfaces of jewel-tone velvet and dark wood, that "ready for your love" was the chorus of the song thumping through the room, not a compliment intended for me.

Behind me, a honk, then tires peeling away.

"BRB!" I said. Could my backpack work as a doorstop? It couldn't hurt to try. There were no guarantees that this door would open again.

It took two trips to get my suitcases through the door, but, I told myself, I hadn't worked out that day, or the day before, so yay. I shut the door behind me and saw that a willowy wisp of a woman had joined the guy I assumed was Miguel in body-rolling around the living room.

"Good times," I said to no one.

The willowy wisp turned to me and burst into giggles. Reflexively, I ran my hand under my nose. She floated to the sound system and turned down the volume. "Anissa, right?"

"It's Anita, actually, but Anissa works, too." I wanted to be easy.

"Riley," she said. She noted how her name rhymed with *smiley* and burst into giggles again. I laughed along, not wanting to be left out.

"Miguel," she called over her shoulder. "The sage, get the sage." She sidled up to me and ran her hands lightly down my arms. You know those women with torsos so slight, you can't imagine how their organs fit? That was Riley. No amount of running or carb cutting could ever make me look like that. She was wearing short shorts that showed off her praying mantis legs and a rose-colored, silky, three-quarter-sleeve kimono that she either got for three dollars at some vintage store or for fourteen hundred at Gucci. I'd tied my Target cardigan around my Target T-shirt that stopped at the top of my Target leggings.

"So weird," she said. She was no longer smiling. She had closed her eyes and kept running her hands up and down my arms. "I can't read your energy."

"Maybe if I get rid of this," I said, unknotting my cardigan. "Or—my skin's really dry from the flight. I could moisturize?" I had no idea whether an extra layer of poly blend or dry skin inhibited the reading of energy, but again, I wanted to be easy.

Miguel appeared with a smoldering bunch of sage. He nudged Riley aside and started drawing figure eights in front of me. "This is to usher you into our humble abode with the best of intentions and brightest of—ugh, I can't, this is making me nauseous." He handed me the sage and collapsed onto the couch with a low groan.

"The universe," Riley said softly, watching him. "Sometimes it do be like that." She shrugged, curled into a yellow butterfly chair, and pulled a sheepskin throw over her head.

Cardigan in one hand, burning sage in the other, I looked around the room and saw, on the coffee table that was either a redwood stump or a very good imitation of one, a clear plastic canister bearing the logo of the mushroom from Super Mario Bros. It was empty.

***

Trip interrupter. Vibe killer. Energetically questionable brown girl with very dry skin. This was not how I wanted to start my new life, but we have to play the hand we're dealt. I found an ashtray for the sage, a fringed blanket to cover Miguel, and an unoccupied bedroom—mine,

I assumed—up a long set of stairs, to the left. By the time I'd dragged up my bags—more unintentional working out, yay—more members of the house had materialized.

They were making sustainable seafood, hacking drone delivery, pioneering virtual reality nightlife, building the Museum of Ice Cream but for Poetry, coaching people on meditation "but also, like, life" (in the case of Riley, who rose from the butterfly chair around sunset). They had calls to jump on, decks to get back to, VCs to meet, sound baths to attend. "You look like you need a drink," said Christina, when she blazed into the Gig that evening. She poured us both goblets of rosé and warmed up two Beyond Meat quesadillas. Immediately, I liked her the best. She had founded a company that supplied under-resourced schools and hospitals with local organic produce, but she still had a sense of humor. "At least they were on mushrooms and not acid," she said, when I told her about my arrival. "Those two." She shook her head and smiled, remembering something. "This one time, Riley swore she'd discovered organic Molly."

"Uh, do tell," I said. I'd finished my glass of wine. I reached over to top her up so that I wouldn't seem like an alcoholic when I poured more for myself.

She put her hand over her glass. "I've actually gotta jump on a call."

Envious of her sense of purpose and ability to stop after one, I poured myself another glass and thought about what I would be doing, if I were still in New York. Preparing for another mind-numbing day at ABN. Laying out some trash biz-caszh outfit. Setting an alarm that I knew I'd snooze though. Steeling myself for yet another ten hours in my dimly lit cubicle, secretly jealous of people like Praveen who had played the game and ascended the ranks.

What happened: I lost my plum campaign reporter-producer position after the sex-tape governor dropped out of the race. My pieces had gotten a lot of views. They'd been linked by all the of-the-moment websites. I had been good at my job, at getting people close to the governor to open up (like her college roommate, whom I'd tracked down at a Chili's in South Florida and taken out to a male revue worthy of *Magic Mike*). I thought I could parlay that gig into a position as a culture correspondent. "Online first, cover what matters to twenty- and thirtysomethings," I had told the head of news gathering, in that period of limbo after coming back from the trail. "Crypto, CBD, crystals." He'd laughed, and I had, too—of course, some of these things sounded ridiculous, but they drove clicks, and wasn't that what the network wanted?

"Sweetheart," he'd said, "if I invented a job for you, I'd have to invent another job for myself, out there." He cocked his head toward the window of his forty-seventh-floor corner office. "Why don't you do crystals"—he sounded baffled, like he couldn't believe these words were coming out of his mouth—"on the side? You'll be good at *American of the Week*. We just got that Metamucil sponsorship. That show needs grinders like yourself.

"Besides," he added, rearranging his face into a performance of sympathy, "given what's happened at home, might be best to carry a lighter load here, yeah?"

I hated him in that moment, using my father's death to sideline me. I'd taken off one week and kept up with my email. Didn't even put up an out-of-office reply.

It dawned on me, fully, that I was never going to make it at ABN. They'd shuffle me around midtier positions until I died of boredom or the next round of layoffs hit. But they had resources. Plenty to use and abuse.

I trailed a Postmates delivery person for a day and covered a Sugar Babies convention, producing my own pieces and uploading them to ABN.com in between logging tape about patriotic dogs and octogenarian Zumba instructors. My most popular piece, about a CBD startup king who blew eighty thousand dollars of investor money on used bathwater from Fashion Nova girls, got linked by the *Daily Mail*, and by that point, I'd figured out Emilia's email address. "Impressive view counts" were her first words to me, via email, the week before we met at that conference.

And now, here I was. The first day of the rest of my life. A chance to start over. A chance to *be* someone, to establish myself as an unquestionable success, one who would make ABN, Neil, and everyone who ever doubted me be like, *damn*, she showed us who's boss.

I refilled my glass and reached for my phone. I'd never posted that shot of the ocean—today, *this day*, deserved to be documented.

As I opened the app, one of those "On This Day" reminders popped up: my dad and me, arm in arm, outside of ABN. The first time he'd visited me at work. The time I'd taken him to my favorite falafel place, the hole-in-the-wall on Fifty-First Street with the owner who was saltier than a box of Maldon. The time he'd patted my back, beamed up at the big brass ABN logo, then back down at me, and said, "This is really something."

My eyes welled up. I put my phone down.

4

The light woke me up. My room had flimsy white curtains and faced east, and it took me pawing around the mattress to remember where I was. This was my room. This was my bed that I'd neglected to put sheets on, that I'd just flopped on top of, drunk and tired, without a pillow, wrapped in the sheepskin throw that had previously graced the silky, poreless epidermis of Riley, that I thought might lend me an iota of her effortless cool-girl energy by osmosis.

Even at this early hour, the Gig hummed with passion. Well, the actual humming may have emanated from twin Nespresso machines and Sub-Zeros in the kitchen, but the degree to which my roommates were booked and busy and I was not felt palpable. Do something about it, I told myself. Check your email. Emilia must've written back by now.

I'd emailed her the week before, kept it casual: Hey, I'll be in LA next week, would love to come by the office and continue the convo. I'd spent a solid ten minutes debating between *convo* and *conversation*. Judging by how effervescent she was when we met—kind of like Riley on mushrooms, it occurred to me now—*convo* seemed like the way to go. I had told myself that it wasn't a big deal that Emilia hadn't responded to my previous messages because no one is ever on top of their inbox and everyone kind of hates email. Now that I was in LA, viable, available—possibly only for one week, for all she knew—surely, she would write back.

I scanned my inbox. Twice. Her name did not appear in bold. I went to my Sent folder and found my last message to her, just in case some glitch in Wi-Fi or the space-time continuum had caused her reply to not show up as new. (It happened, once in a while.) Nope.

Big sigh. To the feeds, then. Perhaps Emilia was on vacation. Perhaps Emilia was dead. But no, eleven minutes ago, she'd posted a photo of her latte, middle finger etched into foam, from Grumpy's on Lincoln Boulevard. It was 1.8 miles away. What if I went there? I wondered. What if I went there the following morning? I could print out a list of story ideas, commandeer a table with a view of the door, wait, wait, wait, and then BAM run right into her when she walked in, throw the list in the air, like in some Drew Barrymore movie. I'd use thirty-six-point font so she wouldn't have any trouble recognizing how stellar my ideas were, even as they fell at her feet.

A tad desperate. Stalkerish. It would also require me to come up with story ideas.

A run. A run would get the ideas churning, would get me acquainted with my new neighborhood, the local culture. A culture correspondent ought to know what was popping. But where? What was the best run to take? This was my first run in LA. I wanted it to be memorable, postable, something I'd look back upon fondly in the future, when I'd run 10Ks every Sunday with my #fitfam and kick back on the beach afterward with a Michelob Ultra.

I scrolled through potential routes on a running app. I mapped out a few of my own. By the time I was done, my stomach was growling. "Eat when you're hungry." Simple enough logic, but then, I'd read somewhere that when you worked out on an empty stomach, your body burned more fat. And then there was intermittent fasting. That defied the whole "eat when you're hungry" thing. But didn't food fuel your brain, too? I was doing this to generate ideas. It was work, kind of.

I went down to the kitchen, where Christina stood, gazing into the depths of the refrigerator.

"You're on a desert island and you only have one choice of milk—go," she said.

Two percent was my honest answer, but Christina seemed like the type of person who drank oat milk, or who probably opposed dairy for tertiary reasons like factory farming rather than taste.

"Almond," I said. I had never had oat milk. I didn't want to come off as disingenuous.

"Really?" she said, shutting the fridge. She held a quart of two percent. "Do you know how much water it takes to grow an almond? A *gallon*. And this drought-plagued state produces 80 percent of the world's supply. It's sick. I mean, don't get me wrong, I used to swear by almond milk, too, before I knew, and then I tried coconut, then barley, then oat—Erewhon has this oat milk that is *fire*, but it also costs, like, half of what I make in a week—and now I'm back to cow." She shrugged as she glugged some into a blender. "Honestly, I think half the people who claim to be dairy averse are just doing it to fit in. You want some of this?"

"What is it?" I came over and peered into the blender. Her knowledge and ease at deploying it intimidated me.

"Acai, cherimoya, guarana, and maca, with a dash of reishi," she said, ticking the ingredients off on her fingers. "Plus milk and a banana, because I'm not that bougie."

"Love reishi," I said.

She turned on the blender and gave me a look. Reishi was a fruit, right? I was pretty sure it was a fruit.

She poured me some, and I asked how her call the previous night had gone.

"Oh, fine. It's funny, though." She leaned back against the kitchen counter. "Part of why I left Google was because I was sick of the pointless calls and meetings. I figured, with Farm to Mass, eventually, the service would speak for itself. Nope. Not yet, anyway. Doesn't matter how many referrals and five-star reviews they've read, all potential new clients want a get-to-know-you call, want to ask for the eighty-third time if the produce is organic, want to know, 'Is there a lot of kale? Our kids can only take so much kale.'"

Wow, I thought. Google. She quit Google. I thought I'd be hot shit, coming from ABN, but no one at the Gig watched ABN—the house didn't get broadcast television—or seemed to care about news in general. "It's bad for your cortisol levels," Riley had said the night before.

It also struck me that Christina was actually a good person, rare as a ripe tomato in February. Reflexively, I wondered: Was I a good person? At my mom's request, I had accompanied her to the Bridgewater Temple the day before I left for LA, followed her as she circumambulated the idols, sat cross-legged on the cold marble floor, and bowed my head whenever the swami conducting the "moving puja" cued. Usually, I would've protested. Usually, I would've come up with an excuse. Usually, I would've pointed out that pujas for such modern flights of fancy as cross-country moves and newly acquired Teslas had to be bullshit, because surely whoever wrote the Vedas could not have predicted all of this.

Did a rare show of obedience count, or did wanting it to count negate any inherent goodness?

"What about you?" Christina asked. "What's your story? I know what you wrote on your application, but some of those questions are so out there, it's like we're actively trying to discourage people."

"Like, 'if your aura had a color, what would it be, and why?'"

"Exactly. Pretty sure Miguel came up with that during one of his trips."

What I'd written on my application, what I think pushed me over the top, was a diatribe about how first-generation daughters were pushed to succeed through school, college, graduate school, and the first years of their careers, only to have to field questions, at the end of all that—sometimes in the midst of it—about when we'd settle down and start a family. It was always about settling down. As if whatever we'd achieved didn't matter. Where was all of our ambition supposed to go? Away? Or were we supposed to drill it into another generation of women, who would be told to abandon their drive once they'd reached a certain age? *What I hope to find at the Gig are other ways of being, of thriving,* I'd written. I wanted alternate models of success, of happiness.

But Christina had read that. She was asking for something more personal. I was afraid of her judging me.

"I just got sick of New York," I said. "The winters really take it out of you. Plus, I hit it off with Gonzo's head of squad at a conference a few months ago, and she said to come by if I'm ever in LA, so"—I did this cheesy flourish of my hands—"here I am!"

Christina cocked her head. "You moved across the country because you hit it off with some HR chick?"

"I mean." Now I sounded like a moron. "It wasn't *just* that. I was phoning it in at a job I hated just so I could pay the rent, and I felt like, unless I took a chance, I'd be doing that forever, and not to be a total cliché, but, yeah, there was a guy, there was a breakup, and it was a while ago, but . . ." I trailed off. She looked sympathetic. I wanted to say more: how it wasn't really a job thing or a Neil thing or even my-dad-suddenly-dying thing, how I had this wild idea that if I changed my surroundings, maybe I'd become a different person, a better person, a success, how if I put three thousand miles between myself and my mom, maybe I wouldn't care so much about disappointing her, about not being a dutiful Indian daughter. Maybe I would spend less time thinking about whether other people liked me and just "do me," like the influencers said and presumably did.

That felt like a lot. I also feared that if I actually voiced how I hoped LA would change me, I'd somehow jinx the process—or Christina would tell me that I was asking too much of this place. I knew I was asking a lot. But it's like playing the lottery—you buy in knowing that the chances of it working out the way you want it to are slim, but *someone* has to win.

So I simply said, "You ever want to blow up your life and start all over?"

She nodded, lifted her smoothie to cheers mine, and excused herself to prep for a meeting. I leaned against the counter for a bit, picking at my cuticles. Had I fucked up? Women talked about the importance of being honest, open, and vulnerable, but it was also possible to be too much of all of those things and simply be a hot mess. No one wanted to associate with a hot mess. Part of me wanted Christina to tell me what to do, how to replicate her success, to share some sort of secret that self-assured women knew that I did not. Part of me wanted to check the Black friend box. I didn't have any close Black friends, and I wanted to change that, but that desire also made me feel gross and racist. Did feeling bad about it make me any better? Did I get some points in an invisible ledger that kept track of how racist everyone was?

Back in my room, I intended to change and go for a run, but I couldn't find a sports bra in the first suitcase I unzipped, or the second, and by the time I had rifled through the third, the amount of poly-cotton in various states of upheaval distressed me to the degree that I had to do something about it.

I tried to do the Marie Kondo thing and fold my shirts into cute, lovable little packets. By the fourth, I reverted to shoveling my clothes into the drawers of the reclaimed-wood dresser by the handful, stuffing in as much as I could because the only thing worse than folding clothes was having to hang them up. So many sweatpants and leggings. Leggings and sweatshirts. It seemed wrong for a human to own this many leggings and other legging-like things. I'd sold most of my "professional" wardrobe, tired nonsense from the Banana Republic clearance rack, to Buffalo Exchange for a grand total of seventeen dollars.

At some point, I caught my reflection in the full-length mirror on the closet door. Yikes, my roots, so kinky and dented. I plugged in my hair straightener—"don't leave home without it," like those old Amex commercials—and started ironing before the thing fully heated up. How many hours had I spent straightening my hair over the past decade? Surely, it counted as self-care. My hair, in its natural state, gave me anxiety. Curly, unpredictable, prone to frizz. Neil hated it. So did ABN's broadcast coach. It was another thing I blamed my mom for. She combed out her curls, amplified the frizz. None of the other aunties wore their hair like that.

After fitting direct-to-consumer sheets on the direct-to-consumer mattress and shoving my direct-to-consumer suitcases in the closet, I assessed the rest of the room. A whiteboard hung on the wall opposite the bed. Below it was a desk. The desk had no chair. No problem: I'd make it a standing desk. Look at me, living healthy in LA. I found some books on the floor of the closet, real thick textbooks for astrophysics or something incomprehensible, and stacked up enough of them so that my laptop could rest at eye level. Was this ergonomic? I wondered. More importantly, was this postable?

New beginnings, I thought, taking twenty-one photos, trying to get the light and framing just right. The first was the best. I perched on the edge of the bed and edited it in VSCO, upping the saturation, toggling back and forth between Q1 and HB2 before settling on C9. Good ol' C9, made everything look straight out of the Amalfi Coast.

New beginnings was too basic for a caption. Too bland.

Home base for taking over LA (Can we say, "trying too hard"?)

NEW ME 101 (Yes caps, because caps communicate confidence, but . . . no.)

MANIFESTING HQ (Does not entirely make sense, but because it's in caps, people will know you mean business.)

Posted. I uncapped a pen on the rim of the whiteboard and wrote *Gonzo.* I opened my laptop and tested out the functionality of my desk by going to the *Daily Mail's* website. An article about Nicole Kidman's "eerily flawless facade" led me down a rabbit hole that stopped at "8

Celebrity Skin Care Regimens That You Can't Afford" and "10 Reasons Why You're Washing Your Face Wrong" before reaching its final destination: me, in front of the full-length mirror, pulling back the skin around my face, wondering what cocktail of products would give me the glowy, dewy look that the influencers seemed to pull off so effortlessly. Or were they altering their photos even when they claimed not to be? You never could tell.

It occurred to me that washing my face wouldn't be a bad first step. I hadn't showered since I'd arrived. I'd tie up my hair, prevent it from getting wet. I'd run later. Magic hour. Way better light than midmorning, would make for way more postable content.

All the rooms at the Gig had en suite bathrooms, and I'd swooned over the photos of mine—teal-blue tile, walnut wood, big copper rainfall showerhead. A huge upgrade from my New York studio, where the calcium deposits around the waterspouts were developed enough to have teeth and second cousins. But inspecting the shower now, with my hair in a topknot and a direct-to-consumer towel around my torso, I realized I had no idea how to turn it on. There were five different knobs and six more spouts, all facing me, besides the rainfall showerhead and the handheld attachment.

I tentatively turned one knob. Nothing. Another. Still nothing. I tried one more, twisted it hard to the right.

Ice-cold water blasted out of all eight spouts. I screamed.

I vaguely registered the sound of someone running up the stairs as I attempted to turn off the water without going into hypothermic shock (bad) or getting my hair so wet that I'd have to wash, dry, and straighten it from scratch (worse). "Are you okay?" I heard outside the bathroom door. "Do you need help?"

I cried out something affirmative from the corner of the stall. Maybe the shower was possessed. Maybe a previous resident who dabbled in witchcraft had put it under a spell.

The door creaked open, and a guy with aviator eyeglasses poked his head in. "It's not your fault," he said. "This shower trips everyone up. Did Miguel not show you how to use it yesterday?"

"Miguel was incapacitated," I said, wrapping my water-splotched towel tighter. Who was this? I wondered. We hadn't met the previous night.

"Ah, right, mushroom Mondays. I used to think that was a vegan thing, but . . . May I?"

I said "sure," and as he slid in the door, graciously making sure to face the demon shower rather than my basically naked self as he explained how to set the temperature *before* turning it on, I realized that this was Max, who oversaw the Gig in place of its founder, Adil, who had long ago moved to Malibu. Max had interviewed me over FaceTime. He had looked . . . different. Not hot. Not that I thought he was hot—well, objectively, maybe, but not my type. Too hipster. Too . . . seemingly in touch with his feelings. I tended to go for alpha males, borderline douchebag.

"Does that make sense?" he was saying. "Adil insisted on replicating the steam showers from the Aman in Kyoto, and yeah, they're beautiful, but you need, like, a PhD in mechanical engineering to figure out how to use them. Welcome, by the way."

I thanked him and tried to show the enormity of my gratitude by gesturing with my hands, which loosened the towel, which almost dropped. I jerked it back around myself just in time. "Sorry!" I said, because unasked-for nakedness definitely qualified as sexual harassment. "Queen of first impressions, right here!"

He turned a little red and laughed uncomfortably. "I'll leave you to it. I've got a deck to get back to."

"What for?"

He rolled his eyes and did a self-deprecating sneer. "Cauliflower rice."

"You're making a deck about cauliflower rice? For the Cauliflower Farmers of America? Or wait—did the Rice Council of America hire you to create a public-awareness campaign about how cauliflower rice isn't actually rice?" Trying too hard off the bat was a known bug of mine.

"Either of those would be way more interesting than the truth— it's for a new cafe that's opening on Abbot Kinney. They want to do an immersive event for the launch. How do you make cauliflower rice *immersive?*"

"Fill up a swimming pool. Invite a bunch of influencers and have them roll around in it like it's a ball pit."

"That's . . . actually not a bad idea."

"Plus kiddie pools of butter, cheese. Chives, maybe."

It was not lost on me that bantering with this totally-not-my-type of guy in nothing but a towel felt oddly comfortable.

"How's it going with Gonzo?" he asked.

During our interview, I'd told Max that I had an "in" at Gonzo but would need to hustle once I got to LA. "There'll probably be a trial run, face time with the C-suite." I thought using trendy corporate slang would obscure the fact that I didn't technically have a job. But I would, soon, surely—all those emails to Emilia, her invitation at that conference in New York to come to LA, where the magic happens. "Persistence pays off." Something my dad had written in an email when I was in college, applying for internships. It did then, it would now. I'd persist, "be so good they can't ignore you," another quote bastardized by Instagram. Or be so annoying. Either way.

"Great," I told Max. "Should be hearing from their head of squad any day now."

"Huge," he said. "They're a hard one to crack, but if you've already got an in, you're golden." He told me to knock on his bedroom door downstairs if I needed anything, and then left. I stood in the shower, biting my lip. I had an in. I totally had an in. I'd be fine.

***

A few days passed, and I developed something of a routine: wake up, go to the kitchen, make a Nespresso, attempt to strike up a conversation with whoever happened to be there, make another Nespresso, go back to my room intending to change and go for a run, check email and socials, panic about why Emilia hadn't gotten back to me yet, draft and abandon another email to Emilia, social-media-stalk Emilia, look for jobs, get depressed, get hungry, go back to the kitchen, repeat.

After five, Nespressos yielded to margaritas, wine, White Claw, or whatever the house was drinking. I'd bring my laptop down to make it look like I was doing something when the conversation turned to fundraising or cryptocurrency or whatever Elon Musk had just tweeted. I had never felt more out of my league. Did no one here watch reality TV or read (scroll) the *Daily Mail*?

One morning, while scrolling through my feeds, I saw an ad for something called The Goddess Effect. The ad was one of those videos that start playing as you scroll over it, a montage of photos and text. It started with a paparazzi shot of one Hadid and the other Hadid, arm in arm, beaming, glowing. Then, testimonials. "Made me lean into my power," according to an "Oscar-winning actress-slash-director." "Will challenge and change you," said a "startup icon." "Like if crack and green juice had a baby," per a "top-tier content creator." Curious that no names were attached to these testimonials, I thought, but then, some people still valued privacy. There was a photo of a woman with luminescent skin and a flowing mane, standing naked in a seashell, hair and hands covering all that was NSFW, like that Botticelli painting. She was tagged: Venus von Turnen, founder of The Goddess Effect. She was hot. She was a boss. She was the very definition of #goals.

I clicked through.

5

I t turned out that the first class was only twenty dollars. On the one hand, I was supposed to be saving money until a job at Gonzo came through. On the other, I needed to get a feel for LA, figure out what was trendy, trending, do my research. A culture correspondent had to be immersed in *the culture*, had to know what was new, next, cutting-edge. Maybe The Goddess Effect was. The Hadids certainly thought so. It had only been around for a year, and there was only one studio, which happened to be one mile from the Gig. If that wasn't a sign, what was?

Really, this was a work expense. It qualified as networking. What if I met a Hadid, what if we hit it off, what if they invited me to their Hadid palace and asked me to join them on the yachts of oligarchs and I got all *sorts* of unprecedented access and became the modern-day equivalent of Slim Aarons but for storytelling, because, let's be honest, C9 could only do so much? Also, my Capital One limit was fifteen thousand dollars, and the minimum payment was only seventy-three dollars the following month. I had plenty to work with.

I had a thousand dollars in savings and about seven times that in debt. Not student loan debt—my parents paid for college, and I knew that made me privileged—but stupid, inexcusable, I-don't-know-how-to-manage-my-money debt. Went-on-a-trip-to-Vegas-that-I-couldn't-afford debt.

Bought-too-many-rompers-from-Forever-21 debt. Can't-ask-Mom-for-help-because-she's-living-off-Dad's-pension debt. I was too proud to ask for help even when he was alive. I figured, I'll get the promotion, I'll get a new job, I'll figure it out. *Be* the model minority my parents think I am. Or maybe I was just afraid of what they'd say if they knew.

There was always a glimmer of hope, in the seconds between logging in to my Capital One account and the home screen loading, that somehow, the balance would have magically disappeared. The work of a benevolent hacker, maybe. Or a massive banking error. Some kind of system-wide failure that wiped out everyone's credit card debt, and the banks wouldn't be able to figure out who owed who what, so we would all just start with a clean slate again.

I bought the introductory class and signed up for the noon session. I found a pair of gray leggings and a faded tie-dyed sports bra. I threw on a sweatshirt (*Worst Behavior*, a pledge of allegiance to Drake), grabbed my track bag and Allbirds, and blew out the door, power walking, pumping my arms. I made it to the studio with four minutes to spare, sweaty and short of breath. You couldn't see through the ground-floor windows or door, and you had to buzz to get in. I wondered if whoever was on the other end of the intercom would take one look at me and be like, "Nah."

I pressed the silver button. The door unlatched. Yay, I thought. I pushed inside and instantly felt like I had dirtied the place. It was all white, filled with light, and smelled like some beautiful flower. It was furnished with four papasan chairs, several floor cushions, and a low coffee table arrayed with a stone scent diffuser and a single book, *Art and Anatomy: The Work of Helmut Newton*. It looked like a waiting room for a very fancy dentist. A very fancy dentist whose name was Rain or Wind or something elemental.

Harness Your Inner Lakshmi was scrawled across one wall in pale lavender brush font. Sweet, I thought. They liked Indians. Or at least, they liked the Hindu goddess of money and wealth. If you had to pick one, you could do worse than Lakshmi.

Where did the working out occur? I wondered. I saw a narrow stairwell in the corner and went up. More of the same decor, but there was a long desk, and the woman behind it looked like Riley. She was staring at an iPad, brow furrowed. Her eyes glanced up as I approached.

"First time?"

"Hi! Um, yes. But I work out, like, all the time," I said. "Running, mostly. I run a lot. And I've been to a lot of gyms." I felt the need to say this because I wasn't as fit as her.

She smirked and handed over another iPad with a liability waiver. "I think you'll find that we're different than most *gyms*," she said, like *gym* was a dirty word she never used, and now she'd have to go wash her mouth out with yuzu and rose-quartz-infused soap.

As front desk girl pointed out the cubbies and bathroom, I had a sinking realization: I should have put on a tank top. My midsection was not ready for public consumption, certainly not this public's consumption. Turn it into a positive, I told myself. Work out in your sweatshirt, like a boxer, like Muhammad Ali, like Drake himself. He probably worked out in a full-blown Givenchy sauna suit, stud that he was.

I followed front desk girl down the hall, into the studio. There were nine other women, some sitting cross-legged on the floor, some in stretches that seemed impossible and also dangerous.

I tried not to stare at a woman in gold lamé leggings as she extended one leg over her head. I failed. Front desk girl deposited me in the back right corner, where I set down my water bottle, rolled my shoulders, paced in a circle, tried to pretend that I belonged.

"I hear we have a virgin." The voice, sonorous and sultry, resounded from unseen speakers. I looked up and saw its source, Venus von Turnen, floating toward me. Tall and lithe, with shelves for collarbones and cascading waves of hair, she wore cream-colored Lululemon from head to toe. Bodysuit and leggings. It took a brave woman to wear cream-colored leggings. Not a hint of a dimple in that fabric, from top to bottom, smooth as butter.

She came in front of me and placed one hand on my shoulder. "You will work. You will sweat. You will feel. You may even break down—in this room, anything goes. In fact, we *want* you to break down. That means the work is working."

"Okay, cool!" I nodded like I got it. She hadn't tilted the microphone away from her face, although I probably wouldn't have asked for clarification even if she had.

She swanned over to the front of the room and told us to sit cross-legged, close our eyes, and "summon an intention to guide you through the work your physical being is about to do for your soul. Know that you are here for your soul—not to lose weight, not to tone up, not to fit into that Mara Hoffman cutout one-piece when you go to Cabo." I choked on a laugh. After a pause, she continued, "And *certainly* not to disrupt the process of other Goddesses who are doing the hard work to blossom into their truest selves." I bit the inside of my cheek and willed myself to stop smirking. Okay, wonderment aside, this was a little ridiculous. I wished that Praveen was with me. Praveen would laugh.

"Time to work," she said, as the opening strums of "Gimme Shelter" filled the room. Weird, I thought. This was not what I'd put on a workout playlist. This was music to do cocaine to at eight o'clock on a Saturday morning when you'd already been doing cocaine all night. Clearly, The Goddess Effect was just a bunch of hype. A waste of twenty dollars. But of course, I had to stay. Get my money's worth. I couldn't leave. Leaving would be awkward. I didn't want to be *that* person.

We started with skaters. That led to burpees, which led to "bounding jumping jacks"—like regular jumping jacks, but with a jump squat in the middle—which led to jumping lunges set to Alanis Morissette screaming about the mess you made when you went away and Venus saying, "The pain you're feeling is just the *real you* struggling to come out into the light, struggling to break free of the bonds of your corporeal body. Let it. Let the real you come out. Don't stop. Stopping is submitting to who people think you should be. Who do you want to be? The real you, or other people's version of you?" Fuck, I thought, I want to be the real me. The best version of me. Sweat streamed from my face and pooled on my mat. Fine, I acknowledged, this was a good workout. A great workout. Possibly due to the Drake sauna suit, but still.

We did "commandos"—elbow, elbow, palm, palm—and "propeller," in which we whirred our arms in frenetic circles while doing high knees. "We've reached it, that point I know you've been waiting for," Venus said, after propeller. The cooldown, thank God, I thought. Gotta hand it to you, Venus, you showed me who's boss. I wondered if this was one of those classes where the instructors came around during the cooldown and rubbed your lower back while you sank into child's pose. I hoped so.

But instead of putting on something from Coldplay's first album, she turned up the volume on "Killing in the Name" by Rage Against the Machine. Weird song choice for a cooldown, I thought. But okay, Venus, you do you. I can do child's pose to anything.

She faced us, squatted down, and pitter-pattered her feet like a football player gearing up to charge. "Shake it out. Fast feet. Get ready. You know what's coming." Everyone else mirrored her. Confused but not wanting to show it, I did the same. We were at that point in the song where Zack de la Rocha harps on about doing what they told you.

"Take this moment, make it your own," she said. She closed her eyes and kept talking. "We call it the guttural cleanse because that's what this exercise does. It clears your gut, your intuition, of all the gunk and junk that stops you from saying what you truly mean, that makes you cower in the face of a challenge, that makes you meek and little, *lesser than*, when really, you should *tower*, *you* should make people cower, you are *more* than, you are a big, screaming, *greater than* sign shining as bright as that trophy you're reaching for, as bright as *all* the trophies. Yes, you *can* sweep this season. Yes, you *will*." Gold lamé leggings nodded vigorously. Was she in that Marie Antoinette biopic, or was I just imagining it?

"You don't need to sound like the person next to you, you don't need to do what they do, you just need to let that monster inside, that demon dragging you down, out into the world, out of your system. Give it a voice and make it loud . . . four, three, two . . ."

On "one," the beat dropped, and sound shook the room. Guttural screams, high-pitched shrieks, elongated groans. Gold lamé leggings howled. A woman in a leopard-print sports bra threw herself on her mat and banged her fists. My mouth hung open. I stopped squatting and pitter-pattering my feet and gaped at everyone. I managed to start moving again and let out a whinnying "ehhh" before Venus closed her fists like a conductor. Whatever demon I had inside did not come out. Probably, my demon laughed at me.

After class, I crumpled onto a birchwood bench by the cubbies and chugged water from my S'well. I looked around. I watched the women sling cool lavender-scented towels around their necks, their faces placid and unlined. They had it all, or at least, they looked like they did. I felt a sudden, overwhelming urge to be them—not to be *like* them, but to transmogrify into a rich white woman between the ages of thirty-two and fifty, beyond juvenile meanderings, seasoned enough to have figured out life to the extent that I could escape to this place at noon on a weekday and not give it a second thought.

I grabbed my phone and texted Praveen. He said the *Daily Mail* had called The Goddess Effect "ayahuasca meets SoulCycle." Then he went into an interlude about how he hadn't met any hot guys at SoulCycle since Kevin, the real estate influencer from last spring, and should he maybe rejoin Equinox because perhaps they'd all migrated to the new one that had opened by Hudson Yards?

I mean who doesn't want 24/7 sauna access, I typed. But wait, should I join Goddess Effect even though there's no way I can afford it?

Praveen: I mean?

Praveen: You could just run?

Praveen: How's it going with Gonzo btw?

6

I lied and told Praveen I had a meeting at Gonzo that week. Then I asked if he'd ever figured out if his segment producer had allergies or a coke problem, and he launched into a whole spiel about that. Praveen had his knight-in-shining-armor moments. After my dad died, after I returned to work, he would show up at my cubicle every afternoon with some tidbit of office gossip that he just *had* to tell me over drinks that night, drinks that he paid for, more often than not. There was a high probability that he made up most of what he said, but it didn't matter. He knew what to do to distract me, to make me feel, for a few hours, like a normal, bumbling millennial.

Most of the time, though, Praveen was salty. But I liked him because he was salty. He was my mango pickle, my kimchi, my deli-style dill. You don't need mango pickle's permission, I told myself. Hello! Do you!

Sitting on the birchwood bench by the cubbies, thumbing mindlessly through my apps, I realized that I ought to gather myself and go, but I didn't really want to. The Goddess Effect smelled so nice. I felt cleaner just being there, despite the fact that there was a bib of sweat above *Worst Behavior* and random strands of hair were plastered around my face in wet curlicues. Sure, some of what Venus said was hokey, but something about her left me in awe. Besides her looks, besides her physique, some combination of assertiveness, confidence, and a seemingly innate ability to lead. The way the other women respected her, moved on her command, no questions asked. You didn't see that every day. And girl did know how to lead a workout. I hadn't had a sweat that satisfying in months.

Wasn't I supposed to prioritize wellness? I felt more well than I had an hour ago. That had to count for something.

Maybe they had a new client special. I raked my hair into a high ponytail and walked up to the front desk.

"What'd you think?" front desk girl asked. She was leaning back in a swivel chair, holding her phone in front of her face.

"I mean, amazing. You were so right, it's like no workout I've ever done."

"Yeah, I don't really think of it as a workout. It's kind of like"—she put her phone down and looked up thoughtfully—"a way of life. Like Hindi, you know?"

What I thought: Like *Hinduism*? You're comparing this boutique fitness class to a four-thousand-year-old religion that you appropriated for your wall art? What I said: "Oh my gosh, totally. I can *totally* see that. So, I was wondering, do you have any promos for new clients?"

She blinked at me, no longer thoughtful. "Promos?" she repeated. I pictured an error sign on her forehead.

"Yeah, like, new year, new you type of deals? I just moved from New York, and the Pilates place by my apartment was offering one of those." I thought if she knew I came from New York, she would take me more seriously. "Anything besides the forty dollars per session or eight-hundred-dollar unlimited monthly class pack?"

"We don't really do . . . *promos*." Another dirty word that would require another rinsing of the mouth. "If you want, you can buy our founder's book. It's only $35.99."

It was on a stand next to the iPad: *Effected*. The cover was that photo of Venus naked in a seashell. According to the blurb on the inside flap, Venus grew up on a potato farm. She attended the Business

College of Idaho on scholarship and then the Institut d'administration des Finances, in Paris. Fancy, I thought.

Chapter five, "Epiphany," began, "One day, bullied out of a board meeting and on the verge of a breakdown, I planted my heart center on the carpet of my office. I turned my head to the side and closed my eyes, willing the tears to fall. Instead, I pushed myself up into a plank. Then I did it again. And again. I did 150 pushups in a Lauren by Ralph Lauren pantsuit that momentous October morning, the Freedom Tower outside my fifty-second-story window signaling what would soon be my truth: freedom from finance. Freedom from male-dominated, misogynist corporate America. Freedom from how women ought to behave in the workplace. I stormed out of my office that day, sweat drenching my armpits and the power source between my legs. 'Fuck you, and fuck the Greenwich office, too,' I told my boss. I grabbed a term sheet off his mahogany desk, blotted my power source, balled it up, and threw it in his face along with my parting words: 'You want this pussy? Grab that.'"

"Super inspiring," I said to front desk girl, placing the book back on its stand. "I'll think about it and maybe come back later." As if front desk girl cared. She was no longer looking at me.

I exhaled deeply, tugged on the straps of my track bag, and turned toward the stairs. Okay, forty dollars per session wasn't so bad, I told myself. Think of all the money you're saving on coffee, on alcohol. Make it a reward, pay in cash. That'll keep you accountable, though they probably only take cards—

I felt a tap on my shoulder. I whipped around to see the taut, glowing face of leopard-print sports bra, the one who banged her fists on the ground during the guttural cleanse.

"They never have sales, but you're new, right? You should do the heaven-sent special. Three months unlimited for six hundred dollars." She leaned in closer. She smelled like jasmine and generational wealth. I wondered if she'd had some advanced type of plastic surgery that made her pituitary glands produce sweat that could be bottled and sold at Le

Labo. "They don't advertise it. You have to have an existing client refer you to get that rate, but I'm happy to do it." Before I could respond, she turned to front desk girl. "Ophelia, my friend"—she looked at me, and I chirped my name—"would like to do the heaven-sent special."

"This is your friend?" Ophelia asked, unbelieving.

"Of course," leopard-print sports bra said. "We go way back. I'm the one who told her to come check out class." She gave me a wry smile, like we had all this history. Why was she doing this? I wondered. Was I getting scammed? But she seemed too genuine to be a scammer. Although, the best kind of scammers worked hard to appear authentic.

Ophelia sat back and crossed her arms. "You know you can only refer one friend per year to the heaven-sent special."

"I know," leopard-print sports bra said.

Ophelia turned to me. "You realize this takes commitment. This isn't, like, some 24 Hour Fitness that you join and then forget about. We take our community incredibly seriously. You have time for this? You have time to show up?"

"Of course," I said, nodding. Truly, I had nothing but time. There were other factors: the random act of kindness, the knowledge that I was being offered a (relatively) good deal that not everyone got, the fact that, in exercise as in sex, I'd rather have someone tell me what to do than have to figure it out on my own. But there was also something drawing me to The Goddess Effect that I couldn't quite put my finger on, or maybe I felt shallow for putting my finger on it. It was aspirational. Leopard-print sports bra and the rest of the women appeared to have their shit together in a way that I did not. Maybe I would learn something just by being around them. "Lean into my power," like that actress-turned-director. Possibly, I could find my tribe. Maybe I'd find my abs.

"Charge it to the card on file?"

"Yes, thank you. *Wow*, this is so awesome." My eyes darted from Ophelia to leopard-print sports bra. "I can't believe—"

Leopard-print sports bra grabbed my wrist. "*So* glad you finally came, babe," she said, dragging me away before I could further ingratiate myself and confirm Ophelia's suspicion that we were not, in fact, friends. "There's this to-die-for café down the street. Wanna grab something?" As I followed her out the door, she said, "By the way, I'm Stacy. Tell me your name again? I want to make sure I'm pronouncing it correctly."

7

P eople often asked if they were pronouncing my last name correctly—Kathlikar—but never my first, which my parents stra-
tegically gave me because it was familiar to Americans. As far as
my last name, most Americans said "*KATH*-li-car," and most Indians,
"*KUTH*-li-khur." I wavered but, more often than not, went with the
American version. I'd heard my parents do this, too; it seemed like the
path of least resistance. In any case, I didn't define myself by my last
name. I'd never met either of my grandfathers. They died before I was
born.

Anyway, I only repeated my first name for Stacy. No one introduces
themselves with their full name unless they're about to give a TED Talk.
Maybe not even then.

As we walked, Stacy asked what brought me to LA.

"I needed a fresh start," I said. This didn't feel like enough. "And
there's a job out here that I'm up for." Not exactly a lie. I was technically
up for anything.

Stacy asked about the job, and I gave her a brief rundown. "Good
for you," she said. "I was just listening to this podcast about women of
color in media, the lack of representation."

I flashed back to senior producer Andrew, who, during my first
month at ABN, offered to take me under his wing and out to lunch at

the Japanese place across the street. "It's hard in there, for folks like us," Andrew said, breaking apart his chopsticks. By "us," I figured he meant people of color. I still believed that my employer had my best interests at heart and hesitated to publicly gripe about them. But I also didn't want to disagree with Andrew, so I said, "Yeah, I don't know a lot of Indian people in media."

"So you're *Indian*. I've been trying to guess. Could've sworn you were Dominican, by that ass." And then, when I turned the color of pickled ginger: "Oh, I meant that as a *compliment*, Anita. Don't take it the wrong way."

He proceeded to tell me how he'd once had an Indian girlfriend and that she said he fucked her better than any of the Indian guys she'd ever been with. That was what came to mind, whenever the subject of women of color in media came up.

"Thanks again for hooking me up with this heaven-sent special," I said. "I haven't had a real workout since I got here."

"Honestly, The Goddess Effect has been so transformative, I just wanted to pass it on. It's really helped me work through all this pain and anger I didn't even know I had."

Stacy's gym bag was a Gucci tote with a snake on it. Her diamond was the size of a Ring Pop. She wore leopard-print leggings that matched her sports bra, coral-pink sneakers that looked fresh out of the box, and a frayed sweatshirt that could've been twenty years old but was more likely new-season Monrow. I wondered what kind of pain and anger she could possibly have.

"How long have you been going?"

"About a year," she said. "I used to have a personal trainer and a running coach and a Pilates instructor and a yoga teacher, and now"—she snapped her fingers—"none of it. Just Goddess Effect. Well, Goddess Effect and my fascia guy. And my chakra opener. And there's a reiki person who comes over once a month to rebalance the energy of the house, but that's, like, home maintenance. It's like having your gutters cleaned." She saw my face and laughed. "Now *I* sound like the crazy person. Believe me, I was not always like this. Before I came to LA, my version of a workout was *actually* cleaning gutters."

I doubted she'd ever seen a gutter, but okay. She'd grown up on a farm in Sonoma. "My parents were total hippies. I didn't even own a blow-dryer before I got to college." She pushed in the door to Provisions and strode up to the register. "Aaliyah, *love* the new 'do, are those—do you call them box braids?" She and Aaliyah engaged in a momentary interlude while I tried to decipher the menu. Were adaptogens a type of sprout?

"I'll have a power greens smoothie and a collagen toast, please," Stacy said, "and would you mind, if it's no trouble, doing that on the gluten-free multigrain? And Anita—oh gosh, I'm sorry, I barely gave you a chance to look at the menu."

"No worries. I'll have the same. Sounds delish." I told myself to focus on wrenching my Capital One from my wallet and not on what collagen toast could possibly be made out of, but Stacy beat me to it.

"My treat," she said, batting my hand away. "You just got here." As she pulled her piece of plastic out of the swiper, I saw that it was a black card. I had never seen one in real life. How? I wondered. She had none of the snobbishness that I would've associated with someone with a nonexistent credit limit. Also, she couldn't have been that much older than me, and I still used age as a barometer for how successful, i.e., rich, one could be.

I followed her to a table by the window, one of those rickety wood-and-scrap-metal affairs. While we waited for our food (assuming that whatever we were about to be served counted as food), she told me about the third Goddess Effect class she'd taken, the one that got her hooked.

"It was Venus's 9:30 a.m., and there was this beam of sun that came in through the window and lit up the whole studio. We were doing burpees, which, I mean, talk about torture—they probably don't even do those at Guantanamo. The sun didn't help, it was getting in my eyes. I was this close to running out to the bathroom or just leaving, never coming back. It sounds wild, but I think Venus sensed that. She came over and stood right in front of me, hands on hips, and said"—Stacy lowered her voice a register—"'This is you. This you at your most pure. Your most natural. Your animal essence. Embrace your animal essence. Embrace who you are, without your Gucci, without your Alo, without the Porsche hybrid that I'm sure you drive, without your second home in Maui and your third home in Aspen, without all the shit that you adorn yourself with, that you do to yourself, to make yourself feel better. This is all you need to do. Do the work. Do this work.'"

She seemed shook, recounting the memory. "Our second home is at Hualālai and our third is in Deer Valley, but everything else, she nailed. It's rare to have someone read you like that, you know?"

"Yeah, that's"—I searched for the appropriate sentiment—"insane." I was reacting more to the fact that she had three homes than what Venus had said to her. I wondered what Venus would say to me. I wondered what Hualālai was and whether I was supposed to know it.

A server put down our "toasts" (seeds) and smoothies. Stacy asked where I lived.

"It's called the Gig," I said. "Sort of like Soho House meets *The Real World* but without the cameras and confessionals and unhinged people throwing stuffed animals off of piers. How about you?"

"Oh, I'm just up the 405, but wait, tell me more about the Gig." She put her elbows on the table, took a bite of her toast, and smiled as she chewed, as if genuinely eager to hear more. I was explaining the concept of the beta run when my phone, facedown on the table, just like Stacy's, started vibrating. Could it be Emilia? My phone number *was* in my email signature.

"Sorry." I smiled apologetically at Stacy and glanced at the screen. It was my mom, FaceTiming. The fuck? We had a ritual: I would FaceTime her for approximately five minutes every evening at six o'clock. She never called me during the day, given how busy I was at "work" (an excuse from my time at ABN that I was happy to carry across the country, to a job that I did not actually have). Was something wrong? Was she dead? "One sec," I told Stacy. I apologized again, trying not to sound panicked as I dashed outside.

I was bracing for sirens as I pressed accept. Instead, I heard my mom, jubilant: "Happy Varalakshmi Puja day!" The screen showed her puja place, a kitchen cabinet reincarnated as a shrine, with burning incense and an array of brass figurines the size of Hot Wheels cars, dotted with the red kumkuma powder that never failed to stain your skin, even if you only kept it on for the amount of time it took to press your palms together and press your forehead to the floor (four seconds).

"It's an important puja for young, unmarried women," she said. "I was doing arti and then thought, why don't I FaceTime, so you can do a namaskar, too?"

"Mom, I'm *busy*." I had no problem with her praying the day away, but she couldn't expect me to join her on command. I'd rarely joined her growing up. She'd rarely asked. Did she think that now that my dad was dead that I'd be a born-again Hindu, too? It didn't make sense. You'd think that you'd abandon religion once life proved itself to be cruel and unpredictable, not go all in.

Filial piety prevented me from saying any of this. Oh, the thoughts I could think. Deep down, I knew I had to play two roles: my father and myself. I had to let her lean on me and tell me what to do.

It also meant that I could not clue her in to anything going awry in my own life. Rocks can't crumble. Well, they *can*, but then there's a mudslide, complete and total havoc, cleanup crews, fundraisers. No one wants that.

"Everything okay?" Stacy asked, as I sat back down.

"Just an HR person from Gonzo, confirming a meeting." Stacy raised her perfectly arched eyebrows. I told myself not to feel guilty.

By the time we'd finished our toasts and smoothies, we'd exchanged numbers, followed each other on Instagram, and signed up for the next day's noon class.

"Can I give you a ride home?" Stacy asked as we stood up. "I'm parked right by the studio."

It all felt too good to be true—the class, the deal, the budding friendship with this fabulous woman, even the collagen toast, remnants of which were stuck between my teeth. I worried that if she saw where I lived, something would burst the bubble. Maybe Riley would be summoning a spirit in the driveway, and Stacy would recognize Riley as one of her kind, realize that Riley was the one she should be friends with, not me.

"You know what, I need to run some errands, so I'm gonna walk, but thank you, seriously, for everything," I said, following her onto the sidewalk.

"It was nothing. Gotta spread the wealth, you know?" We hugged goodbye, and I started walking in the opposite direction from her, even though it was the wrong one, because a second goodbye would've been awkward. I tugged on the straps of my track bag and smiled like a fool. Stacy Gibson, fancy, pretty, owner-of-three-homes Stacy Gibson, had taken me under her wing. The big sister I always wanted.

8

Annalisa taught me how to properly do a skater, how to keep my chest up while reaching down to the floor. Saffron taught me how to properly plank, how to squeeze my glutes and tuck my tail. ("I have one?" I'd asked. "Your tailbone, dear," she'd replied.) I stopped working out in sweatshirts. I had a brief flirtation with tank tops before I took the cue of the other regulars and winged it in a sports bra. Remarkable, how freeing that was. I'd never worked out in just a sports bra.

They started taking me seriously when they saw me coming and going with Stacy. Whoever got to the studio first would grab mats and save spots. She liked front and center, I alternated between right and left.

It only took me a few classes to understand why Venus was Venus and the rest of the instructors worked for her. When she was at the helm, one exercise practically melted into the next, so seamless were her transitions, and her playlist, a mix of funk, alternative rock, and weird electronica, made every move seem revelatory, like hip bridges were meant to be done to the Dillon Francis remix of "Purple Rain," and doing them to any other song would be blasphemy.

I would watch Venus, in her unscripted moments—winding her hair into a high bun before class, applying lip gloss afterward—trying to decipher what made her tick. She didn't do small talk, as I learned when I went up to her after class and asked where in New York she used to live, and she just squeezed my shoulder and walked away. "Don't worry," said Stacy, who was wiping down her mat. "She did the same thing when I asked how she knew we had a place in Hawaii."

I saw, in Venus, a version of who I could be: she left corporate America and charted her own path. I left corporate America, too—check. She created The Goddess Effect, I did The Goddess Effect—check. What other boxes could I tick off? How else could I level up?

"Ugh, I'm so bloated today," Stacy said one morning before Venus's 9:00 a.m., pinching a sliver of skin above her ombré leggings (indigo on top, baby blue at the bottom, matching sports bra). She had her legs tucked under her and was staring at her reflection in the mirrored wall at the front of the studio. I wondered what she saw. "So bloated," for me, meant my most stretched-out Target leggings, not what was very likely new-season Michi.

"You definitely don't look like it," I said.

"You know what, I'm going to do the 5:00 p.m. today, too," she said, turning to me. "I was in the best shape when I was doing two-a-days back in the fall. Wanna come with?"

That's how two-a-days started. I figured I only had the unlimited package for three months, might as well use it.

Goddess Effect was a thing to do. A place to go. A place where I was told that I was progressing, "so strong," "badass," "killing it." Stacy kept me accountable and always suggested Provisions after the a.m. class. Eventually, I gave up on offering to pay. Not only was I making the most of the heaven-sent special, I was also getting a free meal, which added up to me saving money, when you thought about it. Gonzo would come through when Gonzo came through.

Emilia, I'd concluded, didn't want to meet with just anyone, she wanted to meet with people with ideas. Slam-dunk story ideas. I'd hesitated to send any because of that whole "why buy the cow when the milk is free" thing, but I realized that you wouldn't buy a cow without tasting the milk, or at least confirming that it could, indeed, produce milk. I'd sent her three. The best was about a series of raves happening below highway overpasses in downtown LA. I'd heard about it at the Gig: the ravers paid the people they temporarily displaced in exchange for using their "sick acoustics" and sometimes brought donations, like expired ashwagandha supplements and gluten-free carrot cake. "I went to one, and it was fire," said Miguel. "Tragic, but fire."

It was a story of the haves vs. the have-nots and privileged guilt gone awry, a total home run. If Emilia was going to respond at all, it would be to this idea. Still, nothing.

Her social media confirmed her continuing existence. I thought about direct messaging her, but I didn't want to seem desperate. No one wanted to hire desperate. I cast a wider net, copy/pasting my résumé into LinkedIn postings for ninjas and wizards. No follow-ups, but I doubt I would have responded. Any job would get in the way of two-a-days. Why shouldn't I prioritize an activity that made me feel good? Why shouldn't I prioritize The Goddess Effect? While I was saving money and living rent-free, anyway.

One afternoon, early for Annalisa's 6:00 p.m., I got the perfect shot of the reception lounge at magic hour, a honey-colored beam of light across the *Harness Your Inner Lakshmi* graffiti. Upstairs, sitting on the birchwood benches by the cubbies, debating captions—*GODDESS MODE: ACTIVATED* vs. three flexed-bicep emoji vs. nothing, just the picture—I overheard Ophelia grumbling into the phone.

"No, of course I *want* to, Venus."

My attention shifted.

"It's just, between all the usual stuff, and the front desk, and freaking Calabasas, I'm kind of swamped, you know?" She picked at the cuticles of the hand that wasn't holding the phone. "Maybe it's time to bring someone else on board."

I could be the one, I thought. Just like that Avicii song. I didn't know what they were talking about—cleaning the bathrooms, mopping the floors, who knew—but wasn't the first prerequisite for working at a startup—and what was The Goddess Effect but a startup—to be a consumer? I was as passionate a consumer as they came. Startups were always carving out roles, investing in talent. Maybe my dream job was right under my nose. What was that saying? "Do what you love, and you'll never work a day in your life."

Ophelia ended the call in a huff. Noted, I thought. Something to follow up on.

In New York, the Gig seemed like a reason to move. It seemed like the type of place to which I should want to belong: a house full of "changemakers," young people who were thinking different. Getting in, and getting the beta run—"like a Harvard scholarship for postcollegiate hipsters," said the *New York Times*—appealed to all of my Ivy League sensibilities. But it turned out, The Goddess Effect was where I *actually* wanted to belong. If this made me shallow, well, fine. I couldn't deny that, in my heart of hearts, I wanted to be a rich white woman. I wanted to move through the world with Venus's drive and Stacy's ease. Obviously, I could not be reborn as Venus or Stacy (not in this life, anyway), but I could, physically, obey Venus and move like Stacy. Order lunch like Stacy. Maybe one day, lounge poolside at Hualālai like Stacy (in a nude bikini and banded straw hat that said *Rosé All Day* on its brim, per Instagram). I could fake it till I made it, like the influencers said and did.

I was thinking about how to broach the topic of working for The Goddess Effect the following morning, as I walked home from Saffron's 9:00 a.m., sipping the remnants of a Provisions smoothie (blueberry, oat milk, hemp protein—same as Stacy's), when I got a FaceTime. I glared at the caller ID. Did she have no respect for our routine? For my time?

"Hi, Mom."

"I'm sorry, calling you in the middle of the workday—are you outside? What is it that you're wearing?"

"A sports bra."

"You wear that to work?"

"Yes, it's LA, and it's hot, and no one gets to the office before eleven."

She made a face. "Maybe pull this part up." She tugged at the crew neck of her sweatshirt, like I didn't know what she was talking about. God forbid the greater world know that I had breasts.

"What's up?"

"I was just talking with Rupa Auntie, and she mentioned that she has a niece in Irvine, Smita. I thought it might be nice for you to connect with her."

"Why, because she's Indian? There are, like, a billion Indian women in the world. Should I connect with all of them, too?"

"You might enjoy spending time with her. Rupa says she's a lot like you. She's working at a law office, steady job, nine-to-five."

"For the millionth time, I don't want to be a paralegal. I'm not going to law school. That ship has sailed."

"In any case, I'll send you her contact info. Maybe we can all meet when I come to LA for the wedding." I said "whatever" and told her I had to go.

Pooja's wedding was a little more than a month away, and whenever I thought about it, my stomach curdled. So many people from my past to face. So many people to whom I had to prove my betterment, my evolution, my good decision-making skills. "Trust the process," Venus had said the other day. "Trust that the more time you spend here, processing, the more equipped you'll be to deal with the hellscape out there." Who knew? Maybe by the time the wedding rolled around, I'd be the VP of comms for The Goddess Effect. Or a Gonzo correspondent. Or a Goddess Effect brand ambassador. Or—

My phone pinged with Smita's contact card. Her address: 8000 Euclid Avenue, Irvine. Where was Irvine, even? What did my mom expect me to do? Put on a bindi, spend a bunch of money on an Uber, and show up to Smita's starter town house, where I'd have to take off my shoes, do a namaskar, and sip room-temperature water out of a steel cup while spooning up glob after glob of bisi bele bath? Say things like "Mmm, so nice, just like home"? Smile for the picture that would be taken in the middle of the meal by Smita's husband with a selfie stick, in which none of us would be looking in the same direction, and then like all the Facebook comments from the aunties? "So nice!" "Keeping tradition alive 🙏." "May God bless you all." Fuck that. Not my idea of a good time.

Of course, if I didn't text Smita, my mom would find out, and we'd have to have this conversation all over again.

I tapped out the most anodyne, noncommittal message I could think of.

Anita: Hi Smita, it's Anita, Meena Auntie's daughter, the one who just moved to LA. Wanna hang sometime? No pressure

My plan was to cite prior commitments for every date that Smita suggested and be overly apologetic for being so busy. She'd give up, eventually, and I could say that I tried.

9

I was riding high on postworkout endorphins when I got back to the Gig on Friday evening, carrying a salad from Sweetgreen. Christina, Riley, and Constance (of the Museum of Ice Cream but for Poetry) were gathered around the kitchen island and an open bag of cheese doodles made of chickpeas. "We were just talking about you," Riley said. "How about a girls' night?"

Girls' night. Two words that called forth a gleeful mental montage of sequins, metallic eye shadow, and pink drinks. But yikes, those pink drinks. Always so expensive, always full of sugar. The two-a-days had broken me out of the routine of 5:00 p.m. drinks that led to more drinks that led to me not quite remembering when I fell asleep and waking up with a head full of static.

A thought: What would Venus do? Did Venus do girls' nights? I tried to imagine what Venus and Ophelia would do for fun. Ayahuasca? A silent retreat?

In class, Saffron had harped on recognizing forces that drive you down. Would girls' night drive me down? Would girls' night lead me to drown my internal organs in sugary cocktails and Doritos and spoil the progress I'd made so far? I could see, on either side of my belly button, indentations that suggested the presence of abs. I had taken to looking in the mirror once an hour to make sure that they were still there, a new mom checking in on her baby.

But what would I do if I stayed home? Wonder what I was missing out on? Eat Sweetgreen and sip lemon water? On a Friday night? Was there anything sadder?

I had been waiting for Stacy to suggest grabbing a bite after evening class—or better yet, drinks, I would absolutely break my streak of alcohol avoidance to drink with her—but she always had a dinner, an obligation, or a thing to go to with Colt, her real estate developer husband. From what she'd shared thus far, they'd met when she was working as a bottle-service girl at 1 OAK; he'd scooped her up, swept her off her feet, and demanded a not insignificant amount of her attention. "I mean, he pays for everything, so," she'd said, rolling her eyes. "Could be worse!" This struck me as defeatist and sort of sad, but I was in no position to comment on her relationship.

Given what I knew, it would be unwise to put all my eggs in a Stacy-shaped basket. My eggs needed options. Diversity.

I tried to imagine posting a photo with Christina, Constance, and Riley. I could see it. Hashtag girl gang, hashtag no boys allowed, hashtag the future is female.

"What's the plan?" I asked, edging my elbows onto the island.

"So there's this new place called Retro," Riley said. "I know the owners. They said they'd throw in a few rounds if I came by with some friends. And by friends, they obviously meant girls."

"Down," said Christina, crunching down on a chickpea (chick-cheese?) doodle.

Constance screwed up her face. "Isn't this, like, the patriarchy doing what it does best? Giving us free vodka sodas so that we'll shut up and smile and be happy with our eighty cents on the dollar?"

"It's not always about the patriarchy, Constance," Riley said.

"Why don't we go to that arts district salon that I told you about? Tonight's topic is"—Constance consulted her phone—"'Can Robots

Fall in Love?' It's a panel discussion between researchers from Caltech, MIT, and the Joshua Tree Institute of Love and Sex. There's complimentary kombucha and music from deejay A.I.In.Love after." She squinted at her screen. "Apparently, the deejay is one of the researchers. Or a robot. Maybe both? I'm not sure."

"That's gonna be a hard no for me," said Christina.

"Salons are so two years ago," said Riley.

"I'm sorry, Constance," I said. I had been wrong about Sweetgreen and lemon water. There were worse ways to spend a Friday night.

"Ugh, fine," she said. "But I'm not getting all dolled up. Or shaving my legs."

"Love that for you," said Riley. "Whisper"—the owner of the meditation studio where Riley worked—"says body hair has pheromones that lower your resting heart rate. Meet back here in thirty?"

***

I did a mental inventory of my wardrobe as I soaped up in the shower, trying not to get my hair wet. Retro sounded like a club. Clubs meant something fun and formfitting, something that strode the line between "here for a good time" and "here to get date raped." Wrapped in a towel, pawing through my closet, I brushed my hand against a stiff, ribbed fabric I'd forgotten I still owned—an Hervé Léger bandage dress, bought at deep, deep discount from Century 21 before a New Year's Eve party at Marquee.

I laid it on the bed. It was ombré, just like Stacy's leggings and sports bra, but it went from pale pink at the top to deep red at the bottom. It had a plunging neckline, three-quarter-length sleeves, and hit just above the knee. Was it too much? Or was it just right? This *was* my first real night out in LA. What if there was a red carpet? What if there was paparazzi? What if this was my chance to take that photo that would prove I'd finally arrived?

I told myself that if I found my Spanx, it would be a sign. I dug through my top drawer, throwing everything that was not Spanx on the floor. I yanked them on, zipped up the dress, and turned to the mirror. I could hardly breathe. Hervé should've called it the tourniquet dress. But if I sucked in and the Spanx stayed in place and didn't roll down at the waist or up at the thighs, I looked *good*. Really good.

Given the maximalism of the dress, I thought it best to go minimalist with my shoes. My Allbirds matched one of the shades of red. Unconventional, for sure, but wasn't everything in LA? I did a three-quarter turn and looked over my shoulder. Had my ass ever looked better? Fuck my shoes. No one was going to look at my shoes. They'd all be blinded by my ass.

I plugged in my flat iron and went to work, straightening the kinks caused by the high buns mandated by The Goddess Effect. Well, The Goddess Effect didn't mandate them, per se, but that's how Venus and Stacy wore their hair, so. The iron sizzled when I went over this one bump near the crown of my head, which meant that either I had burned my hair or inadvertently gotten it wet in the shower. I went over it a few more times, pressing harder.

Hair suitably straight, I arched my back, pouted my lips, angled my phone below my chin, and took fourteen mirror selfies. The fifth was the best.

Painting the town red
Painting the town ombré
SATC but make it LA

I figured there would be so many postable moments, why blow my load this early? Better to post something with the girls, to show that I had a #squad.

"Whoa," Christina said, as I came downstairs. She had been talking to Max. He turned, eyes bugging. They regarded me the way you might a centaur at Costco.

"Yeah? It works?" I asked. Not wanting to be told no, I kept talking. "How's your deck going, by the way? I've barely seen you since you saved me from a lifetime of biohacker showers."

Panic overtook Max's face. "Deck? You know about the deck?"

"For the cauliflower rice cafe, yeah, we talked about it? Butter, cheese?" I looked at Christina like, "What's with this guy?"

"*Ah*, right." He said something about another client whose "deliverables" had become "action item number one," which made me wonder if he always talked like this and our banter in the bathroom had just been a fluke.

"What's going on with him?" I asked Christina, after he walked away.

"Girl," she said, raising her eyebrows, "don't even get me started. Adil gave him some project, and Max is struggling. He was asking how I define ethics. Not the type of conversation I'm trying to have tonight." She pulled out a bottle of carnation-pink wine from the fridge and poured some for us both. Constance came out in a taupe cocoon dress, the sartorial opposite of what I had on. Riley came out in a duster, ripped jeans, and a white bralette.

"Oh my God, *Ani*," she squealed, delighted. "A bandage dress—*so* retro! I haven't seen one of those since, like, middle school."

Was that a good thing? Like how chokers were out but suddenly in again? I smiled awkwardly and did a little shimmy.

Riley ordered an Escalade and, once we were all in, announced that she had a surprise. From her Cult Gaia purse, she pulled out four vape pens and unfurled them like a fan. "Samples from that cannabis nootropics startup Adil just backed. He gave me a bunch to hand out at the studio, but these are sativa. Not on brand for meditation, def on brand for girls' night."

"Yes please and thank you," said Christina, grabbing one.

"Is it organic?" asked Constance.

"Organic, sustainable, ethical, renewable—it is all of the things," said Riley. The one she handed me was pale pink. "It matches your outfit, Ani. Meant to be."

I turned the vape over. "It's weed and what? Nootropics?"

"Yeah, you know, drugs that make your brain work better," Riley said. "This one's got aniracetam, which makes you more creative. That plus THC, it's a vibe."

"Huh," I said. "Aniracetam" sounded like a prescription drug for racism. Marijuana made me paranoid. In the maybe twenty times I'd gotten high, I'd had a grand total of five minutes of feeling relaxed, happy, and comfortable in my own skin. But who knew what I'd been smoking? The vape seemed high quality. It had a matte finish and a rose gold–plated tip to indicate where you were supposed to inhale. The other end was engraved with a tiny kissy-face emoji. Cute, I thought. It reminded me of those pictures of 1920s flappers with their fancy cigarette holders. It might make me smarter. It *did* match my outfit. It was something to post about.

"Let's all try it on three," said Riley.

"You can smoke in an Uber?" I asked.

Riley gave me a look. "We're not *smoking*, we're vaping, and yes." She stuck her head in the space between the back seat and the driver. "It's prescription. For my anxiety." She counted down. The vape tasted like strawberry Quik and vibrated once you'd taken a hit. I took another. I sat back and imagined weed and rosé waltzing in my stomach.

The Escalade pulled to a stop in front of a large parking lot; beyond it was a ramshackle Victorian house. Clusters of people milled about in front of the entrance, which was blocked by a single velvet rope and two beefy bouncers with iPads.

"Should be on management's list," Riley said, sashaying up to them. She turned to us. "So, the reason it's called Retro is because they serve drinks in copper mugs. Super old Hollywood. Like, Prohibition vibes.

Oh, and also, you can't use your phone or take photos." Wait, what? I thought. No phone? No photos? What was this, prison?

"What?" I assumed my outrage was shared. "What if you're a doctor on call?"

Riley laughed. "Who's even a doctor anymore? Western medicine, such a scam."

The bouncers said we were good to go. I walked with Christina.

"The phone thing's kind of weird, huh?"

"Honestly, I'm into it. No selfies? Sign me up."

"Right," I replied, lamely. I allowed myself a moment to mourn for the #girlgang post that would not be.

"By the way, how's it going with Gonzo?"

I'd been waiting for an opportunity to try out the words. "Actually, I'm exploring other options."

"Oh yeah? Such as?"

"The Goddess Effect."

"That boutique fitness place where you've been spending all your time?"

"Not *all* my time," I said, defensive. "And I'm still talking to Gonzo. Negotiating. You know how it goes. But The Goddess Effect needs help, and as an engaged consumer, I'm thinking, if they can carve out a role—"

"Douchey MBA terms ain't gonna save you, sis!" She said it in a good-natured way, and she had a point. Still, though. I hung on the conversation I'd overheard between Ophelia and Venus the way that I had hung on my five-to-eight minutes with Emilia, back in New York. It kept me buoyed, a boogie board of hope.

We followed Riley down a dimly lit hallway that spat us out onto a dance floor. Banquettes with tables and bottles of Tito's lined the perimeter. A few people wiggled their hips to Fleetwood Mac. Many vaped.

"Question," Christina said, as we surveyed the room. "How many women like you—like us—go to The Goddess Effect?"

"You mean, women who are not white?" Did it always have to be about that? I wondered.

"Yeah, but not just that. Do they have to work for a living? Or have they turned their personal wellness regimens into full-time jobs? Not to be a downer, but I think there's something wack about the whole wellness industry, the idea that you have to spend all this time and money on classes and supplements and treatments to be the best version of yourself. And that best version—it's like the pot of gold at the end of the rainbow. It's always just out of reach. They *keep it* out of reach, so you keep giving them money. There's nothing 'well' about it."

I resisted the urge to say, "Okay, Mom." Before Goddess Effect, I might've agreed with Christina, if only to be agreeable. But The Goddess Effect made me feel good. Worthy. Proficient. Like I had accomplished something, like I had progressed. I felt the need to defend it.

"I don't know who 'they' is, but I do know that The Goddess Effect has helped me. Who knows—maybe I could bring it into disadvantaged communities, like what you're doing with Farm to Mass."

She hooted. "If my kids start carrying rose quartz in their Pokémon backpacks, I'm coming for you."

I laughed along but felt slighted. Who was she, the wellness police? What did she know?

***

Riley led the way past a long bar—packed, three people deep—outside, into a cobblestone courtyard arrayed with more bottles, more banquettes, and another bar. Two tall guys with their shirts unbuttoned to their sternums descended on her, and she introduced them as the owners of Retro. They were the dictionary definition of handsome. They looked like the Hemsworth brothers. *Were* they the Hemsworth brothers? I wondered.

I watched Constance sneak one hand behind the small of her back, grab a handful of her cocoon dress, and pull it taut around her waist. Things change when the patriarchy looks like Thor.

Talk about Retro quickly led to the dreaded chatter about VCs and decks and UX and experiential pop-ups. It's not that I found the conversations themselves dreadful, I just hated that I had nothing to add besides the occasional "Oh yeah, I think I saw that online." After Christina's soapbox moment, there was no way I was going to bring up The Goddess Effect. Even Riley had let it be known that she found boutique fitness to be "kind of vulgar" and "sort of fascist."

I couldn't shake what Christina had said. I drained one comped tequila soda and then another. I took one long pull of my vape and then another. I wanted to get lost in my phone, but no one else had theirs out. Everyone had so much to talk about, I thought, bitterly. So many passions. So many pursuits and projects. So many people to link other people with, to connect other people to. Everyone except for me.

"I'm gonna get another drink," I announced. "Anyone want?" Polite smiles and shakes of the head.

Stupid dress, I thought, walking inside. I could feel the waistband of my Spanx rolling down, could picture the roll of fat poking out above it. I leaned up against the bar and assessed the crowd. Lots of bubbly blondes. Lots of bubbly brunettes. Lots of perfectly done beachy waves and deftly applied false eyelashes. Gel manicures. Leather jackets. Mom jeans. Fake tits. Balloon lips. Was Pooja right? Was this place never going to work for me?

I watched as the bartender served a woman on my right and a woman on my left, twice. Like a tennis match. His hair, down to his chin, was partially slicked back, and he wore a denim shirt with the sleeves rolled up. He addressed everyone as "babe." He looked like a cologne model. I wondered what I would have to do to get his attention. I wondered if I took off my Spanx and threw them in his face, the way girls took off their underwear and threw them at Mick Jagger, if it would compel him to take my order, or if the bouncers would show up and lift me off the ground, dump me in the parking lot.

It would be nice to be free of the bounds of Spanx. It *would* get his attention. A thought: Was I drunk? Nah. This was smart. This was a modern woman, taking charge.

Had I gone to the bathroom, I would've lost my place in line (if you could call the scrum in front of the bar a line) so I just reached under my dress and tugged my Spanx down, momentarily kicking off my Allbirds to get them over my feet.

"Heads up," I said. He was talking animatedly to a blonde babe to whom he had served four shots of tequila long enough ago that her friends had come to claim three of them while she remained, full shot in front of her, dazzling him with her personality.

My Spanx hit his left cheek. In my head: fireworks, pom poms, glitter explosions.

"Seriously?" He smirked as he came over.

"An offering," I said, "to the gods of tequila, along with a prayer that I may be blessed enough to receive another tequila soda in this lifetime." I pressed my palms together and did a namaskar on the bar. When I looked up again, he was grinning.

"Well, that's a first," he said, upending a bottle of Don Julio—an upgrade from the well stuff. "Are you always so generous, or am I special?"

He put my drink down and leaned in, on his forearms. Wait, was he flirting with me?

"I've been known to be a giver," I said. I wrapped my lips around the straw, seductively, I imagined, and took a long pull.

"That's nice. You wanna give me your credit card?"

"Oh, uh, sure." I fumbled for my Capital One.

"Open or closed?"

"You can keep it open."

He nodded, took my card, and walked to the other end of the bar.

You idiot, I told myself, of course he wasn't flirting with you. He's a bartender—he just wants a tip. And now you've left your credit card open when you said you weren't going to spend money on frivolous things, *and* you lost your only pair of Spanx.

I went back to Constance and Christina. The Retro founders were gone, and the girls were talking about some investors they'd met at some female entrepreneurship dinner. I stopped sucking in. I focused on my drink, watched how the soda bubbles clung to the clumps of lime. There was a whole universe in that glass, a whole universe that seemed more interesting than the one that I was currently in, a whole universe that was quickly turning my paper straw to mush. I drank faster. I announced I was going to get another. "This round's on me. Anyone want?" Blank looks, more head shakes.

"You okay, Anita?" Constance asked. She held the remnants of her second drink, which was pretty much melted ice at that point. What a lightweight, I thought. These were not my people. This was not my tribe.

"You wanna go home?" Christina asked.

"I'm *fine*," I said. I shook my empty glass. "BRB."

This time, the definitely-not-flirting-with-me bartender came right away. I got a double tequila soda and a tequila shot, which I knocked back at the bar. Getting obliterated felt like a thing to do, a way to make the night worthwhile.

A drinkless Riley appeared. "Want one? I've got a tab," I said.

She shook her head. "I'm off alcohol this lunar cycle." She squeezed my shoulder and said she'd be right back. I ordered another shot. The bartender raised his eyebrow but brought it anyway. Fuck him, I thought. Fuck LA. Fuck Gonzo. Fuck the Gig. Fuck Pooja. Fuck Pooja *especially*. Fuck Pooja for being right.

10

The last thing I remembered was Christina making me eat a bacon-wrapped hot dog. Was it in the Uber or on the sidewalk? Or in bed?

My hands were sticky with ketchup. There was a plastic carafe of water on the nightstand and a garbage can next to my bed. Nothing in it, thank God. My bandage dress and bra were draped over the barstool I'd repurposed as a desk chair, and I was wearing sweatpants and a T-shirt that I had no memory of putting on.

Goddess Effect. I needed Goddess Effect. Sweat and endorphins and the knowledge that I had done something good for my body. Hopefully, I had enough time to mainline some Nespresso before running to the 10:00 a.m. Yes, I would run. Get that sweat going early. I turned over my phone and—

10:38. Three texts and two missed calls from Stacy. *Fuck.* Stacy would be wondering where I was. Venus would be wondering where I was. I pictured the empty spot next to Stacy, Stacy doing jumping jacks, Stacy glowing, Stacy generating all these hormones that I desperately needed flooding my bloodstream, or my brain, maybe both. Who knew how hormones worked? I groaned and collapsed back into bed. What was wrong with me?

A knock, and then the door creaked open.

"She lives," Christina said.

"Ungh," I said.

She had a "girl, you should know better" look on her face, which was better than an "I hate you, you piece of shit" look. That was something.

"I'm so sorry," I said, sitting up. "What happened?"

"You happened," she said, slapping my shoulder. She perched on the edge of the bed. "Honestly, it's all good. I was ready to bounce anyway."

"How bad was I?" I pressed my fingertips against my eyelids. I was afraid for the answer.

"Well, after we dragged you away from the bar and onto a couch, you kept glaring at everyone and saying random shit, something about perfect Pooja and finding your tribe. Then you passed out and knocked over the water we got you, so I figured your time was up."

"Jesus." I dropped my head into my hands. "What a mess. I'm really sorry, Christina. I'm not usually like this." Whatever slight I'd felt at her questioning of The Goddess Effect had been negated by my own bad behavior.

"We all have our nights. Jayson and I are gonna check out this taco truck. Wanna come? Patented hangover cure. This birria will change your life."

Nothing against stewed goat, but what I wanted most in the world was to feel the way I felt after Goddess Effect, pure and toxin-free and proud of the work I'd put in. Was there still space in Saffron's noon class? Probably.

What I wanted second most in the world was idlis, the way my mom made them, with coconut chutney and potato and carrot sambar. That desire embarrassed me. I wanted to want tacos, or a bacon egg and cheese, or pizza—something Americanized and acceptable.

"Gracias, but I think I need to sweat this one out."

"You do you, boo." She ruffled my hair and left.

I signed up for the noon class, glanced at my email, saw something from my mom. Subject: Sutras for Peace and Positivity. The fuck? This was no time for sutras.

I threw off the covers, splashed some water on my face, and stripped off my sweatpants and T-shirt. It occurred to me that Christina must've put me in those clothes last night, which meant she had taken off my bandage dress, which meant she'd seen my thighs, ass, and stomach in their full, dimpled glory. Embarrassment mounted. Girls' night had been a terrible idea. I needed to get it together. Detox, get a job, have something to show for myself when Pooja's big, fat, fuck-you-money wedding careened into town.

Today called for a cute workout outfit. Something to lift my spirits. I rooted around my clothing piles and extracted my Jennifer Lopez for Kohl's leggings and matching sports bra.

Another knock at the door. "One sec," I called. Should I offer to buy Christina dinner? I wondered. Or maybe a case of Erewhon's oat milk? Despite my lack of funds, I operated under the logic that you could buy your way out of misdeeds. There was no wrong that Capital One couldn't help right.

"Okay, I just realized that you must've seen me naked last night," I said, flinging open the door.

Max's jaw dropped.

I braced myself against the door as heat shot up through my cheeks. "I totally thought you were someone else."

"Should I . . . I can come back?" he stammered.

He seemed more flustered than me. That was funny. Kind of sweet.

"It's fine. Just another morning, dying of embarrassment."

"I take it girls' night was a success?"

"It was a lot. Well, *I* was a lot."

"Happens to the best of us," he said. "My first month here, Adil had to drag me out of a launch party for this oxygenated vodka company.

Open bar, of course, and I figured the extra oxygen would save me, but no. Pretty sure they went under when whippits took off."

His empathy scrambled my signals. The cynic in me said that he was only acting this way because he wanted something. The human in me said maybe he's just a nice guy. Honestly, though, who was nice anymore?

"So, what's going on?" I asked.

"Oh, right—you see Gonzo's tweet?"

"Nope." I'd stopped checking Twitter in the morning, thinking maybe Riley had a point about news and cortisol levels.

"They're having an open call at noon. Thought you might want to go. They're calling it 'Fuck It, We'll Do It Live,' their way of subverting the hiring process. They have some marketing positions open, so I'm gonna check it out, if you wanna roll together."

I did a quick accounting. Noon was the last Goddess Effect class on Saturdays. If I missed it, that would be one whole day without Goddess Effect. I hadn't missed a day since I'd started. The unlimited package. I had to make use of the unlimited package. Emilia and I already had a thing going. Well, we'd *had* a thing. At this point, I had to face facts: she'd ignored my emails and my ideas.

My pride hurt from her lack of response, and in my mind, the space between Gonzo and ABN, formerly as wide as the Pacific, had narrowed. Would Gonzo be all that different than ABN? Maybe. Maybe not. If Emilia wanted me, she knew where to find me. And in the meantime, I would explore other options. Like The Goddess Effect (which, notably, did not require me to come up with some sort of vaguely professional outfit on a Saturday, in the midst of a hangover that threatened to hang curtains and take over dresser drawers if it wasn't sweated out immediately).

A tiny part of me knew that the more sensible thing to do would be to go with Max to this open call. I chose to ignore that part.

Today. Today would be the day I broached the topic of working for The Goddess Effect. Ophelia would be at the front desk. I'd run it by her, find some way to allude to the conversation I'd overheard without sounding creepy. If I wasn't going to go to this open call, I had to at least do that.

But after Retro, my ego couldn't handle someone else poking holes in my plan.

"I already have this thing going with their head of squad, Emilia," I told Max. "I don't want to overstep and mess that up, you know?"

"Right," Max said, though his face suggested otherwise. "Should I mention your name, if I see her?"

"Nah, don't worry about it." Communicate confidence, I told myself. Communicate that you know what you're doing. "Good luck, though. Let me know how it goes."

He thanked me and took his leave. Great. Just needed my credit card and I'd be out the door. I checked the card slot in my crossbody bag—nope. Nightstand? Also nope. Floor, desk, under bed—not a sign of it anywhere. A thought: Had I closed out my tab? I had to have, right? I couldn't have been that stupid?

I ran downstairs and found Christina on the couch.

"Have you seen my Capital One?"

She shook her head. "Now that I think about it—you tried to pay for the bacon-wrapped hot dogs but couldn't find it. You kept patting yourself down, like a drunk TSA agent. I should've videoed it."

"Fuck," I said. I'd left it open. Of course I'd left it open.

11

New plan: Goddess Effect, broach subject of working for Goddess Effect, retrieve credit card. Hashtag slaying Saturday. Hashtag Slayturday. Hashtag—stop thinking of hashtags, I scolded myself as I ran to the studio. Not like you're going to post about any of this. But the conventions of social media had infiltrated my offline life to the degree that my internal monologue frequently devolved into hashtags and potential captions, each one quippier, more potentially likable, than the last. Who was I doing this for? I wondered. Whose validation did I crave? Was I that desperate to be liked?

Or was it a function of being fluent in two languages, the one of screens and the one of three dimensions, like multilinguals who dreamed in one language and spoke another? Did other people deal with this, too? Did Venus?

Her social media was, unsurprisingly, utterly on brand. A recent post: an Annie Leibovitz–style, black-and-white portrait of her curled in a ball, extending one sinewy arm, as if breaking through a shell. The caption:

EVOLUTION
can come from within

can come from without
can come
from you

Cryptic, intriguing. I wondered if Venus herself even knew what she was talking about, but the point, I figured, was to position The Goddess Effect as otherworldly, on a different plane than other workouts. As much as I'd balked at Ophelia comparing it to Hinduism, now that I was committed, I saw her point. It kind of was a way of life.

Good thing Saffron's teaching this one, I thought, buzzing in. My pickled insides could not handle Venus's wrath. As I hustled up the stairs, I thought about how good I'd feel in an hour, coming back down. Virtuous, full of potential, praised, and patted on the back.

I stopped dead one step before the landing. That ass, each cheek the size of what one of my hands could grab. I'd know that ass anywhere.

"Well, look who decided to show up," said Venus, whipping around, looking down at me with a sneer.

I apologized and arranged my face into the expression of someone wounded by their own transgressions. "I overslept."

I felt her eyes on my back as I stashed my track bag in a cubby.

"What's that smell?" She sniffed sharply. "Is that . . . Don Julio?"

"Who drinks Don Julio?" Behind the front desk, Ophelia turned down her mouth. "It's not even organic."

I smelled nothing, but I had consumed about a quart of Don Julio the previous night, and given the sweat I'd worked up by running to The Goddess Effect, it was not inconceivable that Don Julio was now seeping out of my pores.

"Girls' night," I offered, sheepishly. "My housemates and I went to Retro. You know, the new club? I may have had one too many. I didn't realize nonorganic tequila was . . . bad." I didn't know that organic labels extended to tequila, frankly.

"Toxins," Venus said. "You should watch those. Both in what you put in your body and who you surround yourself with."

"We'd never let you get to that place," said Ophelia. "Also, you should drink mescal. Way better for you. Small-batch, cruelty-free."

I made a mental note: Fewer toxins. More mescal. Had Venus given me a bullet-pointed list of what to put in my body, how to be, I would've laminated it, photographed it, committed it to memory. Based on *Effected*, I'd started making a list in the Notes app on my phone. I was on the chapter in which Venus called chips "Walmart's heroin" and said that women who guzzled rosé needed to "take a hard look at what that buzz drowns out."

"Don Julio." Venus shook her head. We were still talking about this? On the other hand: this was the longest conversation Venus and I had ever had. "It's just so . . ."

"Basic," said Ophelia. "It's like Barry's Bootcamp." And then the two of them cracked up, and I faked a laugh, not wanting to be left out, even though I swore by Barry's Bootcamp for two years, back in New York. Praveen and I would go together before work and promise we weren't going to drink that night and then drink a bottle of wine, rinse, repeat.

"Well, time to atone for your sins, buttercup," Venus said. "Come, you're front and center." Would you look at this turn of events? I thought. If the cost of a delightful little nickname and the coveted position usually held by Stacy was a laugh at my expense, great. Fine. Charge me double. Never would I usurp Stacy and take her spot if we were in class together, but here was a rare occasion—opportunity, I corrected myself—that we weren't.

There were nine other women in the studio, and I exchanged smiles and nods with the ones I recognized. I felt special, walking in with Venus. I savored the way their eyes followed me as I took my place in front of her. That's right, Venus picked the brown girl. Surprise,

surprise, bitches. I crossed my legs on the mat that had already been put down and looked up at her, awaiting further instruction.

"So, yeah," she began. "I know Saffron was supposed to teach this class. But I need you today—do you hear that?—*I* need *you*, my Goddesses, because I need to be lifted up." She pounded her chest with her fist.

She started pacing. "That's the thing about this work. When you neglect it, when you don't surround yourself with the community, when you let yourself get obsessed with the corporate ladder and who's in what office and when will you get that promotion to product development head or whatever, you lose a little bit of yourself, right?" She locked eyes with the woman next to me, who nodded knowingly. She wore a faded Facebook T-shirt that ended at her rib cage.

"You get wrapped up in the machinations of a world that, more often than not, is just trying to drag you down," Venus went on. "Commit to you. Commit to this. Know that the more time you spend here, the more time you spend on yourself, the less all that bullshit out there"—she waved her arm in the direction of the street—"matters. Okay—plank pose, let's begin.

"How committed are you to realizing your fullest potential?" she asked, snaking her way around the room during a set of propeller. "Are you willing to do what other people won't? Are you willing to be an early adopter? Are you willing to let the naysayers be like, 'She crazy'? I think you are. You're here. You adopted this. I believe in you. But know that to get to the next level, you might have to shrug off those who do not serve you. You might lose some friends. You might make some enemies. You might become the best version of yourself." Fuck yeah, I thought. These were my people. Christina didn't get it. Probably, no one at the Gig got it. That was okay. I got it. Venus got it. Stacy got it.

I made a real scene during the guttural cleanse, pounded my balled-up fists through the air, yelled until my throat felt raw, squeezed my eyes shut. When I opened them, I saw Venus staring at me, nodding, mouth upturned into a hint of a smile.

We ended, as usual, in repose, which was the same as savasana, as far as I could tell, but no one at Goddess Effect called it that. Eyes closed, I did an assessment. Better, yes, I felt better. This had been the right thing to do. Girls' night had been the wrong thing to do. Again, Christina didn't get it. If I could find a way to make money doing this— doing what I *loved*, wasn't that the goal?—I would be content. Golden.

I practiced an opening line in my head.

By the time I got up from my mat, Venus had left the room. I cleaned up my area and drifted over to the front desk for a lavender-eucalyptus towel. As usual, Ophelia was at her post, fiddling with her phone. I took extra long, slinging the towel around my neck, dabbing here and there, waiting for the right moment, trying to catch her eye.

"So, I've been meaning to ask," I began. "The other day, I heard—"

"Hey, so, what do you do, by the way?" she interrupted, as if only now acknowledging my presence. But that was fine. We could broach the topic this way. Reroute, like Waze.

"Journalism. I used to work at ABN, in New York." Her blank stare made me add, "I think it's channel seven here."

"Oh, I don't do TV."

"Right? But I was actually thinking—"

"Would you ever, like, consider doing something for us?"

Okay, she'd interrupted me again, but I couldn't take it personally, Ophelia seemed like the type of woman who'd never even had to wait at Starbucks, a blithe pixie dream girl for whom doors opened and conversations pivoted on a whim, and big picture—was I about to be appointed The Goddess Effect's first vice president of brand strategy? Had I actually managed to manifest something I wanted?

"Um, yeah," I said.

"It's about our next location." Eastside, for sure, but she and Venus were debating between Los Feliz, Silver Lake, and Echo Park. "All sort of grungy but different types of grungy. We need to figure out a block that's right for us, where we'll fit in but also stand out, you know? Would you be down to scope the neighborhoods, feel out the vibe, do some research? Journalists do research, right?"

"All the time," I said.

"And maybe get to know the locals, too, ask where they're working out? Take a week and see what you find. I'll block out time on V's calendar for us to discuss."

"Sure," I chirped, internally cartwheeling. If I'd be presenting my findings for Venus, that meant this had to be an unequivocable, cash-money *job*, right?

She gave me a doe-eyed look of gratitude. "You're a lifesaver, Anita."

Part of me wanted to leave it at that, to hit the Eastside and put together the most smashing deck that she and Venus had ever seen. Part of me wanted to know what I'd be paid, because this was, after all, work, and I hadn't worked for free since that Central Park SummerStage gig when I was eighteen, when I thought, for one brief, glorious minute, that I had a chance with John Legend. (I brought him a water bottle. He said, "Thanks." None of the other stars said "thanks.")

"One thing," I ventured. "How much were you thinking for this?"

"How much?" Her smile vanished.

"Like, compensation-wise?"

She frowned. "Oh, we don't have budget for that. I just figured, you're so committed, you'd *want* to help the brand—"

"I do, of course, but, you know, three neighborhoods, interviewing people, putting together a deck—"

"Just a pro/con list is fine," she said. "But how about this: we'll extend your heaven-sent package another month, so you'll get four months for the price of three. Pretty sweet deal, if you ask me."

What could I say? What else did I have to do? What if this was the only time this particular door would open? A lot of startups tried out employees before officially bringing them on—hell, I'd told my mother that's what Gonzo was doing with me. If I walked away now, I'd be saying goodbye to any future opportunity of working for The Goddess Effect. Four months for the price of three *was* a deal, when you thought about it. This was like an internship. For an adult. Like that Nancy Meyers movie with Robert De Niro. If it was good enough for Bobby, it was good enough for me.

"For sure," I said. "Thanks so much, Ophelia."

12

Outside, I mapped the distance to Retro. About a mile. Google said it didn't open for a few hours, but a place like that would have someone there long before, mopping, wiping down surfaces, getting it set up. The thought of going later and seeing those bouncers and that bartender again made me shudder. Worst case, I'd get in some extra steps.

On the walk over, I thought about Ophelia's offer. My job, I corrected myself. What Ophelia offered was a job, even if there wasn't an hourly rate attached to it. I had to stop thinking about my worth in such concrete, immigrant, dollars-and-cents terms. I had the beta run. I had my Capital One. I had to take a chance on myself, invest in my potential. Another Instagram aphorism: "Your paycheck ≠ your purpose."

Still, I felt uneasy. Like when you agree to go to your friend's improv show, and then the day comes and you show up and discover that it's three hours long and there's a two-drink minimum and all the drinks are terrible yet somehow cost fifteen dollars.

Stop fixating on money, I told myself. Think about the possibilities. Think about blowing Venus and Ophelia's socks off. Think about how Ophelia asked *you*, of all people. She must see something special in you, how Venus put you front and center, how, slowly but surely, LA is opening up to you, like some tropical flower unfurling in the sunlight. I remembered a scene from *Sex and the City*, when the woman from *Murphy Brown* tells Carrie that you can have it all, but only if you stop expecting your life to look like how you thought it would. So what if my first gig with The Goddess Effect was unpaid? So what if it didn't come with some fancy title? It could lead to more. I had to let go of my past expectations, lean into the unknown.

Was it bad that my guiding lights were *Sex and the City* and Instagram?

The parking lot of Retro was barren save for two parked cars, a Honda and a Jeep without a roof. That had to mean someone was inside. I marched into the Victorian house, which, in the broad light of day, looked like a brothel from some lesser *CSI*. Gross, the places where we spend our time and money after dark.

"Hello?" I called out, walking down the long hall to the dance floor.

"Tequila soda!" he bellowed, like it was my name.

Seriously? The bartender from last night? Just my luck. I flipped my head upside down and raked my hair into a high, tight ponytail, the ponytail of a capable woman, a prosecutor or surgeon or something that I was not.

"Hi," I said, matter-of-factly, approaching the bar. "I left my card here last night."

"You sure?" He smirked. He was peeling lemons.

"Given that you were the last person I gave it to, I'm positive."

He leaned over the bar and looked me up and down. I caught a whiff of his cologne. Something musky and brash.

"What are you doing?" I asked.

"Just wanted to see if you had another generous offering for me."

I had to laugh. "I'm sorry, I'm not usually like that."

"Like what?"

"Like an obnoxious, drunk mess who throws her Spanx at strangers and leaves her card at the bar," I said. "What, do I need to beg for forgiveness? You should be thrilled. I'm sure you slapped a 20 percent tip on that thing before closing it out."

"Oh, come on, it's not about the money, I became a bartender because I value human connection."

"Right, and I read *Playboy* for the articles."

"You read *Playboy*?"

"No I don't *read Playboy*. Is that even a magazine anymore? It's a thing people say." My exasperation was fake. I was enjoying this.

"Ooookayy, if you say so," he said, and went to the other end of the bar to thumb through a stack of cards. "What's your name?" he asked. I told him. He came back with my card—I recognized the cheap, plastic rendering of *Starry Night*—and a folded-up receipt.

"Thank you," I said, stuffing them into the side pocket of my leggings. I'd assess the damage later.

"Anytime, playgirl." He laughed. "Wait, wasn't that also a magazine, or something?"

"Google it!" I turned and started walking. "Maybe they're hiring." I felt brazen and carefree. I was never going to see this guy again.

"Heads up."

I turned and managed to catch my Spanx before they hit me in the face. "And the crowd goes wild," he hollered, bursting into applause. Blushing, beaming, I got the hell out of there.

Back at the Gig, back in my room, I uncrumpled the receipt: $238. Jesus Christ, but what's done is done, I told myself. Fine. You went out with a bang. You're not drinking for the foreseeable future, so that was it, your last hurrah. I envied people with self-control, with the ability to stop after one drink, maybe two. People like Constance, people like Christina, people who knew how to rein themselves in before they went off the rails. People who didn't *want* to go off the rails, who felt no need to escape. They probably had so much money in their bank accounts. Crazy-high credit limits and all this self-worth. They were probably oozing with it.

I was about to throw out the receipt when I saw something scrawled on the opposite side. *Wanna play?* then a phone number. Wait, what? Was this the bartender? He'd written a name, Jared. I quickly googled "Retro Jared." Yep, that was him, shaking a shaker, biceps bulging. Of course there were a variety of posed, stylized shots of him. Of course he was all over Retro's social media feeds. He was hot—it made sense. So, he *was* flirting with me? It wasn't out of the realm of possibility; I *was* flirting with him. I bit my thumbnail. I needed advice.

In the living room, I found Riley starfished on the shag carpet, staring up at the ceiling. She propped herself up on her elbows. "Wanna join me? I'm about to do a ball-of-yarn visualization."

"Um, maybe, actually," I surprised myself by saying. I remembered that sutras email my mom had sent that I had yet to open. It dawned on me that my mom and Riley would probably get along, would bond over meditation rituals or preferred brands of turmeric or something. "Can I ask you something real quick?" I handed her the receipt. "What do you think it means?"

"Duh, he wants you."

"You think?" Men like Jared were not usually into women like me. I attracted lecherous older coworkers and Indian mama's boys who said they were five ten but were really five six, never six-foot-something guys with tattoos and biceps and art-directed photographs of themselves all over the internet.

"Why wouldn't he just ask me out directly?"

"Because this is so much cooler. It's old-school. It's *retro*. Who writes on receipts anymore? Who even *gets* receipts anymore?"

"You think I should text him?"

She shrugged dramatically. "I mean, you could stare at those numbers and wait for him to divine himself into your phone. Or, yeah, you could text him. Why not?"

She had a point. What was the harm?

Hey playboy, I typed, it's tequila soda. What's up?

***

Riley made me put my phone under a tiger-embroidered throw pillow while we did the ball-of-yarn visualization. I had to hand it to her: she had the right voice for her line of work, sonorous and warm. I gave myself over to it, imagined finding the tip of the string on a fuzzy ball of tie-dyed angora, unspooling my pent-up tension as the yarn morphed from cream to lilac to rose and back again. A tingling sort of serenity washed over me. I might've fallen asleep.

"Wow," I said, sitting up. "You're good."

She shrugged like she knew. I reached for my phone. One visualization cannot an addiction break. "He texted."

"Let me see?"

I handed her my phone.

Jared: Suuuuuuup

She started typing. "Let me see it before you send it," I pleaded.

"Too late." She handed my phone back. She had sent five eggplant emoji followed by five shooting-star emoji.

"What the fuck, Riley?!"

"Oh, come on, 'suuuuuuup' doesn't deserve a real response. And eggplant doesn't just mean dick anymore. Whisper says it also signifies that you're planting meaning and substance into the garden of your life."

I stared at my phone. She had a point about "suuuuuuup." I had wanted to formulate a reply that was equal portions witty, sexy, charming, and off the cuff, but perhaps an abbreviated greeting with a bunch of extra vowels did not warrant that. Also, I wasn't trying to marry this guy. I was doing this for fun, in theory. Theoretical fun. Maybe eggplants and shooting stars communicated fun.

Gray bubbles, then buzzes. What was up, it turned out, was that Jared's buddy's ceviche spot was having a soft opening that night. Did

I want to come? I didn't have other plans. I was free. It was free. I liked free food. Especially free food that was fancy and arguably healthy.

It occurred to me that ceviche spots generally served cocktails. I could have *one*, sip it slowly. Especially if it was free.

With Jared's invitation, the voice of reason telling me to detox had changed its tune. I must've done *something* right if this guy was into me.

Riley and Miguel insisted on helping me get ready. Given my performance at Retro, I figured that Riley considered me a charity case in the departments of style and conducting oneself, a project she could work on. I didn't necessarily mind.

"Are you, like, sponsored by Target?" Miguel asked, pawing through my clothes. "Because if you're sponsored by Target, we should be getting our cleaning supplies from there instead of Amazon."

"They have some cute stuff," I protested. "And I have tons of Forever 21. That wrap dress is a dead ringer for DVF."

"Don't insult Diane like that," Miguel said, plucking the fabric and letting it go.

Riley stood there, looking at me, looking at the closet, scrunching up her face. After a moment, she clapped her hands together. "I've got it. I'll be back. One sec."

A few minutes later, I was in a bodysuit and silk duster that belonged to Riley and my own wide-legged, factory-distressed jeans (Target for the win). She made me sit in front of the mirror while she used a cone-shaped wand to engineer some "beachy waves" into my hair, which I thoroughly resisted at first. The notion of any kind of waves filled me with panic, but as she worked her way around my head, I had to admit, I liked the effect. Whimsical. Effortless (despite the not insignificant amount of effort going into creating the waves). Livelier than the pin-straight sheet that I had come to think of as my armor.

She also lent me a pair of blocky sandals. "You're really okay with me borrowing all of this?" I asked, meeting Riley's eye in the mirror.

"Totally. It's all last-season Cult Gaia. Can't wear it to work. Whisper said we're supposed to be billboards of the affluence that comes from a regular meditation practice, and she got us all a crazy Net-a-Porter discount, so."

She patted body shimmer on my collarbones and swiped highlighter on my cheeks. "One last thing," she said, picking up a set of false eyelashes.

"No," I said. Then I said it five more times. I was grateful for the intervention—being fussed over and borrowing clothes I could not afford were two of my favorite things—but I also wanted to feel like myself, not like Influencer Barbie. False eyelashes would put me firmly in the territory of Influencer Barbie.

Riley sighed. "Can I at least give you this?" She lifted a pendant on a long gold chain off her neck and put it around mine. "It's orange carnelian. Opens up the sacral chakra. Thank me later."

13

A cough woke me up. Water. I needed water. The inside of my mouth felt like a loofah. One of those beige ones made of natural sea sponge that cost twenty-nine dollars.

I reached for the S'well that I kept, religiously, on my nightstand. Hold on. This wasn't my nightstand. I turned to my left: Jared, facedown, snoring. I lifted up the duvet—*naked* Jared, facedown, snoring. I had on Riley's bodysuit but nothing else, and it wasn't snapped at the bottom. *Oh,* I remembered. That had happened. A smile bloomed. Fuck yeah, that had happened.

It all came back: the plates of ceviche, dotted with cilantro oil and paper-thin slices of serrano pepper, the pisco sours, the tequila shots— "for my playgirl," he told his buddy, wrapping his arm around my waist, pulling me closer to his side, doing enough right things with his body and demeanor and pheromones that I did not mind that the words that came out of his mouth often did not make sense. (Did he know what *Playgirl* was? Did I care?)

My resolve not to get drunk melted like an ice cube in the sun. Or an ice cube in a pisco sour, of which I had three. The resolution that had been so dire and necessary earlier in the day seemed, given all the evidence at hand, stuck-up and lame. Virtue wasn't going to keep me warm at night.

At some point, he intertwined his hand in mine and led me down the street to another place owned by another buddy of his, a sustainable pharmacy by day, speakeasy by night. The drinks came in beakers; he ordered us mescal negronis. Steely Dan played on the stereo, and he alternated between playing air guitar and tapping his fingertips on my collarbones, which glinted under the low lights. I took and posted selfies. (Us-ies? Stories, not Feed.) I tried to make conversation. I asked where he was from and what he studied, and immediately cursed myself for sounding like my mom. I think he said "San Diego" and "babes like you," and then he leaned in and planted his lips on mine, and I don't remember what we talked about, or if we really talked all that much after that.

He lived in a condo building half a block from the sustainable pharmacy/speakeasy. Convenient indeed. I wanted to sit back and revel in every detail I could remember of the rest of the night—making out in the elevator, stumbling through his door, me flinging off my jeans, him brazenly tearing my lace thong (Amazon Essentials, not much of a loss)—but 9:00 a.m. was fast approaching and I wasn't going to stand up Stacy two days in a row.

I ordered an Uber, chugged the glass of water next to the alarm clock on the nightstand—he owned an alarm clock, a nightstand, and glassware, all good signs—found my clothes, and blazed out the door. Emilio awaited in a Honda Civic.

"How are you?" he asked as I got in.

"Great," I replied. "Really, really great."

***

In the car, I patted myself on the back. Thoroughly. What an upgrade from Neil. Neil who didn't like sex. Neil who refused to do it at his parents' house on Long Island, where we spent so many weekends, him golfing with his dad, me making palak paneer with his mom. I didn't even like palak paneer.

He'd gone to college with Pooja's fiancé, and we'd met, at an East Village bar crawl, when we were twenty-three and new to New York. In many ways, it was an easy relationship: we had the same friends, we both worked a lot, we both liked to drink. He worked in finance. I knew, if we got married, that we'd never have to worry about money. He said so often enough.

But I couldn't get over the sex part of it. *Sex and the City*, after all, was basically my Bible, my sequined, cosmo-soaked guide to life. I had to believe some women really had it like that. Maybe only white women. Maybe Indian women were destined to lives of lackluster sex. Maybe the Kama Sutra was meant to be ironic. Sex was the one topic that Pooja and I never talked about. My mom changed the channel anytime a Victoria's Secret commercial came on.

The few times I brought it up, he got defensive and said, "What do you want me to do, treat you like a whore?" Well, yeah, actually, I wanted to say. But I didn't. I figured no relationship was perfect. How shallow was I, to be so fixated on the physical? Could I not see the bigger picture?

We looked great in photos. He had an Ivy League degree. I never had to explain what Diwali was, or why I had so many aunties and uncles to whom I was not actually related. He knew about 401(k)s and stocks. I did not. I got a Hitachi Magic Wand, told myself to suck it up.

It finally ate away at me to the degree that I cheated on him with a blogger for a right-wing website at the Renaissance in Detroit. We were the last ones at the hotel bar; this was during my stint covering the North Dakota governor. He made this show of walking me to my room, and by that point, it was obvious where the night was going. I kept waiting to feel scandalized, for that moment in which the transgression would be too much to handle. Maybe when I hovered my keycard over the sensor, I'd suddenly turn around, brace myself against the door, and say, "Connor, I'm sorry, I can't. I hope you understand." Then I'd pour myself a drink from the minibar and sit in the hideous side chair by the window, stare forlornly at the parking lot, and imagine what might have been.

That moment never came.

The sex was whatever. We were drunk. I barely remembered it in the morning. What stuck with me was the feeling of being wanted, and that mattered more than anything. With Neil, I always felt like I was doing something wrong, like I wasn't living up to the vision of the subservient Indian girl he had imagined marrying. Or maybe I just wanted to know what I was capable of, and once I realized that I could cheat on a guy I'd been with for years and not feel a hint of remorse, I knew I had to end it.

I wasn't strong enough to tell him why. He got mad and told me I was crazy and selfish, which was not untrue.

My dad died a few weeks after we broke up. Neil came to the funeral, even though we weren't speaking. Pooja must've told him. In a moment of weakness, I leaned my head on his shoulder and forced some tears onto his Brooks Brothers suit; he let me stay there for a minute before gently, but decisively, pushing me away. I got the message: "Still hate you. Only here out of respect."

What comforted me, after that half-hearted Hail Mary: the fact that my dad never really liked him. He thought Neil was a drone, a mama's boy, a classic example of a first-generation kid bred to care about grades and money but nothing else, who lacks taste and only reads if he thinks there's going to be a test. My dad never said this, explicitly, but I could tell. "Not much to him, is there?" he observed, the first time I brought Neil home. I'd defended him at the time—which, looking back, was really an attempt to defend my own judgment—but, it turned out, my dad had been right. I took some solace in that.

Neil started dating Kirtee, a family friend from the same part of Long Island, soon after. I had, from time to time, felt that tug of regret, looking at her photos, thinking about how it could've been me in couture Indian bridal, on the Brooklyn Bridge, if only I'd been happy with what I had.

But not after Jared. Not in that Uber. Not after finally having realized that a Samantha Jones sex life was my God-given right. (Well, Samantha would've skipped the ceviche and cocktails, but still.)

I wondered if The Goddess Effect had anything to do with it, if it had made me more confident, more alluring not only in a physical way but also in the way of a woman who sees what she wants and goes after it.

"Keep the trip going," I told Emilio, as he pulled up in front of the Gig. "I'll be right back."

Water, brush teeth, change, mirror—glowing, I was glowing—more water, back in Uber. I clocked four minutes and twenty-three seconds. That had to be some kind of record. Upon arrival, I thanked Emilio profusely and skipped up the stairs. Ophelia had her feet kicked up on the front desk; Stacy was standing by the cubbies, looking at her phone, shaking her head.

"It's just so unfair. It's unconscionable, is what it is." She showed me her screen, a news story about a study that found that women of color in the workforce made 67 percent less, on average, than white men in the same positions. "How do you deal with this?" I shrugged, sheepishly. For once, money was the last thing on my mind.

"Wait a minute," she said, stepping back and assessing me anew. "Something's different. Not your hair—well, it is your hair, I like it like this, Bali surfer girl vibes—but something else." She tapped my collarbone, still glimmering from the body shimmer.

"I may or may not have slept in my own bed last night," I said, letting the smile playing at the corners of my mouth take full rein of my face. She squealed and insisted I tell her everything. I started to but stopped when we heard, from the back room, a snarl unmistakably belonging to Venus: "Belly up? Is that some kind of pathetic joke about planks? We agreed on exclusive distribution. *Exclusive.*" Stacy and I exchanged a "WTF was that about" look, then Venus stormed past us, into the studio, and we realized that we'd better grab spots.

"You'll have to tell me the rest after," she said. "Oh, and I have a surprise."

14

Venus's spiel that morning focused on trauma, naysayers, and science deniers. "There are some people who don't want you to progress to the most advanced form of yourself, who don't want you to upgrade, who want you to keep the same operating system that you were born with—fuck 'em. Download the upgrade. Run faster. Run stronger." We were doing high knees.

Yes, I thought, silently cursing Neil, ABN, even Gonzo. Who needed them, when I was forging my own path, carving out a lane in the world of wellness, just like Venus? My plan, for the rest of the day, was to research places to scope out on the Eastside, places where I might meet people who'd help me home in on the precise right location for The Goddess Effect's second studio. I wondered if Venus had asked Ophelia to solicit my help. Surely, that decision would've come from the top. I felt a little rush knowing that people I admired had talked about me, had said nice things.

During a set of skaters, Venus bounded into a beam of sun, which glinted off the little gold hoops in her ears. Were those new? They reminded me of the little gold hoops my mom had bought for me in Bangalore, when I was ten. Had I brought them with me?

After class, Stacy and I chugged water by the cubbies. She asked if I thought Jared was boyfriend material.

"I mean," I began. Doesn't every woman picture walking down the aisle with someone after a great fuck? Even an average fuck? Not that I'd had that many fucks in general, or any as good as Jared. Come to think of it, given that I had been pretty drunk, I couldn't say whether it was the fuck that was great or the fact that such an objectively hot guy picked me *to* fuck, made me *feel* great.

"Who knows? I need to figure out my life before I think about a relationship." That seemed like the feminist thing to say.

"Right, you have that Gonzo meeting soon, yeah?"

Stacy kept asking about Gonzo. I kept telling her that my HR meeting had been postponed for one reason or another, cursing myself, every time, for having lied about it to begin with. Why did she care so much? Nice of her to be so thoughtful, but still. For reasons I could not put my finger on, I didn't want to tell her about my job with The Goddess Effect. Not yet. Maybe after my sit-down with Venus, once it was more official.

"What was that thing that Venus said during plank jacks?" I asked, wanting to divert her attention. "Something about removing what's inside you to be born anew?"

"She's been saying stuff like that a lot lately," Stacy said. "I think she means you need to let go of what doesn't serve you, banish past traumas, that sort of thing."

"Mm," I said, taking another sip of water. Something about that particular soliloquy stood out. I remembered another line: "What if a piece of you could help someone else? Could help your fellow Goddesses?" Maybe she meant *piece* as in *peace* as in *compassion*. Even if I had the nerve to ask her about it, she'd vanished as usual into the back room after class. If you listened closely enough, you could hear her groan or curse every so often; the source of her frustration remained unclear. Clearly, she was stressed. Clearly, she needed me to come on board and help.

"She really knows what to say to make you work harder," Stacy went on. "This one time, I came in hungover. Colt had had a brokers' open house for this fifty-million-dollar mansion in the hills, and I'd had, like, eighteen glasses of Veuve. Did you know that they donate 1 percent of their profits to this period charity in Africa? Honestly, I think Ruinart tastes better, but I don't see *them* making sure that girls in Mozambique can continue going to school—anyway. I was just phoning in my jump squats, I didn't even jump for half the set, and she called me out, from the other side of the room: 'What, we don't get your best effort, Stacy? You only bring it for the brokers' opens? Stop slacking. Stop denying yourself. Stop cheating your way through. Show up. Your body showed up. Make your *mind* show up. Make your *heart* show up.' I nearly burst through the ceiling, I was jumping so hard after that."

"Insane," I said. Part of me really did wonder how Venus did it—it couldn't possibly be a coincidence. Part of me was jealous that Stacy had experienced this super specific brand of motivation while I had not. When would Venus drill into me?

"Shit, I didn't realize the time," Stacy said, looking at her phone. "I've gotta run, but wait, your surprise—come down to the car with me?"

***

From the trunk of her burgundy Porsche Panamera, she pulled out an enormous Gucci shopping bag. "What the," I heard myself say. Was she giving me a brand-new version of the snake-embossed tote she used as a gym bag? I couldn't accept it. It was too much. It cost $2,300; I'd looked it up online. Or I could accept it and sell it on Poshmark? Or I could accept it and use it, treat it like a child, rub it down with oil every night—

"Ta-da!" she said, handing me the shopping bag. It was filled to the top with Lululemon and similar-looking athletic apparel that appeared to have been worn before.

"Don't take this the wrong way," she was saying, "but I noticed that you sometimes repeat leggings and sports bras, and while the ones with the glitter stripe down the side"—Jennifer Lopez for Kohl's—"are *super* cute, maybe you'd like more options. I just ordered the entire new Ivy Park line and told myself that I could only do that if I gave away some of what I already had."

While I owned a lot of leggings, I only had three that didn't sag and weren't ripping at the seams or the crotch or were in some other way embarrassing. None were as nice as these. Besides Lululemon, there was Alo, Koral, Koio, other brands I'd never heard of, and a bunch of sports bras and tops. It wasn't a handbag that cost more than the average monthly mortgage, and it was mildly mortifying that she noticed I repeated workout outfits and felt the need to do something about it, but hell if I wasn't going to accept her offer. I ran my hand over a pair of orchid Alos. As soft as a baby's cheek.

"Thanks, Stacy, that's really kind of you."

She beamed. "And one more thing." She reached into the trunk again and unfurled a black garment bag. "Because you can't wear Lulu to that big Gonzo meeting." She unzipped the bag, revealing a black double-breasted leather blazer with shoulder pads and shiny silver buttons. "It's Veronica Beard," she said, matter-of-factly. "Last season, doesn't fit me, never fit me, actually, and I waited too long to return it. I was telling Colt, I want to get this into the hands of someone who needs it, and then I realized, Anita—Anita needs this!"

I ran my hands down the front of the blazer. The leather felt sumptuous and rich. It gleamed in the sunlight. "It's gorgeous, but"—I stopped myself before saying that I had no place to wear it—"what . . . would I even wear with it?"

"These, silly!" She thrust open the jacket to reveal a pair of matching, boxy leather shorts. "It's a suit. Well, it's a blazer and culottes, close enough. No one wears suits anymore, anyway."

I tried to imagine showing up anywhere in this outfit. What statement would it make? I want to be an extra in a Rihanna video? A Rihanna video set in an office tower, where she storms in with a bunch of bad, blazer-and-culotte-wearing bitches, takes the elevator to the top floor, ambushes the corner office, and shoves the old white dude behind the mahogany desk out the window?

"Just try it," Stacy said. "I promise, once you put it on, you won't take it off."

***

It was easier to just accept the outfit than to tell her that there wasn't a Gonzo meeting, that there would probably never be a Gonzo meeting. I'd just keep it in my closet until she stopped asking about Gonzo or I grew a pair, whichever came first. She insisted on giving me a ride home, said it was on her way, and I finally let her, mostly because walking with all that clothing would be (a) difficult and (b) a surefire way to get mugged.

"So this is the Gig," she said dreamily, pulling up in front of the house. "You'll have to give me a tour sometime. It sounds so cool."

"It probably looks like a refugee center compared to a fifty-million-dollar house in the hills."

"I mean, I'd *die* for a refugee center," she said. "You wouldn't believe how boring some of Colt's places are. Once you've seen one infinity pool, you've seen them all."

Highly doubtful, but I kept that to myself and thanked her for the clothes and the ride. "This is a sick car, by the way." The interior leather was the color of peanut butter. I wanted to lick it.

"It's a hybrid," she said. "I would've been fine with a Prius, but Colt, being Colt, insisted I get a Porsche. We compromised on the Panamera, it's not 100 percent electric, but it's something. At least it's in the right direction. I was driving a G wagon before—do you know how bad those are for the environment? The gas mileage? I saw this documentary about fossil fuels, and I could barely look myself in the mirror after that."

Stacy cared about fossil fuels? I hadn't seen that coming. Her habit of making excessively woke offhand comments struck me as both weird and endearing. If I knew her better, I might've shaken her and said, "Stace, it's just me, you don't have to convince me that you're a good person." She'd been good in my book from day one.

But as it was, I wondered what else lurked beneath her polished exterior, what she thought about in her darker moments. Although maybe she didn't have darker moments. Maybe she just cruised around town bestowing ninety-eight-dollar leggings on the needy, the Athleisure Fairy.

We air-kissed goodbye, and I hauled my bags into the house.

"Who was *that*?" asked Max. He was standing by the door, watching Stacy drive away.

"Stacy Gibson. We go to Goddess Effect together."

"Colt Gibson's wife?"

"You know him?" I went to the kitchen to make a smoothie.

"Sort of," he said, following me. "He's infamous in LA real estate. Tried to be a movie producer, but all of his movies flopped so he switched to producing houses. It used to be all gargantuan McMansions, but he's from Dallas, so I guess you can't blame him. Build what you know, right? Now his style is anything that looks like it could be on *Million Dollar Listing*—all clean lines and concrete."

"Mm," I said, stirring a jar of almond butter, half listening.

"He's worth a hundred million dollars, supposedly," Max was saying. "Big Republican donor. By the way, that Gonzo open call was dope. Hundreds of people. I met Emilia."

"Oh?" I pretended to be really interested in the ingredients label of a canister of hemp protein powder. Jealousy bloomed within me like one of those sped-up videos of growing mold.

108

"Yeah, she seemed really into some of my ideas for how to market this mobile-only news app they're about to launch, GonzoDrip. She's cool. Super friendly."

"Super friendly." Emilia had once been super friendly with me, too. Now she was, what? How do you describe someone who does not respond to a dozen emails? Aggressively indifferent? Borderline hostile?

"How does an open call work, anyway?" I asked.

"It's like speed dating, except you only get to 'date' three people from Gonzo, and they get to date, like, whoever they want. But this director of strategic marketing gig sounds promising, and I'm glad I'm not just another name in their inbox now."

"Nice," I said, throwing a bunch of strawberries into the blender. I pressed the pulse button and Max sauntered off, leaving me to watch the ingredients whirl into a gray-pink sludge.

Doubt roiled inside me. Should I have gone to that open call after all? Had Emilia even gotten my emails? Did they all go to spam?

But then, I had this gig for Goddess Effect. While they were not able to pay me in cash money at the moment, surely, if I went above and beyond, exceeded their expectations, they'd find room in their budget to hire me. I could help with their social media, influencer outreach, community outreach—really, the sky was the limit. What could be more fulfilling than exposing new people to this method, the way Stacy had done for me?

15

I spent most of the week Ubering out to the Eastside, indulging in the performance of a Person with a Job to Do, charging a grand total of $356.78 to my Capital One. I figured it was okay, because it was an investment in my future, kind of like "dress for the job you want, not the job you have."

While Ophelia had said that a pro/con list would suffice, given my intention to blow her and Venus's minds, I asked Christina to show me how to make a deck.

"You're doing this for who?"

I told her.

"They paying you?"

I told her.

"Please don't come crying to me when they grind you up and put you in a turmeric latte."

"If they did that, I wouldn't be able to cry, now would I?"

As a thank-you, I brought her a bagel sandwich from this place in Silver Lake that supposedly made better bagels than all of New York. I got one, too, and I convinced myself that it was the best bagel I'd ever had, because if it wasn't, and I had still waited in line for an hour to get it, I wouldn't be able to live with myself.

My reconnaissance led me to several conclusions: the Eastside was essentially the same as Venice, minus the tourists and ocean breeze. Los Feliz was bougier than Silver Lake, which was bougier than Echo Park. All LA coffee shops served oat milk. This was probably the most vegan-friendly city in the world, including the many cities in India where being vegan wasn't notable because everyone just was.

Most importantly: Silver Lake was the ideal location for The Goddess Effect 2.0. Specifically, 4120 Santa Monica Boulevard, a ground-floor retail space next to a brand-new Erewhon and around the corner from an Intelligentsia coffee shop. I camped out in front of both, eavesdropping on the conversations of strangers and occasionally forcing myself to butt in. I felt like a proselytizer, asking every third person in athleisure whether they'd heard of The Goddess Effect and explaining the method to the roughly 50 percent who had not. (My default: "It's not fitness, it's a way of life." I only realized afterward that the reason that phrase came so readily to mind was because I'd seen a pithier version of it on an Equinox billboard.)

"It sounds like calisthenics but . . . annoying," said a woman in Birkenstocks.

"Can't you do the same stuff at home, on your own?" asked a guy in Erewhon sweats.

I'd cite Venus's uncanny ability to make you work harder, face your innermost demons, strengthen yourself from the inside out, and when that didn't work, I'd mention that she'd recently been named to *Fortune*'s Most Powerful Women list and was one of *Forbes'* Ones to Watch. (Often, the names of these publications drew blank stares.) But removed from the idyll of the studio—the ceramic diffuser, the birchwood benches, all the soothing tones of white—I had to ask myself the same thing. What made The Goddess Effect special? Beyond giving me something to do and my compulsion to squeeze all that I could out of the heaven-sent deal, like a juicy wedge of lime, why did I keep going?

I did feel stronger. I had made a new friend. I had not magically transmogrified into a rich white woman, but I knew that wasn't going to happen, certainly not overnight. It was a process. It took time to see results. I believed in it. Jared—there was an example of something The Goddess Effect brought me that I might not have been able to get on my own.

Immediately after that thought came another: if anything "brought me" Jared, it was Riley. Or my abandoned Capital One. But I pushed those rationales aside and chose to believe in the magic of The Goddess Effect. I treated it like religion, wary that if I poked too many holes in it, it wouldn't hold together. I needed The Goddess Effect to stay intact, to anchor me to LA, to give my days shape and purpose.

All told, the reconnaissance wasn't half bad. It gave me something to do (besides going to class). It gave me a distraction from wondering when Jared would text me, or if I should text him, what the absence of a text from him meant, how take-charge a modern Samantha Jones ought to be, etc.

At one point, I thought I saw Praveen come out of Intelligentsia and my heart seized. I jumped behind a traffic sign. It wasn't him, of course, but it did make me think. How would I explain my new "job" to my old work husband? To all the people from my past who would be at Pooja's wedding? To my mom, who still thought the reason I could never FaceTime for more than five minutes was because I was so busy with my Gonzo trial run?

Exactly twelve women said they'd be interested in checking it out. Some asked if I had a card. I gave them my social media handle and said The Goddess Effect didn't believe in confining the function of its team members to a finite piece of paper.

There was one off-putting interaction with a woman who had an evil eye tattoo on the nape of her neck and a yoga mat under her arm.

"That place is sick," she said, disgusted.

Confused, I asked what she meant.

113

"Oh, they haven't asked you yet, huh? If you're out here shilling for them, they will soon enough."

That was hard to shake for a variety of reasons, mostly jealousy over not knowing whatever it was that evil eye tattoo knew. Had she been an instructor? What had she been asked that I had not? She'd crossed the street, and I was too stunned to call after her. But when nothing like that happened again, I filed it away as a fluke. Maybe she was unhinged. Maybe she mixed up The Goddess Effect with something else. Who knew?

***

On Friday, I Ubered straight from Silver Lake to meet Stacy for Saffron's 4:00 p.m. She had missed Friday afternoon classes the past couple weeks on account of dinners and charity events. But the day before, she texted:

Stacy: Hiiiiii! I'm signed up for 4pm 😘

Stacy: Wanna come over to my place after? Just us, Colt's out of town.

Did I!

I wondered where Stacy lived. I wondered if I should bring a change of clothes. But it seemed weird to show up to someone's house for the first time with a duffel bag and a toiletry kit, like you were sleeping over. Don't get your hopes up, I told myself. You're probably just going to get Postmates and eat by the TV.

"I know," Saffron said, as she led us through a series of jump squats that lasted as long as Massive Attack's "Teardrop" (five minutes and thirty-one seconds). "I know your butt hurts. I know you feel that twinge of pain where your legs meet your hips, the cradle of your essence, your womanly power, but know this, know it at your core, that you are doing the work that needs to be done to unfurl the full intensity of the strength within those bones, and we need your bones to be strong, to be so full of collagen that they make you glow from the inside out, that they make *all* of us glow, simply by knowing you, by being in your presence, by being part of this community."

Interesting, I thought. Was that how collagen worked? If I did enough jump squats, would I glow to the degree that I'd be, like, radioactive?

After repose, I saw that Venus had joined Saffron at the front of the room. "I have an announcement," she said, smiling coyly, "and I wanted to tell you all—the hardest of the hard-core, look at you, Friday afternoon, you could be anywhere, but you're here—before the email goes out."

We sat, rapt.

"We've been thinking about how we can deepen your experience," she went on. "For most of you, The Goddess Effect is just a break in your day. But what if . . ."

Ophelia strode in and joined Venus and Saffron at the front of the room.

"What if The Goddess Effect was all day?" Ophelia said.

"For four days," Saffron said.

"What if"—Venus paused for effect—"we did a getaway?"

Stacy and I exchanged a look. Excited murmurs rose up across the room.

"Right here, right now, we're announcing the first-ever Goddess Effect retreat," Venus said, "four days and three nights of everything you know and love about this method, but turned up to a thousand. Full immersion. We will work together, we will dine together, we will drink together—yes, I said *drink*, there *will* be drinking on this retreat." More anticipatory gurgles from the floor. "And we will grow together. It will be an experience unlike any other. If you are serious about your practice, and if you are serious about expanding your horizons, your definition of who you can be, this is an absolute must. It's mandatory. I'm biased, obviously." She chuckled. "But the change we're going to create in Ojai"—she put a hand over her heart and swept her gaze over all of us below—"it's going to be epic. Magical. Momentous."

"And it's limited," said Saffron. "First come, first served."

"Check your inbox," Ophelia said. The three of them glided out of the room.

"We *have* to go," Stacy said, turning to me.

"I mean, yeah!" I said, entirely unsure. How much would this thing cost? Could I put it on my Capital One?

The email arrived during the drive to Stacy's, shortly after the point on the 405 where it dawned on me that she lived nowhere near the studio. The subject line was THE RETREAT, in all caps, as if there existed no retreats on earth besides this one.

I read it aloud: "Anointed Goddesses, the time has come to expand your practice beyond the studio, beyond the confines of one hour and four walls. We invite you to the Ojai Valley Ranch—"

"Oh, I *love* that place," Stacy cooed.

"For four days during which you will work your body, mind, and soul to degrees previously unknown." I looked over at Stacy. "What do you think soul work is?"

"I don't know, but sign me up. Does it say anything about capacity?"

I scrolled. "Limited to twenty-five."

"We'd better reserve our spots now, right?"

The matter of how much this thing cost filled me with dread. I clicked on a button that said "Commit." It led to a page that outlined the various pricing options. The cheapest: four thousand dollars, half of which was due up front, via cash, check, or wire transfer.

"Fuck," I said, under my breath. A thought: Who wired money, besides people in heist movies?

"What? No more spots?!" Stacy looked at me, frantic, and for a moment, I wondered if we were going to hit a truck and this was how I would die, on the 405, looking at an email.

"No, it's just—ugh." I flattened my back against the seat. "I hate to even bring this up, but until I get a job, I'm living off my savings and Capital One, and I can't drop four thousand dollars on a retreat right now." Generally, I'd be embarrassed to admit that I couldn't afford something, but the cost seemed so ludicrous that it didn't matter—I might as well have been looking at the price tag on a yacht or a small island nation.

"Oh," she said quietly, "of course, gosh, *sorry*." She cast a glance at me. "Sometimes my privilege clouds my vision. I didn't even think about the cost. I once went to a yoga retreat at the St. Regis Deer Valley, and there was a caviar-and-Krug bar every day after the second session. I don't remember how much that one cost, but it can't have been cheap. *Caviar*. Gosh. It was sustainable, though. From Sacramento, I think."

We kept to ourselves for the rest of the drive. A sense of defeat seeped through me. I would never reach Stacy's level. I would never know the kind of wealth that allowed you to commit to five-star wellness retreats without caring about the cost. I would never reach the point where money didn't matter. How many generations would it take for my descendants to have Stacy's level of privilege? Would they ever? I had my fair share of privilege, sure, but you never really knew where you stood until you met someone with so much more. Of course, the opposite was true, too, and maybe if I had a gratitude practice, I'd feel less bad, but early morning journaling about what you're thankful for can't close the wealth gap. Not on its own, anyway.

I wondered if I could extend my gig with The Goddess Effect to include attending this retreat. For research's sake. Or if I could work it, hand out lavender-eucalyptus towels. That would be humiliating. Option one was better. I'd ask. Never hurt to ask.

The Panamera cruised off the freeway and onto a wide boulevard. After a couple of turns, we pulled up at a glowing white cube flanked by two iron gates. It looked like a tollbooth, if there were a Kanye West/James Turrell collaboration dedicated exclusively to tollbooths. The gate slid open as we approached.

"We used to live in Venice, this gorgeous Kevin Daly place with abstract walls, trippy architecture, and this incredible tropical garden out front," Stacy said. "I loved mornings there. That's when I started going to Goddess Effect. But then, one of Colt's clients came over and fell in love with it, would not take no for an answer. He offered way over market, all cash, so here we are, a gated community in Bel Air." She gave a sad little laugh. "I never thought I'd say that. We're basically barricaded from the real world."

"This is Bel Air?" I looked out the window, expecting to see a line of waiters with champagne trays. "This is nowhere near the studio—you do this drive four times a day?"

"It's against traffic. It's not so bad," she said. "Gives me time to think, call my representatives. Do you know my councilman voted *against* mandatory composting? Not gonna let *that* happen again."

We cruised up one loping bend after another, passing turreted mansions and a Tuscan villa large enough to be the Olive Garden Institute. We pulled up to another gate, where Stacy tapped a code into a keypad.

From the front, it looked like a modest ranch-style house, modern in design—a series of rectangles and perpendicular angles—but otherwise quaint. Stacy pulled onto the lawn.

"Here we are," she announced. I followed her onto the grass, then she pressed a button on her key fob, and the car lowered itself into the ground.

"Car elevator," she said, as if car elevators grew on trees. "It was the only way we were going to be able to keep Colt's collection here. He really wants a Bugatti." She turned and started walking toward the house. "I like them and all, don't get me wrong, but like I said, I'm all-in on electric. Renewable energy in general, actually. We get so much sun, I want to install solar panels, but Colt hates the way they look, so." She shrugged.

As we approached the vast teak front door, it swung open, revealing a young man in a crisp gray T-shirt, black jeans, and white leather sneakers. He held a heavy-looking tray.

"Good evening, Mrs. Gibson, and good evening, Anita," he said, bowing. He had a trace of an accent that I couldn't place. "May I offer you some cucumber water and cold towels?"

"Kris, I told you to call me Stacy," she said, playfully slapping him with one hand and reaching for a towel with the other. She turned to me. "Kris recently joined us from Thailand, which I'm *dying* to visit. He ran the butler training program for all the Four Seasons there, so he knows the best spots."

I followed her down the long hall into the living room. What looked like a modest ranch-style house from the front was, in fact, a vast, multistory mansion built into a cliff. Amber track lighting, warm wood floors, paint-splattered canvases, a dining table that could accommodate twenty, a sectional as long and fluffy as a cumulus cloud. My eyes locked on the view beyond the floor-to-ceiling windows—city lights that came to a stop where the sky met the ocean. As I approached the glass, it slid open, soundlessly.

"It's something, isn't it?" said Stacy, behind me.

"This is . . . you *live* here?"

"Yeah, I can't believe it, either. Who knows for how long, though. Colt does this—develops insane homes, irons out the kinks while we live in them, and then inevitably, some client or friend of a friend will get obsessed with it, offer an absurd amount of money, we'll sell and move out and start all over again."

"What a life," I said, leaning back against the wraparound balcony, gazing into the living room, all creamy light and right angles.

"You could say that," Stacy said. She faced the view and braced herself against the railing. "Or you could say it's just the rich getting richer, the top one percent widening the gap between themselves and the rest of the world." She paused and glanced up at the darkening sky. "Shall we get a drink?"

Kris stood next to a marble island in the open kitchen, holding an iPad, awaiting instruction, like Siri come to life.

"Kris, really, I can do it," Stacy said, opening a Sub-Zero that had the same wood grain as the rest of the cabinets. "Oh." She peered at an assemblage of Smartwater and some kind of energy drink. "Where's that bottle of wine that we opened last night?"

"Replaced in the cellar, Stacy. Why don't you just tell me what you'd like? Really, it's easier."

She relented and ordered a spicy mescal margarita. Dumbfounded by the notion of ordering something in your own home but trying not to show it, I asked for the same. Stacy added on crudités. And chips, and guac. She suggested we get comfortable outside, by the Bluetooth-enabled firepits.

She led the way down a set of floating stairs into another living room, this one slightly more lived in than the one above. On the flat-screen: the new Marianne Williamson doc, paused, forty-seven minutes in.

"Oops, must've forgotten to turn this off," Stacy said, grabbing the remote. "Have you seen it?"

I told her I hadn't.

"*So* inspiring," she said. "I'm actually watching it a second time. She's exactly what our country needs. There's a passage of hers that I just love." She closed her eyes, clasped the remote over her heart, and launched into a monologue about how our deepest fear is that we're powerful beyond measure and how your playing small does not serve the world. (I recognized it from a three-month fixation with Yoga to the People in New York, where the instructors recited it so often, I wondered if memorizing it was a requirement of working there.)

"I want to get that tattooed on my wrist," she said when she finished. "Or embroidered on a pillow. Or one of those Lingua Franca sweaters. Maybe all of the above. Sometimes I feel like the world expects me to be one thing because I look a certain way, but inside I'm this whole other person whose wants don't fit into a perfect little box. Like, do I want to end income inequality? Yes! Do I also want the new Dolce mules? Yes! Can I have both? I think Marianne Williamson says I can.

Anyway, I'd walk you through the rest of the floor, but they're redoing the spa tubs in the guest bathrooms, and it's a mess. Let's go down."

The thought of Stacy ending income inequality while wearing Dolce & Gabbana mules. I bit the inside of my cheek to keep my mouth from turning up. Did she think income inequality was a thing she could hit with a stick?

Another set of floating stairs led to an entertaining room with a pool table, a semicircular couch, a fully stocked bar, and a floor-to-ceiling bookshelf haphazardly stacked with books and the Amazon boxes in which they came. One stack included *How to Be an Antiracist*, *If They Come for Us*, and *White Fragility*.

"I'm building out the library," she said, following my gaze. "Work in progress."

She breezed through to the glass wall, which slid open soundlessly, revealing a vast, lounger-lined deck and an infinity pool that seemed to cascade down the cliff below. She tapped her phone, and along the perimeter of every edge in sight, low flames shot up against the night sky. I resisted the urge to take out my phone and take a picture. Hashtag made it.

We settled in a pair of cocoon chairs that hung from beams by the far end of the pool. They had been draped with soft throws, like they'd been expecting us, and a low table in front of them was arrayed with two crystal glasses containing our drinks and a spread of snacks that could feed a family of ten. Kris was setting down a plate of neither chips nor guac nor crudités.

"I thought you might enjoy some traditional moo sadoong, grilled pork—"

"With basil, lemongrass, fish sauce, lime, cilantro, onions, rice powder, chili, and garlic? Yes we *would*, Kris. How did you know that I was also craving some spicy Thai?" Stacy exclaimed. "Next time, tom yum, promise?"

"As you wish, Stacy," Kris said with a wink.

"Kris is teaching me how to make Thai food the traditional way, the way his family does, not the watered-down stuff they serve here," she said to me. "I memorize all the recipes. It's such an honor."

Wow, I thought, and said.

"Of course, Colt can't handle spicy, so we only do our sessions when he's out of town." Her tone conveyed that she saw this as a character defect.

"Where is he?" I asked. The can of worms was begging to be opened.

"South Beach Art Week. 'Client liaising,' he calls it. He goes to these events that people who are supposedly into art and design attend, to talk about his work, to drum up new business. But really, none of them are into art or design. They're into money—showing off how much they have, what they can afford that the next guy can't. It's sickening, all the one-upmanship, like, 'Oh, you got the Legacy 500? I got the G500, you should fly with me to Davos, try a real PJ.'" She shook her head. "Colt can't stand flying commercial. Even though he's ConciergeKey, it kills him."

I took a sip of the margarita. It had one of those spicy, salty rims. As the first sip slid down my throat, I mentally tallied how many more I wanted. Five? Seven?

"I'm lucky if I get upgraded to Economy Plus," I said.

"Right?" She took a slug of her drink. "I swore by Southwest when I was getting my master's. Seventy-nine dollars to Santa Rosa, round trip. No first class, board like cattle. The airline of the people."

"Wait—you went to grad school?"

"I never mentioned? For social work. I was getting my MSW at USC when I met Colt."

"And working as a bottle-service girl on the side?"

"Yep. *Great* tips. I made enough, actually, to spend a summer at an ashram in India, volunteering." She gave me a meaningful look as she reached for some kind of heirloom carrot. "Have you ever been?"

"Every other summer, growing up." An *ashram*. And she went willingly?

"Isn't it magical? All those colors, the food, the people, even the way the air smells." She looked up at the sky, dreamy. "I'm so jealous. You've probably seen so much of it."

I thought about how I dreaded every trip to India, how it meant three solid weeks without Nickelodeon or Doritos. The never-ending stream of trips to visit distant relatives who lived in houses without "Western toilets," who would ask the same boring question—"Do you remember me?"— before turning to my parents and giggling about my American accent.

"I can't say I appreciated it," I said. "It's different, when you're young and you're going to visit family you barely know."

Stacy nodded. "I get that. Whenever I tell people I grew up in Sonoma, they think I'm from some kind of wine resort. Really, it was a farm. A farm that produced pretty unremarkable chardonnay. My parents were real salt of the earth—well, they still are, I assume. We've sort of fallen out of touch. They didn't approve of me abandoning my MSW or marrying Colt."

"You never finished?"

"Colt saw how stressed I was and suggested I take a semester off. One became two. Then there was the wedding to plan. Then the kids we tried to have. Then"—she shrugged—"you wake up and a decade's gone by."

My first impression of Stacy was that she led a life of extreme comfort and zero friction, existence in the form of an Ugg boot. Clearly, though, she'd struggled, and she had ambition that surely could not be fulfilled by binging social-good docs and doing Goddess Effect twice a day. I felt guilty for casting her as the Athleisure Fairy. Well, she was that, but the Tinker Bell of Tencel for sure had some dark moments. I wanted to reach over, rest my palm on her arm, and tell her to tell me more, but I worried that the gesture would come off as disingenuous, prying. I didn't know if we were at that level.

We talked about other stuff for a while, like this charity she had been donating to but wanted to pull back from.

"The thing is," she said, "I never know where my money's going. They *say* it's going to help young women in economically disadvantaged communities get involved in tech, finance, and the arts, to 'expand the pipeline'—so many of these women don't even know what jobs are out there, what their options are. But I never get to see the results. Are they getting recruited by Google? Are they interning at Facebook? All I get are stats—'thanks to your donation, we've been able to increase the internet speed in the Compton school district by 54 percent.' And then they trot out twenty of them at the annual gala, which gets more extravagant by the year—the last one was at the Waldorf—and these amazing young women stand there like deer in headlights, and no wonder. Talk about a power imbalance."

"What about organizing your own fundraiser? Something grassroots, so you can actually be the change that you, uh, wish to see in the world." I realized as the words came out of my mouth that I was paraphrasing a Gandhi quote I only knew because of Instagram.

It was like a light bulb flicked on. "That is a *great* idea, Anita. Really, really great. Let me think. Maybe you can help! This is why I need you in my life. The other women I know, they'd just tell me to stop bitching, maximize my tax write-offs."

After three margaritas, Stacy stretched her hands above her head, yawned, and announced how fun the evening had been. I took that as my cue to order an Uber, but when I asked for her address, she flapped her hand and said, "Don't worry, Kris will drive you."

"But it's so far—"

"It's not at all. I insist. Ubers always have trouble finding the house. It's easier this way."

She walked me out; Kris was waiting in an Escalade. As he jumped out to open my door, she wrapped me into a hug. "This was *so* gratifying." A funny way to put it. I chalked it up to the Marianne Williamson doc.

16

The following Monday, I bounded into The Goddess Effect with three copies of a twenty-two-page deck, an anthropological analysis of the Eastside through the lens of wellness. I was to meet with Ophelia and Venus in the back room after class—which was why I signed up for the noon session, Venus's last of the day, rather than 8:00 a.m. with Stacy—and I figured giving Ophelia time to look over the deck beforehand couldn't hurt.

"What the," she said, taking in the spiral-bound stack. "You did all this?" She picked up the top copy and flipped the pages against her thumb.

"It's nothing," I said, even though I'd gone with the most expensive printing package at FedEx Office (color, on the glossy paper that cost eighty cents per sheet). She raised her eyebrows, which I interpreted as her being impressed.

Flutters of anticipation fueled my burpees and skaters. My plan: Start off by presenting my findings (the notion made me feel utterly official, like someone in a lab coat) and segue into other ways I could help The Goddess Effect, like attending the retreat and chronicling it for social media. Surely, Venus, Ophelia, and the rest of the instructors would be too busy staging the retreat to do that. I'd keep my cool. Go with the flow. Ask how else I could be of service. Radiate competence.

After class, I ran to the bathroom and swapped out my sweat-drenched sports bra for a clean one and a cropped T-shirt. I retied my ponytail and splashed my face with cold water. "You got this," I said to my reflection.

The studio had emptied out, but the door behind the front desk was cracked open. I sidled up to it, savoring the thrill of crossing over— not everyone gets to go back here. This is special. *You* are special.

I rapped lightly against the door and poked my head in.

"She's being a greedy little bitch," Venus was saying. The room was narrow, and she and Ophelia were sitting across from each other at a long, blond wood table like the ones at the Apple store. "Equity *and* we have to cover her costs?"

"Just for the trials," said Ophelia. "Look, I'm with you, she's a grade A cunt, but our only other option is to fly in the guy from Seoul. At least Cheng's in Calabasas."

"Might as well be Korea, the amount of time it takes to get there," Venus grumbled. *"Anita!"* She jerked back, seeing me. "How long have you been standing there?"

"Sorry, I, uh, not long—is this still a good time?"

"A good time for *what*?" Venus looked at Ophelia, flabbergasted.

"Oh, right, location two," said Ophelia. "We're supposed to talk about that." She pushed back from the table, ambled to a birchwood console in the corner that was piled with stuff, and extracted my decks from underneath two half-consumed horchata iced lattes. They'd left wet rings on the cover.

"Honestly, that can wait," Venus said, leaning back in her rolling chair and pressing her fingertips to her temples, like *The Scream* with a topknot. "Sorry," she said, dropping her hands and looking at me, "we're dealing with some bullshit." This was a Venus I had never encountered. She seemed superhuman in class. Now she just seemed . . . tired.

"Oh no," I said, both to the bullshit and to being backburnered. "I can totally walk you through the deck another time, no worries *at all.* I was actually going to ask . . . do you need help with the retreat? Is there anything I can do?" Picture that girl from *Grey's Anatomy*: *Pick me, choose me, love me.*

"Oh, that's sweet," said Venus, "but no."

***

Three weeks passed. Neither Ophelia nor Venus said anything further about the deck. One week, fine. Midway through the second, the sight of them began to gnaw at me. I had to keep going. I had to make the most of the heaven-sent special. I had to believe that I had a chance at a job at The Goddess Effect—they had wanted me, they had given me a task, I hadn't made that up.

But the gnawing continued. I kept thinking about what I'd overheard: Who was Cheng? What was the deal with Calabasas? Calabasas was where Drake and the Kardashians lived. Why would they talk about it in such disparaging tones?

Venus's comment about equity made The Goddess Effect seem more startup-y than ever, which made the prospect of working for them—unlikely as it might be—even more attractive, even as I started to notice strange things around the studio: a discarded Doritos bag in the trash by the front desk. No one who attended Goddess Effect would dare come to class with a bag of Doritos. Two regulars, talking in hushed tones by the cubbies: "Did they ask you? Are you going to do it?"

"Was Michaela always that snatched?" I asked Stacy before class one morning, taken aback by a regular's strikingly tiny midsection. A six-pack was one thing. It looked like Michaela had had the sides of her waist carved out by an ice-cream scooper.

"Wow," said Stacy. "I'll have what she's having."

Pooja's wedding week arrived, and with it, a dented cardboard box from Mumbai, addressed to me: the bridesmaid's outfit that should've been delivered weeks before, that Pooja said got delayed because of my change of address, an explanation that seemed less true and more like another dig at me leaving New York. I didn't want to open it. Opening it would mean that the wedding was imminent, which meant the arrival of my mom and a whole bunch of people that I was not yet ready to face was also imminent. Besides the slight indentations in my midsection—not nothing, especially on an Indian woman over thirty—I had nothing to show for myself. No job. No potential life partner. Not even some eye candy that I could bring along as my date.

Jared. Fucking Jared. One evening, after opening a bottle of pet nat with Christina, I'd pulled up our message thread and typed and deleted a series of drafts. First Hey!, then Hey, playboy 😏, then just a winky face, then a bunch of question marks. Then I turned over my phone and shoved it under my thigh.

Two drinks later, I sent the question marks. No reply. I sent four more question marks. Still nothing. At that point, I figured, whatever, one-night stand, not a big deal, fourth-wave feminism, isn't this what we wanted, sex, no strings attached, whoop-de-doo, although running into him would be awkward, never gonna go to that bar again, honestly, fuck that guy, hope he burns in hell, how dare he think I'm not good enough, it's probably because I'm Indian, oh well, shit happens, move on.

Eventually, it came down to the cardboard box or LinkedIn. I blindly applied to three jobs (something-manager, something-producer, something-sorceress), then jabbed a ballpoint pen through the packing tape. Pooja had given her bridesmaids—there were eighteen of us—two options: a maroon-and-gold embroidered lehenga with a crop top that ended just below the boobs, or a maroon-and-gold embroidered lehenga with a long, flowing, boob-and-midriff-shielding tunic top. I'd long ago chosen the crop top, and I'd been aspirational when I sent Pooja's wedding planner my measurements. For once, the odds were in my favor. Given my new life's work, the outfit probably wouldn't need alterations.

I tore open the box. So much fabric. This has to be the skirt, I thought, pulling out a raft of maroon silk. Wait, no. It was the top. The tunic top. The tunic top that appeared to be at least four sizes too big, a veritable muumuu.

This happened with outfits from India. Measurements often got lost in translation. But I had specifically told Pooja and her wedding planner that I wanted outfit option one, and they'd confirmed I'd be receiving it, and given how much time, effort, and money was being spent on this multiday extravaganza, I had a hard time believing that this was a mistake. Pooja did not tolerate mistakes.

She always wanted me to fail. She always needed me to feel better about herself. There was the time we agreed that neither of us would "wear Indian" to that potluck party, and she showed up in a violet anarkali, sopped up the compliments while I glowered in overalls. There was the time she got into the "gifted" society and I did not, and whenever she'd come to my house for dinner, she'd regale my parents with tales about whatever it was they did in there—advanced word puzzles, PSATs, who knew—even though it upset me. Probably *because* it upset me. After I broke up with Neil, she made it all about her: "It would've been so fun, all four of us, getting married, raising kids, growing old together. Are you sure you can't make it work? What's the problem? You have to compromise, Ani. That's your problem—you want too much."

Over the years, countless little slights that I was supposed to overlook because, what? Our moms were friends? We'd known each other for so long?

I laid the lehenga on the bed. An intervention. This lehenga needed an intervention. I ran to Miguel's room, down the hall.

"So (a) you have the best taste of anyone I know," I began, "and (b) you said you can sew."

He followed me back to my room, took a long look at the explosion of maroon silk, and said, "It would take the entire cast of *Project Runway* to make this wearable, and I'm talking old *Project Runway*, Bravo, Tim Gunn."

"Please, Miguel. The wedding is this weekend, and I'm desperate." I showed him a photo of what the outfit was supposed to look like.

"A wedding," he repeated. "Where is it?"

"The Beverly Hills Hotel."

He let out a low whistle. I saw my angle.

"Do you . . . want to come?" Granted, if this were a regular wedding, the invitation would've been inappropriate. To a six-hundred-person Indian wedding, this was par for the course. There would be overflow tables set up for the uncle who brought his colleague's cousin from Ohio State and the auntie who came with her batchmate's granddaughter who was also a doctor. I'd seen Miguel dance. He would fit right in.

"Can I bring Riley?"

"Sure." What was one more?

***

I was standing in front of the mirror with milkmaid arms while Miguel fitted the bodice of my new, drastically cropped lehenga top when Max appeared in the doorway.

"Did I miss the memo about arts and crafts hour?"

"Psh," Miguel huffed, removing a set of pins from his mouth. "This is four semesters of FIT and a year assisting Ariana Grande's stylist."

"Dude, you know I'm kidding. Anita, you look." He paused, as if only now taking it all in—the ruby-colored silk, the gold paisleys glinting under the light, the strategic six inches of bare midriff. "Amazing."

"Thank you." I told him about the wedding. "My mom's coming, it's a whole thing."

"Bring her over," he said. "Austin's out of town. She can even spend the night if she wants. Officially, beta runs aren't supposed to have overnight guests, but we only made that rule because this guy James used his beta run to beta test his idea for a thrupple app, and . . . you can imagine. This one girl was completely naked, making onion rings at 2:00 a.m. Who uses a deep fryer completely naked?"

I laughed. Miguel scolded me. "We've got a room at the hotel, and there are, like, seventeen events. I don't think there'll be time. Plus, I don't know if my mom would get it." I tried to picture what she would've done if she'd been in my shoes that first day, when I arrived at the Gig. Probably called the police.

"I hear you," said Max. "My dad—well, long story, but he wouldn't be caught dead here. Anyway"—he clapped the doorframe—"Gonzo's having another open call on Saturday. All day, nine to nine."

The bridesmaids were due in Pooja's suite at 9:00 a.m. Saturday. I'd stopped looking at the feeds of Gonzo and Emilia altogether. When something from either of them would surface, I would blur my vision and keep scrolling, as if I hadn't seen it, as if not processing the post would mean that it didn't exist, that Gonzo itself did not exist, that I had not been thoroughly rejected. Worse than rejected: forgotten about, ignored.

I said I wouldn't be able to recuse myself. He said he understood—his sister's wedding was also a whole to-do. After he left, I appraised my reflection as Miguel continued to pinch and prod. Yes, this was drastic, but it was necessary. In this outfit, I'd be ready. In this outfit, I could face them all. The job would come. The job would materialize. The job would manifest. But first, this.

17

Rosette or paisley?" the henna artist asked.

"Whatever you think is best," I said.

She nodded and began painting minuscule petals on the back of my left hand, deftly connecting one to the next, no pausing, no second-guessing, no sign of doubt, even though she was working freehand, presumably making up the design as she went along. I wished that I could do anything with that kind of self-assuredness. I could learn from her. I wondered how much she got paid.

Perched on a gold Moroccan pouf, I surveyed the top floor of Soho House West Hollywood. Plenty of Indian men, bearded and clean-shaven, in suits and sherwanis, potbellied, gaunt, and everything in between, but none of them mine, none of them the one I longed to see.

Earlier, I'd caught sight of a man in a blue-gray suit with the same build and salt-and-pepper swoop of hair as my father. My heart stopped. Then he turned, and I saw his face, and of course, it was just another uncle. I wondered how long I would keep searching for my dad in crowds like these, whether I would ever fully accept that I would never see him again, whether some part of me would always be hoping for a glitch in the space-time continuum that would bring him back to this world.

I had to hand it to Pooja. Or her wedding planner, Aparna Mukherjee, who was apparently Mindy Weiss for monied South Asians. From the henna artists to the bartenders to the decorators who'd transformed the rooftop garden of the private club into a scene out of Marrakesh, no expense had been spared, no detail overlooked. On one end of the vast glass cube in the sky: a hookah lounge, where turbaned attendants turned glowing cubes of charcoal with golden tongs. On another: a "living wall" composed of exotic mosses and Pooja ♥ Amit, spelled out in red roses. The Kardashians' photo booth director had set up shop in front of it, and the flurry of flashbulbs was constant. Moroccan lanterns hung from the trees improbably planted on the fourteenth floor of a glossy corporate tower; candles burned on seemingly every flat surface. A brigade of servers circulated with kebabs, little bowls of warm nuts, and the signature cocktail: Kiss from a Rose, owing both to Seal—*Batman Forever* was Amit's favorite *Batman*—and Morocco's national flower. It was an amalgam of vodka, rose liquor, and rose water, finished with a rose petal. I was on my third.

I deserved all the drinks, for having kept it together for this long. I'd met my mom in the lobby of the Beverly Hills Hotel that morning, weekend bag packed. She was giddy from the private jet—"The opulence," she gushed, "the candy, baskets upon baskets, and all of it *free*"—and the weekend to come.

"What a blessing," she said, hugging me tight, "that we get to spend time together in a place like this." She took in the gilded lobby, the red carpet that ran through it, and shook her head in disbelief. "To think, we have Pooja to thank for this Hollywood treatment, to think that you grew up with someone as *grand* as this."

And then something inside me shriveled and died, because, as usual, I would be held to the unsurmountable standard set by Pooja and found to be lacking.

After she was done marveling at every last thing—the Illy coffee machine, the bedspread, the welcome basket, which was the size of one of those Ikea bags in which you could hide a body—she sat down on one bed and motioned for me to sit next to her.

"So. Tell me." This was her way of asking me to tell her everything.

I shrugged. "I'm good. Things are good. LA's great."

"How is it going at Gonzo? Do you think we can stop by there, or the Gig? There's time now, before the sangeet, or maybe Sunday morning, before the brunch."

"It's too far, and the Gig doesn't allow guests, and people don't bring their moms to the office. No one does that." Well, I had done that, at ABN. With both my parents. Plenty of employees did.

"But it's going well, Gonzo? When will your first piece air? I want to make sure I catch it."

"Yeah, soon, I'll send you a link. I don't want to talk about work. Oh, did you bring those gold hoop earrings I asked for?"

My renewed interest in Indian jewelry pleased her to the degree that she stopped asking prying questions and prattled on for a while about family friends and relatives whose names rang a bell but whose faces I could not picture. "Did you connect with Smita, by the way? I was hoping we could all meet while we're out here, but if there's not even time to see where you *live*—"

"She never texted me back. Guess she's super busy with her steady law job."

She took a nap, and I looked at my phone and debated doing a second workout in the hotel gym. (I'd taken Annalisa's 8:00 a.m.) I wondered if attempting my own version of the guttural cleanse would do me any good, if it might cleanse my insides of the angst that seemed to multiply with every minute I spent in the same room as my mother. I didn't want to be checked up on. I needed more time. Why didn't she get it?

The saving grace of the wedding was the chance to see Praveen. Through me, he and Pooja had gotten close enough, over the years, to warrant a wedding invitation (though, given the guest count, if you had ever met Pooja and you *didn't* get invited, shame on you). We had planned to catch up, just the two of us, over drinks at the Polo Lounge before boarding one of the rose-garlanded charter buses to Soho House. I would come clean to him about Gonzo, The Goddess Effect, my general lack of a plan. I needed help. I knew that. Praveen was a producer. He executed. He knew people. He wouldn't judge me. Well, he *would* judge me, but then he'd help me, which would make it all worthwhile. I'd fall at his feet, he'd make me promise him my firstborn, I'd tell him he'd have to find me a man, too, for that to happen—we'd make a thing out of it, have a good laugh, a heart to heart.

But an hour before our date, he texted that he'd matched with a hot hype house realtor on one of the apps and said he'd just meet me at the sangeet. This might be my only chance to get blown in a TikTok mansion, he'd said, before apologizing in all caps, with eight exclamation points.

This meant that I rode to the sangeet with my mom. After she tried to make me wear a sari that she'd brought for me from home. After I'd refused, said I hated saris, and angrily pulled on the highlighter-pink satin palazzo pants and tiny gold-sequined tank top that I'd borrowed from Riley.

"Too much," my mom said, making a face and gesturing at my midsection.

"Are you kidding? That sari shows more skin than what I'm wearing."

"This is *tradition*," she said, adjusting the pleats of her own sari, six yards of emerald-green silk flecked with gold. "That, I don't know what that is."

"It's a DIY salwar. Sabyasachi's new collection is just like this."

"Who?"

"How do you not know Sabyasachi? He's, like, the Gucci of India. He's what perfect Pooja is wearing for her big Hollywood wedding."

In retrospect, I hadn't entirely kept it together. Still, I deserved another drink. I'd submitted to getting the back of my left hand hennaed at my mom's insistence. "It will look so nice. All the other girls are getting it done. Why not you?"

"Why not *you*?" I'd said.

She looked away, guiltily. "Really, I shouldn't even be here, because of Daddy, one year of mourning. Mehndi, on me, now, it won't look nice." By "nice," she meant right, appropriate, God-fearing, etc. Sometimes, it seemed like she spent every waking hour trying to come up with ways to look more nice.

"All done," the henna artist said. I took a moment to appraise her work, and I had to admit, it was beautiful. Rosettes yielded to vines, which snaked up and around my pointer finger and down the outside of my wrist, creating the impression of a beautiful garden growing on the back of my hand, a bounty that belied my bitter, black soul. I thanked her and got up to get another drink.

By the hookah lounge, I spotted a waiter with a fresh tray of rose cocktails. A couple in a Tom Ford suit and a Falguni Shane Peacock lehenga leaned in to take two. Neil and Kirtee. Neil and Kirtee leaned in to take two. I turned and beelined to the bar.

As two uncles walked away with tumblers of Blue Label and I pushed in to take their place, I saw Praveen. I yelled his name and waved my unhennaed hand. He was talking to a guy about our age, super fit, a dead ringer for Riz Ahmed.

"Finally," I said, as we hugged. "Did you get my texts? What took you so long?"

He launched into a *Titanic*-length retelling of his day—the TikTok mansion (epic), the hype house realtor (huge dick), the flight (whatever, wished he'd made the cut for the private jet)—and segued into ABN: who'd gotten fired, who'd gotten promoted, who'd left under suspicious circumstances. "Does anyone *really* want to spend more time with their family, I mean . . . ?"

I laughed and asked follow-up questions and relished his exuberance until it dawned on me that he still hadn't told me how great I looked. It's a rule: when you see a friend after they've made a major life change, you tell them how great they look. The truth matters not at all.

He was talking about alternating running days with StairMaster days when I interjected, "I basically stopped running once I started Goddess Effect."

"I was going to say, snatched dot com." I put that moment in my memory bank, next to the time that Jared tapped on my collarbones.

"I'm actually kind of working for them," I said.

He frowned. "Seriously? What about Gonzo?"

His expression, his general demeanor, the fact that we were surrounded by a crowd that included my ex-boyfriend, his new fiancée, and my mother—Pooja, too, presumably; Pooja was somewhere in this place—all of it added up to me squashing my plan to come clean and ask him for help. I shrugged and took a sip of my fourth Kiss from a Rose.

He asked what my "job" entailed. I said strategizing expansion.

"Uh-huh," he said, unconvinced. "When in Rome, I guess. They paying you enough that you can move out of that hovel?"

Had Praveen always been so judgmental? I wondered.

Many friendships rely on circumstance, but I thought we had more than ABN in common. Sure, we were both Indian, and sure, we had years of shared experiences, but there are only so many times you can laugh about that time you snuck into the *Call Me by Your Name* after-party and did blow with Armie Hammer's publicist's assistant in the bathroom of the Waverly Inn. At some point, you have to wonder whether your friendship will revolve around the replaying of the highlight reel rather than the acquisition of new footage. Even the best highlight reel gets old after a while.

A more rational part of me recognized that it was pretty hypocritical to accuse someone of being judgmental and unevolved when you were also lying to them. Maybe Praveen saw through me. Maybe I should've told him everything. Blame it on whatever pride I had left: I decided to stick with my story and focus on having a good time, which, in our case, meant drinking too much, ignoring our own problems, and gossiping about other people.

Praveen motioned for Riz lookalike to join us, and I quickly discovered that he was Amit's sole remaining single cousin, the one, presumably, with whom Pooja envisioned setting me up. Judging by the chemistry between him and Praveen, no dowry in the world would compel him to marry me. We got another round and made bitchy comments about everyone's outfits until dinner. While Praveen and Riz lookalike retrieved our table cards, I got in the buffet line.

My mom materialized as I was piling a gold-rimmed cocktail plate with pita. "Did you see how gorgeous Pooja looks?" she said, gesturing at the living wall where Pooja had materialized, resplendent in a sari of sparkling silver beads. Hers was not the stiff Mysore silk my mom had implored me to wear, the kind of sari that made you look like you had a FUPA and a horse's ass. Hers was slinky, sexy, flattering.

She was beautiful. But I thought admitting this would lead my mother to ask when I was going to look like that, i.e., when I was going to get married, so I just shrugged and told her I had to go find my table.

By the fourth speech—this glorified rehearsal dinner had six—the pita and rose cocktails had fused into a sour pit of self-loathing. I did what every unattached individual does during wedding speeches: wondered if and when anyone would say such glowing things about me.

Praveen and Riz lookalike were debating which *Million Dollar Listing* broker was the hottest when my phone buzzed.

Jared: Wanna hang?

18

"H ang" after 10:00 p.m. only means one thing, and the prospect of it was a lot more appealing than going back to the hotel, to the room that my mom and I were sharing. I texted her in the elevator down to the Uber: work emergency, don't wait up, I have a key. I didn't, but I figured I could get one from the front desk when I came back. If I came back.

I lowered the window of the Honda Accord and breathed in the cool night air, watched Sunset Boulevard morph from buzzy bars and gleaming office towers to manicured lawns and Mediterranean cypresses. Quiet. Quiet was nice, after the fourteen-piece Bollywood jazz band (not on theme, but a sangeet without some rendition of "Desi Girl" would not be tolerated, and in any case, they left Morocco behind when they wheeled out the chafing trays of paneer makhani and garlic naan).

Twenty minutes later, she still hadn't replied. Was this a new low, getting ghosted by my own mother? Oh, well. At least hot bartender wanted me. At least I was on my way to get some. Look at me, a regular Cardi B, a bad bitch, getting busy.

The doorman smiled and nodded as I walked in. He seemed to know who I was, a good sign, like Jared owning glassware and a nightstand. Maybe he didn't bring many girls back to his place. Maybe he was waiting by the door with a warm smile and a big glass of wine, eager to envelop me and enquire about my day. The American dream.

The elevator opened, and I could hear French house music coming from the direction of Jared's condo, the melody of a Yoplait commercial over thumping bass. It sounded like a party. Was he having a party? I was not in the mood for a party, did not want to make small talk, answer questions like "Ooh, what's that on your hand?" (I'd used the complimentary Cowshed lotion in the Soho House bathroom to scrape off the dried henna with a butter knife. It had stained my skin the color of rust and smelled like a barn.)

My feet kept moving in the direction of Jared's door because I had come this far. What else was I going to do? The Uber had cost $38.50. I wasn't getting that back.

I rang the bell. Nothing. I pressed down the handle of the door and let myself in. The bass throbbed like a wall of Jell-O. The living room was dark and smoky and smelled like incense, which reminded me of my mom and her puja place. I thought of her, alone, in the hotel room, wondering why her daughter couldn't bear to be with her, because surely, she saw through my lie. I would pay for this, at some point. If there was a next life, I'd be coming back as a slug.

There was no one in the living room. An empty bottle of tequila sat on the dining table along with a half-full bottle of rye. I picked up the rye and watched the amber liquid swirl. I hated rye. I thought about calling Jared's name, but that felt desperate. Maybe I'd make myself a drink, and he'd appear, and I'd be sitting in one of the high-backed chairs along the kitchen island, looking bored, like the Parisian cool girl who I imagined enjoyed this sort of music. I looked in his fridge. Protein shakes, sparkling water, three bananas that were almost black. What went with rye? Did it matter? I took a swig.

His place was opulent yet sparse. Harman Kardon sound system but no pots or pans. Stone Buddha on the mantel but nothing hanging on the walls. Diptyque candle burning in the half bath but no toilet paper. It was like he knew the kind of man he wanted to be but didn't feel like making the effort to get there.

I heard a playful yelp from down the hall and then a woman's voice: "Oh my God, Jared, *stop*!" in a tone that indicated that she most definitely did not want him to stop. I felt a surge of jealousy that I immediately wanted to take back. He wasn't my boyfriend. Maybe this yelpy person was his cousin. Who knew? I walked down the hallway and realized that this was the part of the condo I remembered from our "date" and the blurry morning after. So they were in the master bedroom, and then I was, too, standing in the doorway, watching Jared attempt to use his teeth to pull a lace thong off a woman who looked like Emily Ratajkowski's body double. She giggled and squirmed on his vast, low-to-the-ground, black-duvet-covered bed. She was definitely not his cousin.

"Uh," I said. In another world, I might've stormed up to him, slapped him across the face, and stormed out of there, but I felt none of the outrage necessary to make that happen. In all honesty, it made sense now—the incense, the music, the playful yelp of a woman pretending to resist.

Jared turned and gave me a lascivious smile. "Playgirl, just in time." He pushed back from the bed and sauntered over, wrapped his hands around the small of my back, and pushed his mouth against mine. He tasted sour, like milk that had been left out too long. "Missed you," he said, pulling his face away. He seemed looser, drunker than I remembered him. Maybe I wasn't drunk enough.

"Meet Raven." He grabbed my wrist—either he didn't notice the henna, or he didn't care—and led me over to the bed, which I perched on the edge of, next to Raven's left foot. Her toenails were painted the prettiest shade of orchid, and the skin on her legs had that poreless, even, taut quality that I thought was only possible with Facetune and Photoshop and other apps too advanced for me to know. I thought of my own legs, unmoisturized, a week unshaven. Raven had adjusted her thong back around her hips and propped herself up on her elbows. She half smiled at me, then looked down at her phone. She wore a faded Guns N' Roses T-shirt that cut off around her rib cage. She looked like the type of Instagram model I had expected to see at LAX.

"Hi," I said. I tried to match her nonchalance, but my mind raced: a threesome. They wanted to have a threesome, right? Or was I being presumptuous? Maybe Raven was about to put on her pants, and we'd all go out for pizza.

"Sooo, I'm gonna get us all some drinks, let you two get acquainted," Jared said. "Don't have too much fun without me," he called from down the hall.

Awkward silence. "I'm Anita," I said. Part of me thought it would be funny to reach out and shake her hand, but I decided against it. I did a cost-benefit analysis: yes, I had always wanted to have a threesome, but no, this was not my ideal scenario. What even was my ideal scenario? One in which I felt sexier. One in which I was the hotter one, which was not going to be the case here. I felt late to the party, which, of course, I was. They'd clearly been laying the groundwork for this for hours. As I understood it, in most threesomes, there was an entrée and a side dish. I wanted to be the steak, and right now, I was the steamed spinach.

Jared returned with three tumblers of what looked like straight rye, and I realized that Raven had not said anything at all in the interim. She had gotten up and was ambling around the room, tapping her finlike hip bones in tune with the music, a bored look on her face, peach-emoji ass asserting its status as one of the new seven wonders of the world. Well, fine, I thought. You don't go to a threesome to make friends. I get it. I forced my mouth into a smile and took a tumbler from Jared. "That's against the rules, babycakes," he said, pointing at my palazzo pants. "No street clothes on the bed."

"Oh, well, I wouldn't want to break any *rules*," I said, trying to be sexy. It occurred to me to point out that he was fully clothed and wearing Air Jordans, which were definitely not house shoes, but no one likes a know-it-all.

One zip, and the palazzo pants pooled at my feet. I slid out of my sandals and was about to wriggle out of the tiny sequined tank top when I remembered that (a) wriggling out of sequins is not cute and (b) I wasn't wearing a bra underneath. I wasn't ready to be the most naked one in the room.

A thought: What would Venus do?

Before I could meditate much on that, Jared stuck his tongue in my mouth. He pulled me closer to the bed and then turned to kiss Raven, then kind of pushed me toward Raven. We kissed gently. I wasn't about to go sticking my tongue in the mouth of someone who hadn't even done me the courtesy of introducing herself. I felt Jared fiddling with the waistband of my Target thong and thanked God that I'd had the foresight to at least wear sexy-adjacent underwear. How long had it been since I last shaved? Seven days? Ten? I fretted about the state of my stubble and then thought, Fuck it. I was a modern woman. I didn't have time to constantly keep my bikini line in a state of prepubescence. They'd deal. Or I'd just keep my thong on. Judging by the perfunctory way Raven was kissing, she wasn't about to go down on me, and Jared seemed like the type of guy who'd gotten away with never having to go down on anyone because he looked like a cologne model.

Raven and I pulled away from each other, and she kind of smiled. I felt competent, for a moment.

"Allllriiight, *now* we're talking," Jared said, as he stripped off his clothes. Raven was doing something with her phone. Was she texting? How expert do you have to be to *text* during a threesome? Then he bounded onto the bed in Calvin Klein boxer briefs; she jammed her phone into the alarm clock charger, knelt beside him, and tucked her heels beneath her. He motioned for me to come around and do the same.

I kneeled. I planted my left palm on the bed, anticipating next steps. There was something about seeing my hennaed hand in that position. Next to my naked thigh. Next to everything else. It was lurid. Cognitively dissonant. Did I really want to be here?

Raven looked at me poutily and then looked at the bulge in Jared's Calvin Kleins, as if she wanted me to go first. Oh, how *kind* of you Raven, to leave the first leg of oral to me.

I didn't need this. I wasn't steamed spinach. I was prime fucking rib. I'd left an open bar for this bullshit.

Venus would . . . I still couldn't picture Venus having sex. But she would not do anything she didn't want to do.

"I'm sorry," I said, jumping backward off the bed. "I mean, actually, I'm *not*," I clarified, grabbing my stuff off the floor, "I'm *so* not sorry." It seemed important to reiterate this.

"Seriously?" said Raven.

"Babe!" said Jared.

"Definitely not your babe!" I said, bolting out of his bedroom, mentally tipping my hat to Andy in *The Devil Wears Prada*.

My cheeks were still flushed when the Nissan Sentra arrived. A new low. Except, a voice in my head said, you left. That was something. That was progress. Progress, not perfection, as Saffron liked to say.

19

The thought of sleeping in the same room as my mom after that: I just couldn't. For her sake, really. God forbid the aura of that threesome sully her. She, I knew, would be coming back as a queen or Kris Jenner or whatever happened after you'd attained the highest level of reincarnation. Nirvana? I wasn't going to fuck up her chance at Nirvana by dragging my threesomed ass into the Beverly Hills Hotel.

That's what I told myself as I punched in the door code to the Gig and crawled into bed. The truer part of me knew that I was also doing this so I could go to Goddess Effect.

***

While Aparna's color-coded schedule said that the bridesmaids were due in Pooja's suite at 9:00 a.m., accounting for IST (Indian Standard Time), most people wouldn't start rolling in until closer to ten, and the photographs wouldn't get good until around eleven, when the champagne kicked in. I figured if I went to Venus's 8:00 a.m., I'd still have plenty of time. I needed a reset. I needed no-holds-barred intense physical activity to stem the stream of questions running through my brain:

What made Jared think I'd be okay being a side dish? *Was I* a side dish? Would I ever rise to the level of entrée in anyone's mind?

Related: Was I bad at sex? I felt like I needed to enroll in remedial sex ed, a class that actually taught you how to have sex with other human beings. Probably, classes like that existed in LA. Definitely, I was too embarrassed to enter that into a search bar.

Raven's ass haunted me in my dreams, continued to haunt me as I ascended the stairs to the front desk. Its sheer perfection, the fact that all the squats in the world would not make my ass look like that, although maybe it was CoolSculpting, and if she'd been CoolSculpted, it wasn't a fair fight. It was apples and oranges, or, more accurately, apples and peaches, *genetically modified* peaches—

"Ani! I thought you were at that wedding. Wait, your hand, oh, that's so gorgeous, let me see?"

Of course Stacy would be at Goddess Effect, and in my haze, I hadn't thought of an explanation for why I was here rather than at the wedding that I'd told her would keep me occupied all weekend.

She gushed over the henna. "Mmm, that smell." She planted her nose on the back of my hand and inhaled deeply. "So earthy." The expression on her face indicated that this was a good thing. I gave her a brief account of the sangeet, leaving out the part where I left early to be humiliated.

"And the wedding's today at the Beverly Hills Hotel?" she repeated. "So close!"

You can see it in their eyes, when someone's angling for an invitation to an Indian wedding, visions of Bollywood dancing in their heads. I'd already invited Miguel and Riley. Riz lookalike said his mom had invited her naturopath and his business manager. Surely, I could tack on Stacy. She'd been so generous to me. I wanted to do something for her. I also wanted to have a friend in my corner, and given Praveen's fixation with Riz lookalike and questioning of my life choices, I didn't know if he qualified.

"You want to come?"

She squealed and jumped. Venus, emerging from the back room, gave us a look. "Sorry," I said, trying to catch her eye. I'd given up on her getting back to me about the deck, but some child in me still believed that maybe she'd extend an invitation to the retreat. For free.

She breezed past us without a word, leaving a trail of Santal 33 in her wake.

***

Stacy offered to drive to the Beverly Hills Hotel after stopping at home to grab her makeup bag and an outfit. I followed her to her walk-in "formal" closet and decreed several options perfect, including a one-shoulder, ombré sequin gown by Marchesa and a sleeveless beaded minidress by Balmain. Sequins, beads, a bunch of colors that have no business being together—pick one or select all, and you're a gold-medal contender for best non-Indian-at-an-Indian-wedding.

"By the way," she said, as she cruised down the winding roads to Sunset Boulevard, "I have an idea for a fundraiser." She wriggled in her seat, excitedly.

"Do tell!"

"Well, it's not a fundraiser per se. But basically, I have all of these samples of face masks and skin creams and serums—so many I've lost count. I was trying *everything* before I found Nina, my Ayurvedic facialist. Anyway, I was thinking, I could package them in fun little bags and give them to the girls at the Compton school, and the fun little bags could be those Telfar bags, because I know they're so hot right now and *so* hard to get."

"You'd basically be giving them random skincare products in a Telfar bag?"

"Yeah! Isn't that nice? *Luxury* skincare products. Don't you think they'd love that?"

Who wouldn't love that? I supposed. But the whole notion felt misguided. Like, what was the point of Stacy giving the girls this stuff? To make her feel better? It was like people who volunteered an hour of their time so they could post about doing it, or who bought antiracism books that looked so nice all stacked together, but when push came to shove and it was *Between the World and Me* or *Big Little Lies*, what did they choose?

"I mean, sure," I said. I stopped myself before saying, "But what are you hoping to achieve?" It would make more sense for Stacy to answer that and then backsolve. Maybe I was afraid of what her answer would be.

By the time we arrived at the hotel, it was past ten, and I had three missed calls and one text from Aparna: BRIDAL SUITE PHOTOS IMMINENT. I texted back, Be there in 5. Had Aparna never heard of IST? She was from Mumbai—she ought to know. The ceremony wasn't until 2:00 p.m. Surely, I had time. At least enough time to shower. Would Aparna want me there with the residue of an aborted threesome *and* a workout? Would Pooja? No way.

The other advantage of bringing Stacy was that my mom could only get so mad at my abrupt and inexcusable absence if I showed up with a friend, especially a nice white slightly older female friend. I got a new keycard and led the way to the room, preemptively apologizing for its size (minuscule, compared to where Stacy rolled around) and the presence of my mom. "Just ignore her if she starts rambling," I said.

"*There* you are," my mom said. She was standing in front of the full-length mirror in another sari, cornflower blue with gold paisleys, pleated and pinned, combing out her curls.

As she registered Stacy, I watched her face transform from "I'm going to kill you" to "Ooh, lovely American woman." She introduced herself and asked if Stacy was also attending the wedding.

"Your daughter invited me just now. I hope that's okay."

"You know Indians: the more, the merrier!" She giggled, as if perpetuating stereotypes was fun. "I once went to a wedding with a thousand guests, back in Bangalore."

"Is that where you're from?" Stacy asked, perching on the unmussed bed, the bed I should've slept in.

"I grew up in Mysore, but Bangalore is where I met my husband and did my studies."

"Mysore has that famous palace, right?"

"You know Mysore!" My mom beamed. I hadn't seen that look on her face in ages. Certainly not since she got to LA.

"I'm gonna shower," I announced, to no one.

Body, face, don't get hair wet, shave legs? Why bother? Not getting naked with another human being until the end of time. Amoebas had it figured out. Fuck needing another individual. Just fuck yourself. Everyone leaves satisfied.

Despite my best efforts, the hair at the nape of my neck had gotten wet, as usual, so I blow-dried it straight, wrapped myself in a towel, emerged to get the Miguel-altered bridesmaid's lehenga hanging in the closet, and saw Stacy in a sari. A motherfucking sari. The sari that my mom had wanted me to wear to the sangeet.

"The petticoat is supposed to be tight, but tell me if it's *too* tight," my mom was saying, pulling the drawstring around Stacy's taut abs.

"It's perfect, Meena Auntie," she said. "Are you sure it's okay for me to call you that?"

Speechless, I ducked back into the bathroom and scrambled into my outfit. What was going on? Had I entered an alternate universe? My phone buzzed—another call from Aparna. I'd be there in a minute. Just needed a hit of my straightener.

I plugged it in by the dresser, and as it heated up, I watched, in the mirror, as my mom did Stacy's pleats. The color suited her, I had to admit. Coral pink, like the color of the sneakers she was wearing the day we first met, with a pattern of diamonds embroidered in glimmering gold thread.

"FYI, it's impossible to dance in a sari," I said to Stacy.

"I manage," my mom said.

"And good luck going to the bathroom."

"Anita."

"I'm just saying!"

"Is it supposed to be smoking, like that?" my mom asked, gesturing at the hair straightener clamped below my ear.

"That's how you know it's working," I said.

Stacy grimaced. "I don't know. I once burned a chunk of my hair that way, right before Richard Branson's Studio 54 pop-up on Necker. I had to get emergency extensions ferried in from Bermuda—it was a whole thing. But I paid them double! These island nations are so dependent on tourist dollars, you know?"

I ripped my straightener out of the wall. Turning it off was never enough. There was always the fear that I had not actually turned it off and it would start a fire, or the power would trip and it would start a fire, or it would magically become possessed and start a fire. So many minutes of my life, wasted, because I had to go back and make sure that I'd turned my straightener off.

"I'm late for bridesmaids' stuff," I said. "Stace, I'll text you Praveen's number. You can sit with him. Cue up a podcast—it's gonna be a long one." As the door shut behind me, I heard Stacy ask my mom how a kanjeevaram sari was different from a regular sari. Who'd have thought she'd be so into saris? With all that Balmain. Could I wear the Balmain? I wondered. Maybe I'd change after the ceremony.

Pooja was in the premier suite, and I knew, the moment I saw Aparna's face, that I was in deep shit.

"The one she's been asking for, only two hours and fifteen minutes—*what* is it that you're wearing?" Her eyes went wide. "This is not regulation. This is neither option one nor two."

"Sorry," I stammered. "It didn't fit, and I think I got the wrong one, and—"

"Get in here," she said, grabbing me by the arm. "Selfish child. This is why I charge double for US weddings. Too many stupid Americans who need a good smacking."

***

An hour later, I was sunken into the couch on the patio with a third lukewarm glass of champagne. According to Aparna, Pooja had wanted me, specifically, to weigh in on whether she should wear the Vajra Jewelers imitation of a yellow diamond necklace worn by Lady Gaga or the Vajra Jewelers imitation of a non-yellow diamond necklace also worn by Lady Gaga. Both had pear-shaped pendants; both were rip-offs of Tiffany & Co. designs that had gotten significant red carpet time; both were equally gauche. Why my opinion mattered more than that of the seventeen other bridesmaids and dozen more attendants in the suite, I couldn't understand, but it was nice to be wanted, even though she reamed me out about being late and going rogue on the lehenga.

"You realize that you completely ruined the pictures?" she said by way of hello, as I approached the vanity where she was getting her makeup done. The two necklaces sat in red velvet boxes on the table before the mirror.

"Vis-u-al sym-me-try," she said, clapping on the syllables. "You know what fucks up visual symmetry? An uneven number of bridesmaids and a random-ass outfit."

"I'm sorry, Pooja, I just thought, you know, IST, and there are so many of us—"

"Which makes your little DIY job even more obvious. You are such a child, Anita, honestly. Who are you, Etsy?"

I could feel the eyes on me as I attempted to hold it together—well, I could've seen them, too, thanks to the mirror in front of Pooja, but I didn't have the courage to look. She was right. I got it. I deserved it. If it were my wedding, if I were Pooja, I'd be livid, too. I realized, in that moment, watching a makeup artist glue three-inch strips of mink fringe onto Pooja's eyelids, what I should have done long before: manned up, woman-ed up, whatever.

It wasn't my bridesmaid's lehenga that had needed an intervention, it was our friendship. If I'd felt so slighted, I should've said something, swallowed my fear of confrontation, attempted to salvage our relationship.

Or, if she bothered me that much, I should've excused myself from the proceedings. Told her I couldn't be a bridesmaid. Initiated a breakup. As it was, I'd languished in limbo, disparaging her in my head while getting a blowout that she paid for. That was the worst kind of person. Someone who was fake.

"The yellow one," I said, feebly. It set off the glimmering gems lining the edges of her Sabyasachi lehenga, with its deep V and voluminous skirt, embroidered all over with magnificent red blossoms, like the bedspread of some seventeenth-century European monarch, worthy of a gala at the Met, or a glass case in the Met, at the very least. "You look beautiful, by the way." I excused myself to drink my feelings.

The other bridesmaids treated me like a leper, except for Preeti, Pooja's eighteen-year-old cousin. "I like what you did with it," she said shyly, gazing at the ruched straps that Miguel had ingeniously fashioned for my top. I gave her a sad little smile. Let this child not remember me as an example of how a grown woman ought to behave.

Aparna insisted on draping my dupatta in such a way that the Etsy-ness of my outfit wouldn't be terribly obvious as I walked down the aisle, which was fine. Not like anyone would be looking at me, given the twenty peacocks that would join the procession once we got outside. Disassociate, I told myself. Find something to look forward to. Thinking about The Goddess Effect made me think about the deck, which made me think about the retreat, which made me sad.

"The chef we just signed," Venus had said that morning, chuckling to herself, "what Stefano does with hearts of palm—honestly, it makes me wet." I had gasped and giggled with everyone else, but I couldn't ignore that feeling of defeat, of being left out. The retreat was the following weekend, and the studio would be closed for four days on account of all the instructors being in Ojai. I wondered if I could do one of those phone hiatuses while the retreat was going on, lock it in a drawer or give it to Christina or throw it in the ocean or smash it to tiny bits—something to shield myself from knowing about the fun I would not have.

For a while, I focused on the opulence. The peacocks. The famous sitar player backed by an orchestra. The dancers who preceded us, polka-dotted skirts swirling, towers of clay vessels balanced precariously on their heads. The sea of faces that turned in our direction, like flowers toward the sun, as we made our way down the aisle. I clutched my bouquet and willed myself not to trip.

The ceremony was three and a half hours long. I spent most of it on my phone, scrolling first through my regular feed, then through Raven's (sponsored content galore, most recently for a line of bikinis made of repurposed plastic straws), Jared's, Annalisa's, Saffron's, Ophelia's, and Venus's, in that order. Who was she, really? I asked myself, thumbing back through her posts, scrolling through the comments.

Two underneath her most recent post, another Annie Leibovitz–style portrait of her stretching in the shape of a crescent moon, stood out: *u r unwell*, from one user, and *there's a special place in hell for WOMEN WHO PREY ON OTHER WOMEN*, from another. Weird. Both of the accounts were private. Competitors? Possibly, but they wouldn't be private if they were in the boutique fitness business and had any intent to make money. Trolls? Bots?

They both had several hundred posts and followers, and neither had a bunch of numbers in their username, which implied that they weren't the sort of bots or trolls that shat on people for kicks. What would happen if I requested to follow them? Why not? Maybe I'd find out something that would compel Venus to take me seriously. Or something that would clue me in to what made her tick. Despite what I'd read in *Effected*, and the fact that I saw her pretty much every day, some essential part of her remained a mystery. I kept coming back to that image of her in the back room—tired, spent, dragged down.

Miguel texted that he and Riley wouldn't be able to make it after all. Mushroom ceremony in Topanga got out of hand SORRY. Probably for the best. In retrospect, I was up there with Owen Wilson and Vince Vaughn as the worst wedding guest of all time. I did not need two extra bodies that the bride didn't know on my back.

After the kanyadaan (step 14 of 54), I texted Stacy and asked how she was holding up. No response. No gray bubbles. I turned around and looked for her. Amid the sea of faces and upheld iPhones, I spotted Praveen, talking to Riz lookalike in the way back, by the chai and lemonade station. No Stacy. Maybe she got bored and left. It happened. Half the uncles did it.

As I swiveled back, I spotted her.

Next to my mother. Wearing a bindi.

She didn't see me, transfixed as she was by the chanting pandit and twenty-foot-tall mandap and ten thousand blush roses and Swarovski crystal chandelier and veritable bonfire before Pooja and Amit, who had been joined by a battalion of their extended families for whatever step it was they were on now. (Seventeen? Thirty-seven? Steps in Hindu weddings seemed to multiply, blow past the numbers and order on the program. They had a mind of their own and a not-so-subtle intent to make the distance between you and cocktails as long as possible.)

By the time the pandit gave his final blessing, it was after five, my stomach felt like it was eating itself, and I needed a nap, a vat of chicken tikka masala, or an IV of tequila—maybe all three. The nice thing about Hindu weddings is that there's no recessional, it's just a free-for-all, so as well-wishers stormed the mandap with fistfuls of marigold petals and hydroponically farmed basmati rice, I slipped away.

I searched for Praveen and Stacy as I made my way across the lawn, allowing myself to get momentarily sidetracked by a champagne tower and a kebab platter the size of a South Pacific island.

"Please tell me you brought some Molly," I said, jutting into the line that had already formed for the chaat station and linking my arm through Praveen's, "because I had the worst sexual experience of my life last night, and alcohol alone is not gonna cut it."

"I'm not Praveen."

Neil. I had linked arms with Neil. My ex. My ex who, in his newly slim and trim state, apparently bore a striking resemblance to Praveen from behind. My slim and trim ex who was in line with his *fiancée*, resplendent as ever in another fucking Falguni Shane Peacock lehenga. Good God, was she sponsored by them? Who owned that much Indian couture? She was looking at me in horror.

"Oh, fuck," I said, dropping my arm. "My bad." She continued to gape. Delicate body, delicate sensibilities. "Oh come on," I said, "you've never done Molly? Put it on your registry. Thank me later." I grabbed a champagne off the tray of a passing server and chugged it on the way to Praveen—the real Praveen—who was leaning against one of the gin-and-tonic bars with Riz lookalike.

"What's the word for someone who's beyond shame?" I asked.

Praveen looked mildly annoyed at my intrusion. "Martha Stewart?"

"I should be so lucky," I said. "Speaking of rich white women—I want you to meet my friend Stacy."

"That blonde who's fawning all over your mom? I was wondering who she was."

The overwhelmingly generous big sister I never had, I wanted to say. What I said instead: "We met at Goddess Effect. She's the one who got me into it. You'll love her." I dragged him by the hand, past the vessel-balancing dancers whose shift apparently did not end with the ceremony. Stacy was by the pani puri station, deep in conversation with my mom. She set down her plate to kiss Praveen's cheek.

"Best wedding *ever*," she said to me. "Your lovely mother walked me through every step. I was entranced."

"Seriously?" Praveen said. "I stopped listening after the pandit called out his social handles."

"It's been *years* since I've had a cultural immersion, literal years." Stacy had this dreamy look on her face. "I binged that Netflix series about Indian weddings, but actually *being* at one—"

"I take it it's your first?" Praveen interrupted.

"First of many, I hope," Stacy said. "Meena Auntie was telling me about the unconventional wedding she had, way back when." She turned to my mom to ask her something, and Praveen motioned for me to come with him. My head spun—Stacy and my mom were friends? Stacy knew that my parents eloped? I was supposed to be in control of what Stacy knew about me, but here was my mom, fucking everything up.

"She's using you," Praveen said, pulling me toward the pav bhaji station.

"What? Who?"

"Wannabe Indian Barbie. No one hangs on every namaskar of a three-and-a-half-hour Hindu wedding unless they've got some ulterior motive. *And* she's in a sari? Hashtag desperate. I can't figure it out, though—what could a woman with a rock like that possibly want from you?"

How many slights can you take before you finally snap? How many had I taken in the past twenty-four hours? Had some been self-inflicted? Sure. Was I perfect? Not a chance. But there are times when it seems like the myriad forces of the universe are conspiring against you, when all signs point to the fact that the universe does not have your back, that the universe actually wants you *on* your back, down for the count. Well, fine. The universe could have its way. I couldn't fight it anymore.

"Honestly? Fuck off." I turned and started walking before the tears began to stream.

"What?" said Praveen.

"Ayyabba," said my mom. A Kannada word I hadn't heard in years; it meant fearsome and difficult to tackle. Essentially: the worst.

20

Technically, cocktail hour was happening inside the Polo Lounge as well, but since it was one of those picture-postcard LA evenings, and there were twelve bars set up outside, plus an army of servers passing champagne, the bar inside the Polo Lounge was blissfully empty apart from the two uncles in the corner sipping scotch and talking stocks, the Indian equivalent of those old Muppets in the balcony. It's not a party without them.

I slumped into a high-backed chair that gave me a direct view of the bottles and nothing else. The bartender, probably taking into account my tea-bag eyes, skipped the banter and asked what I wanted. "A mescal negroni," I mumbled.

I dug to the root of my discontent. Praveen, Neil, Pooja, even the threesome—all of it I could shrug off or file away as a thing to laugh about later. What really bothered me was my mom. More specifically: my mom's fast friendship with Stacy. It didn't make sense. My mom and I were so different—her, ever so rule abiding, me, breaking them all.

Although. There was a time when she hadn't been so conformist. When she, a Hindu Brahman, married my father, a Muslim who'd forsaken Allah for atheism, in a civil ceremony in Troy, New York. None of their family attended. They didn't even tell people "back home" until after it was done, and then my mother's parents didn't speak to her for a year. The youngest of ten, she was the only one of her siblings to leave India. At some point, she must've known what it was like to do the opposite of what was expected.

My parents did not trumpet their love story. They did not keep framed photos around the house. I never asked my dad how he and my mom met, and when I asked her, she sort of smiled to herself and said it just happened. They were in the same department in grad school; they were in the same circle of friends. Nothing about it struck me as revolutionary, at the time, but then, it's pretty much impossible to regard your parents as radical when you're living under their roof.

"Anita, what are you doing in here?" I turned and saw Pooja's mom, Payal Auntie, almost unrecognizable in Anastasia of Beverly Hills eyelash extensions and diamond earrings the size of Christmas ornaments. "The party's all outside. I just came in for one of these blue-cheese-stuffed olives." She leaned over me and plucked one from the garnish compartment behind the bar. "The paneer-stuffed olives out there . . . don't tell anyone," she said conspiratorially, still chewing, "but I don't think paneer tastes like anything!" I had to laugh.

She leaned back against the bar and touched my forearm. "I have to say, I'm so happy that you convinced your mother to come. She ought to *enjoy* her life, not live it according to some ancient, misogynistic mourning tradition. Meena is—what's that term you kids use these days?"

I fumbled an explanation of the "I'm not a mom, I'm a cool mom" meme.

"No, not that," Payal Auntie said, batting away my idiocy. "Is it . . . Bad B? Baddie? Bad*ass*? One of those—*that's* what I was thinking." She put her hand over her mouth and giggled. "The things I say after a few champagnes."

She implored me to get up and go with her. I said I needed a moment, but I would be out there soon.

Too funny, I thought, staring at the startlingly clear block of ice in my drink. But maybe Payal had a point. I had never thought of my mom as a person with an identity besides my mother, or my dad's wife. It was possible that Meena was more of a badass than I thought. It was possible that we had more in common than I thought. It was possible that I'd be *lucky* to have more in common with her. By marrying my dad, she risked being disowned. Thus far, I'd risked what? My credit score?

I had been so awful to her. I guess I needed someone to blame, and it seemed wrong to blame the dead guy, even in my own head.

He died on a Sunday. What I remember: the phone call from my mom, sometime after 10:00 a.m., voice shaking, telling me I needed to come to the hospital. Me, on the phone with Praveen, in the Uber, him saying, "I'm sure it's just a minor scare, but say the word and I'll order a car, too.'" Me not saying the word because I didn't want to put him out. How silly would that be, making him Uber to Morristown Memorial on a Sunday when he could be at brunch at Catch? He stayed on the phone the whole time. Me, walking into the ER, seeing Rupa Auntie and then another auntie and then a whole brigade of aunties and uncles huddled around my dad, on a stretcher, and my mother, still in her knee-length tennis shorts, and realizing only then that this was not minor. This was the very definition of major.

The next time I saw my dad—the last time—was at the wake, in his casket. Even though I planned the funeral, I didn't remember agreeing to a wake. The logistics of the funeral were a mess—what do you do for a former Muslim-turned-atheist who married a Hindu? What does tradition mean? Does it matter? Would he have wanted any of this? I kept asking myself.

Besides an obligatory moment, I avoided looking at the casket. I didn't want to remember him like that. I wanted to remember us spending hours at Tower Records, him playing me Miles Davis, me playing him Kanye. Him making me scrambled eggs and asking me, with zero judgment, how my night was, the time I came home at 1:00 a.m. even though my curfew was eleven.

My mom kept breaking down and crying. It annoyed me. They'd grown apart after I'd gone to college. They no longer slept in the same bedroom. They sometimes had, I knew from growing up, epic arguments, slamming doors, shouting. And here she was, at the funeral I'd been forced to plan because she couldn't keep it together, shoulders shaking, face buried in the pallu of her sari. How dare she lose it like that? My dad had told me never to cry. Classic immigrant parent advice: show no weakness.

Maybe that was the problem. I tipped back the remainder of the negroni, sucked the last drops of alcohol through the shrunken block of ice. My mom had felt all her feelings, had grieved in a messy, public way. What had I done?

I put down the glass and started scrolling, seeking an escape from my morass of self-loathing. Venus draped over an olive tree, espousing the healing properties of Ojai. A Kardashian-Jenner. A baby.

A sponsored post from Gonzo: Emilia behind a folding table in a parking lot, beaming as a sprite with purple hair did a kick flip. The caption: *Wanna join this squad? Show us what you got.* Ugh. That open call Max had told me about. My time would've been better spent there than embarrassing myself at this wedding.

A warm hand on my shoulder, and then a voice. "Two more of what she's having, please." I watched, in shock, as my mom eased herself into the chair next to mine.

"Have you ever tried mescal?" I asked.

"First time's a charm," she said.

We watched, in silence, as the bartender made our drinks and set them down before us.

"Cheers," she said, lifting her glass to mine, and her show of grace toward someone who deserved exactly none of it moved me to the degree that, this time, the tears came in earnest.

She patted my back and made soothing sounds as I pressed my face into her shoulder. She didn't even have to ask me what was wrong. It all came spilling out between sobs: "I don't know what I'm doing here. I don't have a job at Gonzo. I'm sorry I've been such a jerk. I'm so mad about Daddy. Why isn't anything"—sob—"working out"—sob—"the way I thought it would?"

I expected her to tell me to pack my bags and join her on the plane home. Instead, once my sobs had retreated and I'd patted my face down with a pile of cocktail napkins, she said, "It's okay to not know the answers all the time. Life is like that. But you can always talk to me. That's what I'm here for."

"Really?" I sniveled. "I thought you wanted me to be just like Pooja. Perfect. Have everything all figured out."

"You are you, Anita. You can only be yourself." Obvious, yes, but from her, it sounded revelatory.

"Besides, none of us have it all figured out," she said. "That's why I've come to rely so much on these religious texts, to make sense of all of this." She gestured around the room, presumably referring to human existence in general and not merely the Polo Lounge.

"I miss him," I said. It was the first time I'd said it, out loud.

"Me, too," she said. "Imagine what he would've said about this wedding."

"'Gross. Gratuitous.'"

She laughed. "'Gauche.' He always liked that word."

"Why didn't you make him take his medication?" I didn't say it unkindly. It just seemed, in retrospect, like an obvious thing that could've been done to prevent disaster, like changing the batteries in a smoke alarm.

She shook her head. "There's only so much you can tell a man to do. Not just a man—any person. He thought he had a handle on his health, he thought he was okay. I had to trust him. After thirty-two years of marriage, you get to that point. It's not all . . . what was that show you used to watch? With the pastor and his wife, and everyone was always happy?"

"*7th Heaven*?"

"Yes. Most marriages are not like that."

I thought, again, of those arguments my parents had had. My mom knew how to stand her ground. If my dad had chosen to go his own way, maybe it was no one's fault but his own. And even then, we'd never know the whole confluence of reasons for why things work out the way they do. I'd been yearning for someone to blame for his death, as if assigning it to a source would make me feel better.

"I just have to believe that there's some meaning, some reason, some rationale to the universe," she was saying, gazing down at her drink. "That's why I've leaned so much on the temple, the Hindu rituals, Gita class. They help me to accept life and all of its mysteries. Not to understand, but to accept, to come to peace with reality."

Everyone had their coping mechanisms. Mine was drinking and Goddess Effect. Hers was religion. Was one better than the other? I filed that away as something to think about later.

"You will find your way," she said. "If not here, if not somewhere else, there's always back home."

I jumped off my chair and embraced her, inhaled the scent of coconut oil and fifteen-year-old Chanel No. 5 and a round, resounding warmth that I could not place. The amount of restraint it took for an Indian mom to discover that her child was unemployed and not lose her shit. She deserved a Nobel.

Aparna's voice came over the speakers, imploring us to find our place cards or flag down an attendant with an iPad and take our seats in the Crystal Ballroom.

"Should I even show my face?" I asked. "Does everyone think I'm crazy?"

"Come on," she said. "There are six hundred people at this wedding. The pandit is crazier than you, asking us to follow him on TokTik or whatever it's called."

I laughed, really laughed, for what felt like the first time in months. "So you hit it off with Stacy, huh?" I said, taking her hand, helping her down from her chair.

"She's very inquisitive. Keeps asking about my 'immigrant experience' and saying that her upbringing was 'so bland.' Seems kind of fixated."

21

y place card put me at table 17, with Praveen, but I ended
up sitting with Stacy and my mom at one of the overflow
tables. Not that anyone spent much time in their seats—
the deejay was India's answer to Calvin Harris, the dancers with pots
on their heads transformed into Bollywood showgirls who beseeched
even the walker-equipped aunties and uncles to get out on the floor, and
after Pooja and Amit's first dance, to a mashup of a ballad from *Lagaan*
and Rihanna's "This Is What You Came For," one thousand foam glow
sticks dropped from the ceiling of the Crystal Ballroom. I made sure
my mom got two. By the time the reception ended, at midnight, I had
dark moons underneath my armpits.

I had a history of avoiding confrontation, of brushing off slights
in the interest of being agreeable. Maybe it was the precedent I'd set
the previous night by walking out of the threesome, maybe "What
would Venus do?" was still in my head, maybe it was the liquid courage brought on by the champagne and mescal negronis, which I had
been alternating, one to one: I was determined to set things right with
Praveen.

I pulled him aside during a dubstep remix of "Chammak Challo."

"I'm sorry for overreacting," I said, "but you've also been kind of a
bitch to me this whole weekend."

He sighed. "I know. I miss you. I miss *us*—ABN us. It's weird, not having you there, and not to be a total drunkle, but what are you doing here, babe? Working for The Goddess Effect?" Behind his haze of several gin and tonics, I saw genuine concern.

Frankly, I had no idea what I was doing. But I still had a month left of my beta run to figure it out, and after coming clean to my mom, I had no problem owning the fact that I was a work in progress or a hot mess, depending on the angle.

"Can you just trust that I'll figure it out? I needed a reset. I need to be here now. And I need you to be my friend, not the guy who pokes holes in everything I do."

"Fine," he said, bringing me in for a hug. "And I'm sorry for ditching you for Vishal." Riz lookalike was engaged in a limbo-type move with Stacy that made his torso go parallel to the ground. We watched his biceps, bulging beneath a Thom Browne shirt that had been unbuttoned to his sternum.

"What does he do?"

"Owns his own *hedge fund*," Praveen said, knuckle in mouth.

"Well, that's it. You're not going to do any better."

"I *know*," Praveen said, visibly stressed. "I really did hit it off with that hype house realtor . . . but Uber stock, versus TikTok mansions, versus Tribeca penthouse, versus—"

I told Praveen to shut up and dragged him back out to the dance floor.

After the farewell brunch—South Indian-themed, dosas, idlis, and appams galore—I squeezed my mom tight, let my eyes get wet. Stacy and I waved goodbye as the charter bus pulled out, bound for Van Nuys and the private jet back to Newark. She slung her arm around me and let me lay my head on her shoulder as we waited for the valet to bring around the Panamera; the next time she spoke was when we pulled up at the Gig.

"You're a true friend," she said. "Thank you for bringing me into your world." She promised to return the favor. I said something to the effect of "That's not necessary." We hugged, and I went upstairs to collapse in bed. I woke up for the amount of time it took to nuke and inhale the five idlis I'd taken home in a cubic-zirconia-studded tiffin (part of the welcome basket). Sober sleep—one hell of a drug.

Monday morning came with new urgency: get a job, any job, stat. I planned to spend the day trawling LinkedIn, besides a break for Venus's 9:00 a.m., which, I reasoned, would arm me with the endorphins and mental clarity necessary for applying for yet another round of positions with titles like "ninja" and "slayer." Stacy texted, Crazy cramps. Not gonna make class. TY again for that PRICELESS cultural immersion, so so special! 🙏🙏💀 She loved that phrase, *cultural immersion*. Was that weird?

I scanned my inbox. Sale, sale, spam, newsletter, another newsletter. What was this from The Goddess Effect?

> Subject: YOU'RE IN.

> Message: Thank you, Anita, for choosing to grace us with your presence at our inaugural retreat. Trust, you will emerge from this cocoon with wings wide open, fluttering with purpose and passion, stronger and more resilient than ever before. We're putting the finishing touches on your itinerary and cannot wait to share it with you soon.

> Divinely yours,

> The Goddess Effect

I sat straight up, clutching my phone. This had to be a mistake. I hadn't signed up for the retreat. I couldn't afford the retreat. Was I being hacked? Was The Goddess Effect being hacked? I looked at the email again, closely. It had been sent from the same address that sent my class confirmations. It looked real. My name was right there.

Then the wheels started turning. I'd asked Venus and Ophelia about attending—maybe they'd found a spot for me after all. Maybe this was their way of carving out a position for me. Regardless, if I had a spot at the retreat and I didn't have to pay for it, there was no way I wasn't going to go. That would be stupid. This was a gift. Maybe it was a gift from God. Maybe he/she/they had observed my show of honesty and gratitude toward my mother and decided to reward me for being marginally less of a shithead. But I had to make sure. I had to get to the studio, ask Venus and Ophelia in person, confirm that this message had not been sent in error.

As I told myself not to get my hopes up, they went airborne. I thought about Ojai, tugging on a pair of Stacy's hand-me-down Lulus, magical Ojai, this mythical place with a mystical name where I would grow wings and learn how to operate them. Stacy had said the resort was to die for. The possibilities made my mind race. I bounded downstairs to the door.

"How was the wedding?" Max called after me. He was in the kitchen, pouring the contents of a French press into a Le Creuset mug.

"Great," I said, and asked about his weekend, more out of courtesy than interest.

"Eh, I ended up going to that Gonzo open call, figured, in this dumpster fire economy, why not? Emilia didn't even remember me. Glad I made such a lasting impression."

I grimaced. "Yikes."

"What are you gonna do?" He took a sip of his coffee and shrugged. "Guess I'll be working on marketing decks for cauliflower rice cafés until the end of time."

"Cassava is the new cauliflower rice," I said, pushing out the door. "Thank me later."

My clavicle was studded with sweat by the time I reached the front desk. Ophelia was looking down, banging on the keys of a laptop that I had not seen before, muttering to herself.

"It's not that hard, *Cassie*. Find a Western Union. Do a bank transfer. Write a goddamn check, Venmo, who gives a fuck—but no, we are not going to accept a *Nordstrom gift card* as a deposit."

Cassie (another regular) was tripping if she thought she could use a Nordstrom gift card to reserve a place at the retreat. But Western Unions were not that easy to find, and it struck me as odd, again, that The Goddess Effect wasn't allowing attendees to pay for the retreat with a credit card. Were they that hard up for cash? I flashed back to the conversation I'd overheard in the back room—Venus bitching about Cheng wanting equity and having to cover her costs.

"*Hi*, Anita. Can I help you?" Ophelia asked, glaring up at me.

At this point, it was obvious that something at The Goddess Effect was off. Over the past few weeks, Ophelia had escalated from generally blasé to generally bothered. In class, Venus kept harping on resilience—"How much are you willing to *give* to *get* the kind of glow that money can't buy?" she'd posited recently—but elsewhere, in the back room, she was about as resilient as a late-autumn leaf. Maybe they were overworked, given the retreat. Maybe . . .

Perhaps The Goddess Effect was something other than what it seemed. But there was the matter of the confirmation email. Regardless of my mixed feelings about *Jesus Is King* and *The Life of Pablo*, if someone gave me tickets to a Kanye concert, no doubt, I would go. You didn't have to love *everything* to take part. You could be curious. You could be hungry for a new experience. You could simply want to know what a four-thousand-dollar (and up) retreat entailed.

I pulled up the confirmation email on my phone as Venus emerged from the back room. "So I got this, this morning," I said, turning the screen to them. "It's like, *beyond*, but I didn't sign up for the retreat. I just want to make sure it's legit."

They exchanged a look. Venus turned to me. "Totally legit. It's actually the perfect place to talk about an idea we've been discussing. How would you feel about joining our team?"

It felt too good to be true. All through class, I tried to make the equation compute. So Venus decided that she wanted me to attend the retreat after all, and the confirmation email was her way of saying so? But if I was working the retreat, why would they put together an itinerary for me? Or did the staff also get to participate? What was going on?

By repose, the questions that seemed so urgent during a set of burpees—anything was better than focusing on the burpees themselves—had lost their oomph. What was that phrase? "Don't look a gift horse in the mouth." (Related: What the fuck was a gift horse?) I worried that if I asked too many questions, they'd rescind the invitation. They'd think I was high-maintenance. Shut up and go, I told myself. What else are you going to do?

On my back, in a figure four, I blinked at the whitewashed wood beams above and wondered if the ceiling would make a good post. It was design-y but not intimidatingly so. What to say?

Beneath these beams, change is happening (Ugh, could you be more basic?)

Women break through all sorts of ceilings, every day (Yeah, no.)

I could tell you what's happening on the ground, but it's so visceral that I'm still processing it, and when we are agents of change, when we are changelings, *it's important to look up, to understand how much more we must grow* (You've got to be fucking kidding me.)

No paragraph-long, "please take me seriously" captions. No ceiling post. It was just a ceiling, after all. But perhaps social media for The Goddess Effect was an avenue worth exploring in a more substantive way. They clearly needed help with it. The Goddess Effect wasn't on all the platforms that it could be, and Venus's Annie Leibovitz portraits, while art adjacent, didn't do a good job of describing what The Goddess Effect actually was. And the critics were vicious.

I'd noticed another weird comment beneath a photo of her in a butterfly stretch: *NDAs? srsly girl? you on that weinstein shit?* Like the others, this user was private, and I'd also requested to follow them. It seemed like there was some other version of Venus out there, one that countered the narrative she'd cultivated in class, one that, if this user was to be believed, dispensed nondisclosure agreements for who knew what reason. Venus might not be able to silence her haters—what woman could?—but she might want to know who they were. Keep tabs on them. As it was, it wasn't even clear if Venus knew she had critics.

If they were serious about me joining their team, and if I genuinely wanted to (though I had no other viable options), that was a thing I could do. I could be The Goddess Effect's head of brand. I could pitch the idea to them, in Ojai. I could own my destiny, manifest it, like those colonists. I could make destiny my bitch.

That was one way the retreat could go. But, as I'd learned, The Goddess Effect was full of surprises.

22

By Thursday, the day before the retreat, I was thrumming with anticipation. Stacy had sent me the entire catalog of excitement-related emoji after I informed her that I'd be going after all—the double exclamation point, the shooting star, the face that's laughing so hard it's crying—and insisted on driving up together. I hadn't seen her since the wedding. IDK what's up with my period, she'd texted, but I'll be good by Friday. In her absence, I took front and center in class and tried to emit an aura of confidence. I imagined Venus sniffing my aura, like a dog.

For reasons I could not fully explain, I didn't tell Stacy about what Venus had said. Part of it was that Stacy kept talking about how great it was that I was "forging ahead" despite being "marginalized" by ABN—"I put a parental block on them," she'd said—and I didn't want to disappoint her. Part of it was that Venus's offer—"How would you feel about joining our team?"—had all the heft of a soap bubble. But another, less charitable part of it was that I didn't want Stacy to somehow steal the opportunity, nebulous as it was. There was no reason to think that she would, but I still regarded her, in all of her white, fit, rich splendor, as better than me, and assumed that anyone, given the option, would pick Stacy over me. For anything. To pump gas, even.

I was counting out no-show thongs and dropping them in my duffel bag Thursday afternoon when Christina knocked on my door and asked if I wanted to come downstairs and help.

"Help?" I repeated, dumbly.

"You know, house dinner," she said. In my post-wedding, pre-retreat frenzy, I'd forgotten about that Gig ritual. House dinner was supposed to be once a month, but because of Adil's travel schedule, there hadn't been one since I moved in. As the Gig's founder, he got invited to a lot of entrepreneurship conferences. According to his social media, he'd most recently been on a panel in New Zealand with the founder of WeWork. They'd gone surfing afterward.

"Miguel's a control freak and said he'd do everything himself, but making dinner for ten is a lot," Christina said. "Also, the Amazon house account is on his phone, so we can order shit while controlling the music." She had a point, and I was low on body wash.

Miguel was freaking out about having accidentally mixed cilantro into the guacamole (Jay and Constance had that condition that made cilantro taste like soap).

"We've got more avocados than Chipotle," Christina said. "I'll make another guac for them." She told me to make Miguel a margarita. "Actually, make a pitcher. It's five o'clock somewhere, and somewhere is here."

I embraced the purposefulness of being given a task I could handle, even though the margarita mix was that Ecto Cooler green stuff filled with high-fructose corn syrup or whatever it was that gave you diabetes on contact.

"Is house dinner always this intense?" I asked. In various states of assemblage: vegan queso, grain-free nachos, red enchiladas, green enchiladas, mole enchiladas, and "rice and beans" except the rice was—you guessed it—cauliflower, and the beans were crickets. I wasn't there yet.

"Yup," said Miguel. "It's one of the"—he dropped his voice and put an oven-mitted hand over his heart—"distinguishing factors of the

Gig, a philosophy of hospitality that set us apart from the start, before Venice Beach became Silicon Beach, when LA was merely for stars, not unicorns."

"I remember the first time I heard Adil do that speech," Christina said. "Boy sure knows how to make himself sound like God."

Adil's claim to fame: buying Cars.com, Pets.com, Hotels.com, and other generic URLs at the age of seventeen, before everyone realized that the internet was A Thing. He ended up selling them for millions, creating the basis of his fund. But lately, according to Miguel and Christina, he'd been on a losing streak.

"I mean, *I* could've told him not to invest in HomeBodies," Miguel said. "But, you know. That's how it goes with investing. Win some, lose some." Miguel mentioned Adil's stake in Smack, the cannabis nootropics company that produced the kissy-face-engraved vape I'd abused at Retro. "And his network is still thick as hell. Half the reason I wanted this job was so that he can recommend me as a personal assistant for one of his buddies when my time is up. Evan Spiegel, the guy from Reddit, Peter Thiel—I don't care. I'll be a blood boy, too, if the money's right."

I wondered if I should have put more thought into making a good first impression on Adil. I dipped a spoon into the margarita pitcher. Too sweet. I poured in more tequila. Maybe Señor Frog's–level margaritas were the key to unlocking Adil's goodwill, or my charm, or both.

Riley sauntered over and launched into a story about how one of her clients brought her Pomeranian to a breath-work class. Constance came down seeking feedback on a draft of the pet policy for the Museum of Ice Cream but for Poetry. By seven, everyone but Max had gathered in the kitchen. His door was closed, but you could tell the lights were on.

"What's up with that?" I asked Christina, nodding in the direction of his room.

"Probably consumed with that project Adil gave him. I heard there's equity involved. Max said he signed an NDA, but I get the feeling that he's set for life if this thing takes off."

"Wait, what? He was just complaining to me about the dumpster fire economy."

Christina laughed. "The economy can't touch Max. His family built Manhattan. They're like the Astors."

"No. Seriously? What is he doing here?"

"A shot at the Southern California dream," she said, gesturing grandly. "Babes, beach, billion-dollar valuations plucked from the sky."

"Jesus. To be a white guy with generational wealth. I hope I come back as that in my next life."

It didn't make sense. Why was Max living at the Gig? Why was he stressing over decks for cauliflower rice cafés and going to Gonzo open calls? Why was he pretending to be poor? It was like when rich people shopped at Target for the novelty of it, when they called it "Tar-zhay" and thought they were so clever.

I was on my third margarita when the front door opened and a warm baritone bellowed, "Anyone home?" I could sense Adil's smile before I saw it: Invisaligned, whitened, possibly made perfect by plastic surgery but perfect nonetheless. If there were a handbook for what a woke businessman should look like, he would've been on the cover: tall and trim, a thick swoop of hair and two days of scruff, a direct-to-consumer cashmere crewneck, and a diversity-quota tan. Attractive but not intimidatingly so. He looked like the kind of person who submitted themselves to 40 Under 40 lists and practiced saying "hi" in the mirror.

Max strode out of his room; Adil brought him in for a one-armed bro hug. "HomeBodies is gonna give me an ulcer," I overhead him say. "Should've seen the red flags flapping around that one."

"Yeah . . . ," said Max.

"Stock price is tanking, institutional investors are pulling out. I mean, look, if you're going to turn your home into a coworking space and invite over a bunch of strangers from the internet, maybe hide your Gucci loafers and don't leave your Chanel wallet on your Cloud couch when you go to get your Postmates. These bitches were *asking* to get robbed. And of course they blame the platform. Blame HomeBodies' vetting process. People should do their own vetting. Fucking babies, expecting tech to do everything for them. What's good here?"

"Jay's VR nightlife venture could be cool if he could get the audio and video to sync—right now, you go to his piano bar, there's a guy playing Billy Joel and a chick twerking in the background."

"That actually sounds kind of awesome," Adil said.

"Right? But about this thing . . ."

I watched Adil nod and purse his lips at eerily regular intervals. It was like he had just watched a TED Talk: "How to Look Like You're Listening When You're Really Not." He wore an Apple Watch and an Oura ring. Why did I want to flirt with him? Because he had power? Because my ego still hurt from the threesome? Because he was Indian, and, whether I wanted to admit it to myself or not, deep down, I wanted to be liked by other Indians?

I sauntered over; Adil flashed his veneers.

"You must be Anita," he said. "Great to meet you. Max sent me your application. How's it going so far? You in at Gonzo?"

"I've kind of changed course," I said, attempting to toss my hair seductively over my shoulder. Pain shot up my neck.

"Oh yeah?" asked Max.

I ignored him. "Do you know Venus von Turnen, founder of The Goddess Effect?"

Adil blinked and jerked his head, almost imperceptibly. "We met at a conference last year."

"I might be joining her team."

"Interesting," he said. "In what capacity?"

"We're discussing it in Ojai this weekend. She's doing a retreat at the Ranch." This, I'd learned, was how regulars referred to it.

"Getting into the experiential extended-gathering market," Adil said, curling up one side of his mouth and nodding to himself. At that point, Miguel sounded a miniature gong on the mantel. Adil came around to my side and touched his hand to the small of my back. "She must've lined up some sick sponsors. Who's on board?"

"Not sure of them all, but she did mention the Warby Parker of vibrators." Max choked on a laugh; I shot him a look.

"*Super* interesting," Adil said, not even flinching at the mention of vibrators. "Save me the seat next to you, I want to hear more."

23

Adil and I talked for a little while. I debated his interest in me. Platonic, mentorial, or more than that? Romantic? He wanted to know lots of specifics about the retreat—how many women would be there, the age range, how many workouts a day we'd be doing. They were the sorts of questions that I couldn't imagine most men asking—hell, besides those of us going on the retreat, I couldn't imagine anyone caring that much. But maybe Adil was different. Maybe Adil cared about women.

Though there was that rant about HomeBodies.

After a little while, Miguel tapped his glass with a knife and announced it was time for house huddle, which involved going around the table and expounding on a conversational prompt.

"Tonight's is 'What's your moral of the month?'" he said. "I'll go first. My moral is that one month of garbage cannot fit in a mason jar. Thoughts and prayers for those antiplastic crusaders, but no. I know we're supposed to be all philosophical and dreamy in these 'sharing is caring' shebangs, but I needed to drop some real talk, because do you know how much space aluminum foil takes up, and do you know how many sheet pan dinners y'all eat?" The table cracked up. I felt a surge of gratitude for Miguel, for reasons greater than his handiness with root vegetables.

I attempted to actually listen to my housemates and not do the thing you normally do during an icebreaker, which is panic, worry about what you're going to say, and freak out when someone else says the thing that was in your head. My turn came. I took a sip of my drink.

"It's okay not to know," I ventured. Riley nodded knowingly. Christina gave me an encouraging look. I said something about the best-laid plans and trusting the will of the universe; no one was more shocked than me. On the one hand, I couldn't believe these words were coming out of my mouth, on the other, I kind of believed them. Maybe LA was changing me. Maybe I was going soft in the sun, like an overripe plum.

Around nine thirty, Adil looked up from his phone, pushed back his chair, and turned to me. "I've gotta run, but hey, let's get dinner after you get back from Ojai? You can give me the full download."

"Sure," I said. Was I in it for the attention, the free restaurant meal, or because I actually liked Adil? Probably a 40/50/10 split.

"And hey," he said, "if anything really crazy happens, let me know, okay?" He laughed, so I laughed, too. Why would something crazy happen? Why would I reach out to him if it did? Strange. It was possible that he was just socially awkward. I thought of his HomeBodies rant again. But his inquisitiveness, pointed like the tip of a freshly sharpened No. 2, struck me as off in the same way as all the weird things I'd started to notice around and about The Goddess Effect.

I pulled out my phone to see if any of the private commenters had accepted my follow requests. Maybe I ought to DM them. And say what? "Why are you trolling Venus?" That sounded like harassment.

One new follower notification, and a DM.

I clicked the tab and nearly dropped my phone.

@GonzoEmilia.

"What?" The din of shifting chairs and stacking plates must have drowned me out, because no one looked my way.

@GonzoEmilia: Heyyyyyyy sorry went on a cleanse, just saw your notes, would LOVE to meet, come by the office tomorrow at 10?

Questions multiplied in my brain like pop-ups in MS-DOS: (a) what type of cleanse involved not checking your email for weeks on end, and (b) *tomorrow*? Of all days? Stacy and I were supposed to leave for Ojai at ten. That would give us time to get settled in our rooms before WARM, or Welcome and Reconstruct Me, the first official retreat event. It would be taking place in the Ranch's newly renovated infrared sauna, which had been lined with cedar sourced from the Himalayas and "imbued with ancient Buddhist spirits purported to accelerate the soul's path to Nirvana," according to the Ranch's website. Did I want to miss the opportunity to have a newly reconstructed, cedar-scented soul for a zero-notice meeting with a woman who'd ignored me for months?

Although. The things I would've done for this meeting, not long ago.

"We're on duty for cleanup," Max said, clapping my shoulder.

I shrugged off his hand and said I'd be there in a minute. I stared at Emilia's message. I'd respond later, make up some excuse.

Or was the smart thing to do to explore all my options? I wondered as I rinsed dishes. Of course that was the smart thing to do. Maybe I could tell Emilia I had a doctor's appointment, ask if I could come by next week. You couldn't argue with a doctor's appointment. Or would this opportunity evaporate if I put it off?

I was debating the merits of starting my message with *Hey!* versus *Hey,* when Max pointed out that I'd rinsed the same mason jar seven times.

"You okay?" he asked, taking the jar out of my hand and placing it in the dishwasher.

"Emilia DM-ed asking if I could come into Gonzo tomorrow," I said, picking up another mason jar. It felt absurd, saying it out loud, and more than a little thrilling. It sounded so official. Gonzo wanted me. Even if I didn't want them, they wanted me. It was nice to be wanted.

"That's awesome," Max said, turning to face me, a mason jar in either hand, a smile on his face.

"The thing is, I can't go."

"What? Why?"

"The Goddess Effect retreat," I said, turning over the last jar in the sink. "Stacy and I are supposed to leave for Ojai at ten."

"So go later," Max said, screwing up his face. "Uber. Gonzo's what you said you were moving to LA for. Why would you turn down a meeting with them to go to some workout retreat?"

"It's not just *some workout retreat*," I said. "I'm also supposed to talk with Venus about working for The Goddess Effect, and Emilia basically blew me off. Why should I drop everything for her now?"

"Because it's what you moved to LA for," Max said, enunciating as you would with a three-year-old. "This is what you said what you wanted."

"What if what I want changed? What if I don't know what I want?" I felt the hinges coming loose. I grabbed a dish towel and rubbed it roughly over my hands.

"You know you'd be going into Gonzo with an advantage."

"What are you talking about?"

"You're a woman of color," Max said, shrugging. "You're all anyone wants to hire. Take the meeting. People would kill for that privilege."

"*Privilege,*" I repeated, suddenly remembering what Christina had said. "You're one to talk about privilege, between your generational wealth and this super secret, super lucrative project you're doing for Adil."

"What?" he scoffed. "Listen—"

"No, Max, I'm done listening to you." The gall of this guy, to question my rationale, to tell me what to do. He had no right. What would Venus do? Venus would not get mansplained. Venus would get the fuck out. I tossed the dish towel on the counter and stormed upstairs.

24

I spent several minutes drafting a text to Stacy that was equal parts apologetic and proactive—I was so sorry for the change in plans! I could totally take an Uber!

But Stacy said it wasn't a problem. She'd pick me up from Gonzo, and we'd ride up from there.

Stacy: We might be a few min late to WARM but that's totally fine
Stacy: I'm your ally, I wanna support you! 😘
Stacy: We're in this together!

Were we, though? But I wasn't going to argue with her. After storming upstairs and pacing for the length of Jay-Z's "Threat," I decided that the best course of action would be to take the meeting. Not because of what Max said, but because if I didn't, I'd spend the retreat wondering what Emilia wanted.

I imagined what my dad would say. He would laugh at the notion of working for The Goddess Effect. He would tell me to go to Gonzo (and pay off my credit card debt).

It only made sense to keep my options open. Best-case scenario: Gonzo offered me a job, I said I needed four days to think about it, Goddess Effect offered me a job, I leveraged them against each other and walked away with an annual salary of a hundred thousand dollars, a corporate card, and unlimited PTO.

I also decided that, given Emilia's total disregard for professionalism, I wasn't going to go through the ordeal of obsessing over an interview outfit. She would get me in leggings and a sweatshirt. Stacy's shiny, leatherlike Takara leggings and an artfully ripped Stella McCartney sweatshirt, but still—leggings and a sweatshirt.

I tried to push Max out of my mind. Calling me a "woman of color." The nerve. I mean, I *was* a woman of color, of course, duh. And sure, I knew that many companies wanted to increase their diversity or at least look like they were trying. But still. To shove my privilege in my face like that. Yes, I had privilege, but so did he—loads, apparently. So did everyone in this house.

You couldn't win as a woman of color. First they ignored you, then they sought you out, then you became the enemy, and the cycle started all over again.

As I walked out of my room the next morning, I saw Max in the kitchen. I stopped and considered going back in, waiting until the coast was clear. But Julio with a 4.98 rating was waiting in a Kia Soul, and if I canceled, I'd get charged a fee.

I looked straight ahead at the front door as I walked past, like I couldn't see him.

He called my name. "About last night—"

"Nope," I said.

I let the front door slam.

In the car, I took five deep breaths, in through my nose, out through my mouth. Max does not get to live in your head rent-free. It's going to be okay. It's going to be *more* than okay. Get excited! You're going to Gonzo. Finally, Gonzo. And then The Goddess Effect retreat. This is, like, your dream day.

As much as I tried to gin up some hunky-dory attitude, I mostly felt dread. Anxiety and dread. What did Emilia want from me?

Julio pulled up at a low, unremarkable brick building next to a smoke shop and Thai massage place. "Have a nice day," he said.

"Are you sure?" I asked. There was no signage for Gonzo anywhere. My map was doing that weird thing where the compass goes diagonal and indicates some other plane of existence.

"Look, ma'am." He pointed to the number on the building, 3501.

"Sorry, my bad." I opened the door. "Five stars."

The windows were blacked out. I buzzed in to one set of doors and then another before entering a narrow hallway with metal detectors and a bag scanner. "This is Gonzo?" I asked the uniformed security guard, who had a gun holstered to his side. He nodded and smacked his gum. As I collected my bags from the belt, a woman in a miniskirt and a Champion sweatshirt burst through the doors at the other end of the hall. Her "hello" was so elongated and high-pitched, it might've been a mating call for an exotic bird.

Her heels made a loud clacking sound on the linoleum floor. "I'm Liza, Emilia's assistant. Super psyched to meet you. How's it going? Ohmygod, you moving in?" She gestured at my backpack and duffel and burst into giggles. She had a long sheet of hair, glossy and straight. Natural, for sure. No flat iron burns for that forehead. I followed her down a long, dark corridor filled with framed stills from past Gonzo specials: *Julian Assange: Man of the Millennium*; *White Supremacist, Age 6*; *The Hipster Bandit, an Origin Story*.

I told her I was going to Ojai. "Ohmygod, *cute*," Liza said. "There's this energy healer up there who can totally reset you. I heard it's where Justin Bieber went after he mooned all those people at the Vatican."

Did my energy need to be reset? Was that what Liza was saying? Was anxiety, like, seeping out of my pores? We reached the end of the hallway, and I lost my train of thought. A cross between a frat house and a playpen, the Gonzo newsroom—I assumed it was the Gonzo newsroom; the Gonzo logo hung from the ceiling, like a mobile, and there were screens mounted along the perimeter—looked like no newsroom I had seen before. Cocoon chairs dangled from every corner; a guy in one had an eye mask on and his mouth open. Some people sprawled out on beanbags, balancing laptops over their faces. A girl with lavender stripes in her hair leaned into a monitor on a standing desk. Was she not wearing a top, or did a ribbed bralette now count as a top? A bong sat on top of an AP style guide.

"Different, isn't it?" Liza said, watching me. "We call it the pit."

"Can I take photos?" I asked.

"Only inside," she said, "and no location tags. We keep our address private. Mass shooters, right?"

I took a quick series of photos, making sure to get the mobile, and posted the best right away. I couldn't resist. No time for filters or over-wrought overlays of text. My current ambivalence about Gonzo aside, after all that time reaching and obsessing, it was thrilling to have finally made it. I wanted to brag. I pictured Praveen tapping through, nodding, going, "That's my girl."

Liza led the way up to a ring of glass-walled conference rooms. We passed Zapata and X. She pushed in the door to Che, told me to help myself to whatever, then left. On the reclaimed-wood conference table: Hi-Chews, kale chips, Pellegrino, Fiji, and caffeinated turkey jerky. I opened a Pellegrino and stuffed three packs of Hi-Chews into my backpack.

The glass door creaked open, and Emilia strode in. She wore high-waist red patent leather pants, platform sandals that looked like Birkenstocks but were probably some much cooler brand, and a cropped white T-shirt that grazed her rib cage. Her lipstick and fingernails—talons, truly, you could tear open a package with those tips—matched her pants, and her blonde hair was in waves that definitely required heat to create. The effect was Scarlett Johansson meets Harley Quinn. I straightened up in my Aeron chair and subtly tugged at the back of my sweatshirt, as if that would help my case in any way.

She sang my name in an Oprah voice as she pulled out the chair across from me. Then she paused, reconsidered, and launched herself on top of the table. One sandal flew over her shoulder, and then the other, as she arranged herself in a half lotus. My vantage point gave me an unobstructed view of her crotch.

"Wait," she said, assessing me anew. "Have we met?"

"In New York, at that future of media conference," I said. She didn't remember me? What about our moment, the A-plus networking, her giggling and touching my arm?

"Oh," she said, remembering. "Right. I was microdosing. Well, megadosing might've been more accurate. New York, amiright?" She laughed, so I did, too, even though this new information called everything—her, Gonzo, my decision-making skills, me in general—into question.

"I'm gonna get right down to it." She reached over for a packet of turkey jerky, ripped it open, grabbed a piece, and tore it in half with her teeth. "Dane, in all his infinite wisdom"—she rolled her eyes and wiggled her fingers in the air, like the founder of Gonzo was someone who read crystal balls and could not be trusted—"has decided that we need to ramp up the launch of GonzoDrip to compete with some Gen Z news service that Facebook's supposedly about to drop."

"GonzoDrip, the mobile-first app?" I tried to ignore that I'd learned this information from Max.

"Yup. Mobile first." I watched a lump of turkey jerky pass down her throat. "Crosspost to IG, Twitter, Facebook, TikTok—whatever else the youths do to distract themselves from the tyranny of existence. Those kids need content. New content, shareable stuff, all day long, and we need people to churn it out. People like you." She smiled. "Where are you from, by the way?"

"New York. Well, New Jersey."

"Right, but where are you *from* from? You look like you could be anything."

I flashed back to ABN and senior producer Andrew. At least he'd bought me a bento box.

"My parents are from India," I told Emilia.

"*Fabulous.* India, emerging market—there's a freaking billion people there, right? And they've all got phones and unlimited data, *I hope.*" She guffawed and looked at me as if this was a human right, and I would know. "Okay, so, GonzoDrip. Any ideas?"

Plenty, but many things about this did not feel right. And yet. Presented with an opportunity, a chance to shine, what's a model minority to do? Since I'd stepped foot in Gonzo, a little, better version of me, Angel Anita, had been tapping my shoulder, asking incessantly, "What if?" What if this *was* my chance? What I'd been waiting for? I thought again of that trope: "Stop expecting your life to look like how you thought it would." So this meeting hadn't happened as quickly as I thought it would, so this opportunity wasn't exactly what I had hoped for. It was still an opportunity.

"Have you heard about the boycott against Plants & Purpose, that chain of vegan cafés? An employee found out that the owners went back to raising and slaughtering cattle after thirty years of being vegan, and people are freaking out." There had been a protest outside the Silver Lake location; someone had thrown a chickpea bomb through the window. "Plenty of outlets have interviewed the protesters, but the owners haven't talked yet. It would take some legwork, but I think I could convince them."

"How old are they?"

"Sixties, maybe seventies."

"Meh, not our demo."

"Does GonzoDrip only cover people in its demo?" I wondered if I was even in its demo.

"No, but like"—she made a face—"I can't imagine they're lookers. It's just not going to work on mobile. And also, ever since that *Wall Street Journal* profile of Dane that mentioned his Friday night ritual of T-bones and Château Latour, vegans have been flaming us on social. What else? What's all that?" She pointed at my bags. I told her I was going to the Ranch.

"*Love* that place. What for?"

"Have you heard of The Goddess Effect? They're doing a retreat."

"The *Goddess Effect* is doing a retreat?" Emilia dropped the package of turkey jerky and planted her palms on the table. "How did I miss this?"

"Do you go?" I asked, pleasantly surprised. Maybe this was something we could bond over, since whatever bond I'd thought we'd forged at that conference had been negated by the triumvirate of psychedelics (her), naivete (me), and time.

"No, I go to Dogpound, but wait, Venus von Turnen is *super* interesting." Her eyes darted back and forth. "It's cult-y, right? Cult-y and self-help-y?"

Funny of her to call it cult-y. Funny of her to put words to a hunch that was in the corner of my mind.

"I mean, I guess you could interpret it that way, but the method really does make you stronger." Ambivalence aside, I felt the need to defend The Goddess Effect, now that I'd revealed that I was a follower.

"That's it," she said, nodding to herself. "Cover the retreat."

"Cover the retreat?"

"Yeah, there's gotta be something juicy to dig into there. Maybe it's, like, bulimia. Contagious bulimia. Or girl-on-girl action—bored, rich housewives getting their rocks off with each other. I'm guessing, besides you, they're all housewives."

"Not exactly . . ." I thought of that woman in the Facebook T-shirt, but I hadn't seen her in a while. Same with gold lamé leggings from day one, the maybe-could-be Marie Antoinette biopic star. Come to think of it: they were the two that had been talking in hushed tones by the cubbies the other week, asking each other if they were going to do "it."

"Just find something scintillating, scandalous. I'm sure you won't have to try that hard," Emilia went on.

"It's not really like that, and also, I don't think Venus allows video—"

Emilia guffawed again. "You don't think these housewives are going to be recording and posting every moment? Half the reason women go to these things is to make other women jealous."

She had a point.

"And how do you know what it's like? Isn't this the first one? Embed. They must've taught you how to do that at ABN. Just pretend you're one of them. You know, like." She angled her phone over her face, pouted, and batted her eyelashes. "Don't be a perfectionist—all the demo wants now is shaky cell phone video—the less professional, the better."

She kept talking. A mental calculation: On the one hand, accepting this assignment felt like cheating on The Goddess Effect. "Once a cheater, always a cheater." But I wasn't officially employed by The Goddess Effect. There were no guarantees. I'd come this far. "You didn't come this far to only go this far." What had I written in my Moleskine? What had I written on my whiteboard? This was my shot. "You only get one shot."

"Our producers will stitch your videos together," Emilia was saying, "but if you want to go live, DM me and we'll crosspost to GonzoDrip. Don't worry about the time—I only sleep four hours a week. It's Tim Ferriss's latest thing—"

"I'm in," I said.

25

Downstairs, before walking out to the parking lot, I checked to see if any of Venus's social media detractors had accepted my follow requests. Still 0 for three. DM-ing them before seemed harass-y. Now, with a story to explore, I had a legitimate reason to reach out. Maybe one of them would lead me down a path. Given the nature of their comments, that path would probably lead to something that I didn't want to know, if I wanted to continue going to The Goddess Effect.

Typical me: act first, assess the damage later.

I tapped out a message and copy/pasted it to all of them: hey, just curious about your experience with the goddess effect, have a sec to talk? The lack of caps and casual abbreviation signaled that I was easy, I was one of them, I could be trusted.

I told myself that it hardly mattered. Probably, none of them would see it, let alone respond. Probably.

"Am I in the presence of Gonzo's brand-new culture correspondent?" Stacy asked as I slid into the Panamera. "You're hesitating—does that mean yes? Don't be modest, Ani. *Own* your success!"

I stalled by opening and closing the passenger side door again, as if I hadn't done it right the first time. On the one hand, covering the retreat while also participating in the retreat seemed ethically bankrupt;

on the other, this was the sort of insider-y storytelling that resonated these days. I had a choice: Tell the truth. Tell Stacy I felt conflicted but also wanted to give Gonzo my best shot. Or: skirt the truth and elaborate later, if necessary, if Gonzo actually aired anything I shot. Or: flat out lie.

"Not exactly," I said. "But I learned a lot about the kind of stories they're looking for."

Stacy gave me a look that was full of hope and promise. "That's huge. And now all you need is a blockbuster idea. Ooh—we can brainstorm. What about . . ."—she tapped her chin with her gel-manicured finger—"that woman who's running for mayor, who wants to turn Skid Row into a greenhouse?"

"That's an idea!" I said. It wasn't; she'd already been profiled and protested and profiled about the protests. "But we've got all weekend . . . and, I believe, two spots in a Himalayan cedar sauna with our names on them?"

She let out a whoop and slammed her foot on the gas. I tore open a pack of pilfered Hi-Chews and offered her one, feigning can't-wait-to-get-there feverishness as my mind swam with questions. How was I going to balance participating in the next four days with finding something salacious to say about it? How could I cover The Goddess Effect for Gonzo and also entertain the idea of working for The Goddess Effect? What if one of the commenters wrote back and said that Venus tried to kill her or something? What would I do with that?

Maybe they'd never see my messages. Maybe I wouldn't find anything. Maybe Venus had a job offer that included a 401(k) and benefits and a housing stipend that would allow me to put a down payment on a new-construction condo on Abbot Kinney, and I could forget about Emilia and Gonzo, and everything would be fine.

We whizzed past a sign for Malibu.

"Music? I'll deejay," I offered. "Any requests?"

"I've really been digging Spotify's Black History Month playlist," Stacy said.

***

We didn't talk much for the rest of the drive, between bobbing our heads to Mos Def, Common, and Black Thought. Midway through "Spaceship," after the verse in which Kanye recounts being trotted out from the back of the Gap every time a Black customer walked in, Stacy shook her head and said, almost to herself, "The nerve."

We exited the 101 onto a series of picturesque country roads. Fields led to farms that led to orange groves that blanketed both sides of the road, which wound up and down and back up again. Stacy lowered the windows, and the intoxicating scent of orange blossoms filled the car. "I love Ojai this time of year," she said.

"It's like Bath & Body Works," I marveled, "but real life."

The roads kept getting narrower until we reached a gate with a metal plaque hung on a flagstone: THE OJAI VALLEY RANCH, EST. 1920. A man in a booth beside it raised his hand and waved as the gate slid open, and we continued up the winding path, past a golf course and more orchards, before reaching a circular driveway in front of a grand, white-walled, mission-style hacienda. The moment Stacy put the car in park, two men in cream-colored polo shirts opened our doors.

"Welcome to the Ojai Valley Ranch," my guy—Beau, according to his name tag—said. "Are you ladies here for the retreat?"

"We are, and we are due at the infrared sauna, like, ten minutes ago," Stacy said. "Would you mind taking care of all of this"—she gestured at the Panamera and our luggage, which her guy, Chip, was already unloading from the trunk—"and sending our room keys to the spa?"

"Of course, Mrs. Gibson. My colleague Dan will take you over in a golf cart right now." Beau nodded at another polo shirt who'd pulled up behind us.

Dan drove us up and over the rolling green hills of the golf course, past an umbrella-laden patio on which veritable Ralph Lauren models ate leafy green salads and sipped fishbowl-sized glasses of rosé. On the left, a huge infinity pool lined with loungers; on the right, in the distance, a range of craggy, pink-hued mountains. There was a massive oak tree with lanterns hanging from its limbs; as we passed it, I twisted myself around to get another look. Charming. So charming. It ought to be illegal for a place to be this charming.

"That's the perfect spot to watch the pink moment," said Stacy, watching me. "At sunset, the light bounces off the mountains and bathes the whole ranch in this incredible rose glow. It's unreal. They say the east-west orientation of the range makes Ojai a vortex of good energy. You never know what can happen here. Ooh, I'm just so excited to bring you to this place." She squirmed happily and squeezed my hand.

Wasn't The Goddess Effect bringing me to this place? I thought. But whatever, semantics. Stacy had driven me here, after all. The golf cart slowed to a halt in front of yet another white stone hacienda complex, this one with a three-story tower and a little dome on top, like the place had been airdropped in from some Spanish colonial village.

Stacy grabbed a bill from her beige Birkin and hopped down in front of Dan. "Thank you, Dan, for everything you do, everything you've *done*." She attempted to slip the bill under his palm, which was still on the steering wheel. When he politely protested, she said, "I insist. Reparations."

Dan's eyes widened. She dropped the bill—one hundred dollars— in the cup holder by his side.

"We owe you," she said, "and I, for one, am not going to forget that." She planted her palms together and bowed her head. "Namaste."

My mouth hung open. Dan and I made eye contact. I shrugged in a way that communicated "I don't know this woman," except I very much did.

She waved goodbye to Dan and linked her arm through mine. "I decided, recently, that if our government isn't going to entertain the idea of reparations, I'm going to do what I can to make up the difference," she said.

"I guess that's something?" I ventured. I pictured myself in Dan's shoes, the absurdity of this Birkin-toting blonde bringing up reparations. But a hundred dollars was a hundred dollars. He probably made, what, sixteen dollars an hour, at most?

Stacy breezed past the spa reception desk without a glance at the three women—white, I noticed—behind it. "Mrs. Gibson?" one of them called out. "Can we help you?"

"We know where we're going," she called back. To me: "They want to tell us how to work the keypads on the spa lockers, but honestly, no one here steals anything. And frankly, I think it's insulting to the people who actually work in the locker rooms—most of whom are disadvantaged people of color, as you might imagine—to suggest that the guests don't trust them. Who even steals anything anymore? Everyone has an iPhone."

Uh, no, I wanted to point out. In my mind, I was doing an accounting. Dan, the Black History Month playlist, *ally, cultural immersion.* I thought about how solicitous she was with Kris, her Thai butler, Aaliyah, who worked the register at Provisions, all of the Indian servers and staffers I'd seen her interact with at Pooja's wedding.

Was Stacy reverse racist? But she idolized Venus and was married to Colt. If she were really, inappropriately, perversely into people of color only *because* they were people of color, she would have found a husband and workout guru to match, right?

Or were people of color her extracurricular activity, a hobby, a thing for her to engage with when she had the bandwidth and interest? Was she making up for something? Was she trying to make herself feel better? And if the answer to any of these hypotheticals was yes, what did that make me?

Then we were in the locker room, and Stacy was flinging open a birchwood locker and stripping off her leggings, and I did the same because it did not seem like the time or place to have a race reckoning, and frankly, I also wanted to see what WARM was all about. I wondered how many other conversations about race did not take place because of some other, more urgent desire, which generally boiled down to not wanting to feel uncomfortable or arouse discomfort in the other person.

She grabbed a towel, and in the moment before she wrapped it around her torso, I thought I caught sight of something strange about her waist—it looked tinier than I remembered, tinier than it had been when my mom was tying a sari on her, a week before. But then the fluffy blue terry cloth obscured it all, and Stacy was saying, "Come, let's go" and acting like we were about to miss the moon landing, so I followed her quick steps down the indigo-tiled hall. Maybe it was just the light.

Stacy reached the cedar door and looked back at me, eyes sparkling, before pushing it in. "Here we go," she whispered.

A wall of steam hit my face. It felt like being lost in a cloud. Venus's voice resonated, bouncing off the sauna walls. "And it is this deep sense of commitment that I want you to—oh, *hello*," she said, pointedly. "Nice of you to join us."

"Sorry," said Stacy. "Anita had a very important meeting."

"Is that right?" asked Venus. The steam had cleared, and I could see her staring straight at me. Her long, lustrous waves fell over her breasts, into her lap. She sat ramrod straight against the back wall, on the sauna's highest bench, one leg crossed over the other, a queen addressing her subjects.

"What's more important than us?" asked a voice I recognized as Ophelia's. She was sitting one level below Venus, elbow on knee, hand under chin, *The Thinker* meets Kate Moss.

"Anita had an interview for her dream job," said Stacy, taking a seat on the bench across from Venus. "Frankly, all of your teachings probably had something to do with her getting the interview, right, Ani?"

"Um, yeah," I said, sitting down next to Stacy, hoping that Venus wouldn't be peeved that I had gone on an interview when we were supposed to talk about me working for her.

"How nice," Venus said, in a tone that conveyed she did not find it nice at all. "That's what we call the actual Goddess Effect," she said, "and it dovetails with what I was just getting to. If you all want to truly benefit from the bounty of programming we've lined up for this retreat—if you want to feel *the actual Goddess Effect*—you will need to give yourselves over totally to us. Trust the teaching. Trust the struggle. Trust me." She laughed to herself. "Obviously, trust me. You may hit a wall over these next four days. You may encounter demons that you didn't know you had. You may hear a little voice in your head telling you that you can't do it. That you shouldn't do it. That it's weird. Do not, I repeat, do not listen to it."

"Silence that shit," said Ophelia.

"Put it in sleep mode," said Annalisa, next to Ophelia.

"Also," said Venus, "put your phone in sleep mode. Do not disturb—whatever it's called. Your partners and pets and kids, they can wait. You are becoming your best self."

"Make it your autoresponse," said Ophelia.

"The only acceptable use of your phone, over the next four days, is to document this journey for yourself," said Venus.

"And for social media," said Saffron, opposite Annalisa. "I'll send out hashtags."

"The reconstructive vibes coursing through these planks of Himalayan cedar and into your central nervous system are the perfect— how shall I put it—*pregame shooter* for what we have in store this week-end," Venus went on. "You'll find a full schedule in your room, along with some provisions intended to intensify your retreat experience. Is it mandatory to take them? No. Would you strongly benefit from taking them? Would you make the most of your time here by taking them? Would you, I don't know, unlock physical and mental capabilities that you didn't know you had by taking them? Yes, yes, and very likely, yes. Don't quote me on that last one, though." She gave a wry little laugh.

"Results may vary," said Ophelia.

Stacy nudged me excitedly. "Let's take them," she whispered. "Let's take them *all*."

26

My room felt like a page ripped out of a Restoration Hardware catalog. King bed. Too many pillows. A marble bathroom with double sinks, a Jacuzzi tub with jets, and a rainfall showerhead twice the size of the one I had at the Gig. A sitting area with a fireplace. A sliding glass door that led to a balcony that looked out onto the verdant knolls of the Ranch's golf course and the mountains beyond. A Nespresso machine.

The first thing I did was throw all but one of the Nespresso pods into my duffel bag. Lately, Miguel had been getting the off-brand ones from Trader Joe's, and the note by the machine said that housekeeping would replenish the pods twice a day, so.

I popped the remaining pod into the machine and, mug in hand, addressed the welcome basket on the bed. It was smaller than the one for Pooja's wedding, but measurably more chic: the shape of a wicker basket, it was made of creamy slate-gray leather that felt cool to the touch, the sort of vessel that Gwyneth Paltrow might use for dirty dishrags.

On top was a printed-out schedule, individually customized. While we'd all work out, eat, and engage in "immersion" activities like a gluten-free vegan marshmallow roast together, everyone had their own one-on-one, "ask me anything" session with Venus, and we'd had the option to sign up for add-ons like a crystal-guided chakra healing, anti-gravity sound bath, or acupuncture fertility facial. Well, other attendees had had the option. Given that I still wasn't sure who had paid my way into the retreat—Venus? Ophelia? The benevolent hacker I fantasized about when I logged into my Capital One?—I hadn't opted for any of the add-ons. I didn't want to seem greedy, to The Goddess Effect or to whatever force in the universe gave me access to this thing.

My one-on-one was scheduled for the following day at five o'clock in the afternoon. There was a handwritten note by that bullet point:

*We'll talk about u joining the team. Smooches 🖤

Fantastic.

Schedule assessed, I overturned the basket and pawed through the contents. Carb-free granola bars. A nighttime cream made of caterpillar larva. Gabrielle Bernstein's latest book: *A Toke of Hope: How to Ditch What Drags You Down and Get High on Your Own Supply*. A solar-powered vibrator made of sustainable silicone. *Os for All*, it said on the side.

The solar-powered vibrator was funny. I'd mention it in my Gonzo piece. *If* I did a Gonzo piece. (Was it anti-feminist to make fun of a vibrator? Any vibrator?)

There was more: a pack of Goddess Effect–branded hair ties, a Goddess Effect–branded jade egg, a clear cylinder of gummy bears. The label: dāna. Huh. Never met her. There was another label, on the opposite side: *A proprietary blend of herbs and supplements to promote youthful exuberance and magical thinking.* Interesting. This must've been what Venus was talking about in the sauna. I opened the canister and pulled out a piece of paper inside.

DIRECTIONS: Take one thirty minutes prior to each workout and immersion. If you really want to feel it, take two. 😊

The first workout was in half an hour. I took three.

***

For the occasion of the retreat, the Ranch's great room, normally a prized wedding venue, had been transformed into something out of a wellness wet dream. Long bungee cords with handles on either end dangled over the wood beams of the A-frame's ceiling. Mirrored panels covered all the walls except the one at the back, which was glass, with panoramic views of the rolling hills and pink-hued mountains. In the corners, fat candles clustered with succulents in squat ceramic pots. The smell of smoldering palo santo hung thick.

The first workout, Rebound, required the use of a minitrampoline. Stacy was sitting cross-legged on one in the front row when I arrived; I recognized her rhinestone-encrusted water bottle on the trampoline to her left.

I glided over. It actually felt like I was gliding—not merely walking fast, but walking on air. I felt alert in a way I hadn't before. Must've been the Nespresso. The pods in the room were ristretto, and the Trader Joe's knockoffs I'd gotten used to drinking at the Gig were way less intense.

"How 'bout those welcome baskets?" said Stacy.

"I'm obsessed," I said. With what, I didn't know, but it seemed in the spirit of things to say. I sat down on my trampoline and asked if she'd tried the gummy bears.

"Oh yeah," she said. "Love the little kissy face on their bellies. So cute."

The kissy face—why did that ring a bell? Probably because Stacy texted them to me all the time. **Heading down now!** 😘 **Running late, save me a spot!** 😘 The kissy-face emoji was an easy way to communicate goodwill without having to get specific: "I come in peace, and I'm gonna go in for an air-kiss because I'm fancy like that."

A low drumbeat started thumping from the speakers. I knew the song: "Diablo Rojo," by Rodrigo y Gabriela. The bass was turned up to the degree that it felt like the band was in the room with us. I closed my eyes and bounced, lightly, to the beat.

"To rebound." Venus's voice reverberated through the room, converging with the rhythm as if her words were meant to be lyrics. "To bounce back. To cleanse the lymphatic system, to flush it out, to slam the heel of your hand on the lever and make that shit swirl. On your feet, squat position, four, three, two, one, bounce."

There were trampoline jumping jacks and shoulder-tap planks. There was an exercise in which we had to squat on one side of our trampoline, jump on top of it, and come down in a squat on the other side, which I thought would trip me up but that I nailed on the first try. Damn, girl, I thought. Slaying them with your finesse.

Midway through class, Venus appeared in front of me and stood, hands on hips, as I pumped down the bungee cord with my palms while simultaneously squat bouncing. "Bullet with Butterfly Wings" pounded through the room. She wore a low-cut, sage-green leotard, matching high-waist leggings, a Madonna headset, and a messy topknot.

"I know where you've been," she said to me, but also to the entire room, because she didn't bother to angle the microphone away from her face the way Annalisa and Saffron did when they came around to correct your form.

She does? I thought. Is she talking about Gonzo?

"The thing about ambition," Venus continued, turning away from me and pacing, "that type-A, corporate, 'How will this look on my résumé?' type of ambition, is that it can obscure who you really are. Yeah, your ego wants this title and that salary, but what about your *soul*? What does your soul want? What does your soul *desire*? Does it want to toil away in some office until midnight? I'm gonna say no. Does it want to clock in and clock out? Nah. Probably not. Does it want to be beholden to some executive overlord? I know mine didn't. That's why I left Russet Capital and became my own boss. Built something I believed in. Built something to feed my soul, to feed *your* souls."

Part of me wanted to believe that it was all in my head, but it was too much of a coincidence.

"And the way we're going," she went on, "we'll soon be feeding souls across the country." Someone in the back woo-ed. "Which is why it's more important than ever that all of you in this room, our most devoted members, stick together, stick with us. If we're gonna take on the Barrys and Souls and Pelotons, we're gonna need to be thick as thieves. With your strength, we can dominate. We can start a revolution. We can help women around the world harness the power within and feed that power to their fellow sisters. We can build a tribe that *cannot be broken*." Another yelp from the back.

She turned back to me. "If you have to adjust your life, your goals, your values, to fully commit to this method, do it. Your soul will thank you. This"—she pounded her fist on her heart—"will thank you."

Finally, Venus had dug into me the way that she had dug into Stacy. It didn't feel the way I thought it would. It felt creepy.

Out of the corner of my eye, I saw something on the floor vibrate: my phone. I'd forgotten to put it in sleep mode. The room was loud enough that no one noticed, but I saw the name before the screen went black: Max? The fuck? What did that guy want?

***

By the time we were done, I had two missed calls from Max. Probably wanted to apologize, "feel heard." Whatever. Not a priority. Not my concern.

Stacy was sitting cross-legged on her trampoline, ruffling her sweaty hair with one hand and holding her phone above her face with the other, just as Emilia had predicted she would.

"How do you go live?" she asked.

"Press that button, above your thumb," I said.

"And then you just, like, broadcast yourself to the world?"

"That's how it works, yep."

She put her phone down and dropped her hand from her hair. "I really want to do a video diary or something, but maybe I'll start later. I need a theme. Like, 'Why The Goddess Effect Is the Solution to Inequality,' or something."

That rivaled latent periodic amnesia as the biggest stretch I'd ever heard.

"Dinner's in thirty, but is it weird that I'm not hungry?" I said. It was definitely weird: I was always hungry. But I had been conditioned to ask if hunger was weird because I was a woman who had grown up in America.

"I'm not, either," she said. "Maybe we just get ready and meet at the vegan marshmallow roast? There's supposed to be a tasting of cruelty-free mescals, too. Agave counts as a vegetable, if you think about it."

As we walked back to our rooms, I asked Stacy if she felt more on point than usual during the workout.

"Now that you mention it, yes. Everything just clicked." She snapped her fingers. "It's like I knew what to do before Venus even told us. Must be those gummies."

"The gummies," I repeated. The fact that I still felt wired indicated that something more than ristretto was at play. Supplements had always struck me as a scam, but maybe I was wrong. I made a mental note to google dāna.

The path wound down to the oak tree hung with lanterns, and Stacy grabbed my arm as we got closer.

"Look," she said, pointing at the mountains, awash in a bath of coral light. "Perfect timing."

We stood there, soaking in the pink moment. I took out my phone and took thirty-seven photos. At one point, I looked at Stacy, cheeks glowing like a cherub's, and wondered, again, why she'd picked me. I had encountered so many women like her in New York who didn't give me a second look, who pushed bathroom doors in my face, who swung their twenty-pound Goyard tote bags into my shoulder on the A train and didn't so much as glance back in apology. Why did Stacy bother? Why did Stacy care?

Cultural immersion. India. "All those colors."

I had wanted to check the Black friend box with Christina. If Stacy was doing that with me, was that an issue? Maybe we all had ulterior motives.

After the sun set, we continued walking. We passed a housekeeping attendant pushing a cart in the opposite direction. "Gracias, señora," Stacy said, whipping a bill from the pocket of her leggings and placing it on the cart of the attendant, who bowed and said thanks. I smiled awkwardly. Stacy got to show her gratitude. The woman got a hundred dollars. Everybody won, right? So why did watching that exchange make me feel kind of sick?

On the third floor, we parted—our rooms were on opposite ends of the hall, which I assumed meant that hers was markedly more fabulous. We agreed to text each other when we were ready. I took a scaldingly hot shower, generating a cloud of steam thick enough to bite. Robe on, hair in towel, I settled into the armchair by the fireplace and FaceTimed my mom.

"Look at you, in the lap of luxury." She sounded delighted. I gave her all the mom-friendly details about the retreat, which meant the solar-powered vibrator went unmentioned. She told me about her latest trip to the temple and a festival that was coming up.

She asked if Smita, Rupa Auntie's niece with the steady law job in Irvine, had ever texted back. She hadn't. "Pity," my mom said. "Rupa said she's been busy with a project. Maybe try her again, when you have a chance."

I shrugged and said sure. It was of no consequence to me. The animosity I'd felt toward Smita, or the idea of Smita, had dissolved. No one was asking me to have a steady law job, certainly not a law firm.

As we talked, I tried to figure out how to vocalize my hunch about Stacy. None of the PC workarounds cut it, so in the midst of my mom recounting why the temple decided to change the hours of the lower-level canteen, I blurted, "Do you think Stacy's, like, perversely into people of color?"

She smiled knowingly. "She does seem bent on understanding cultures besides her own. But is that a bad thing? She might come on strong, but her heart is in the right place."

A fair assessment. I felt the urge to gnaw on something and reached for the gummies.

"So," my mom ventured, "this Goddess Effect, are you still . . . pursuing a position with them?" I could feel her apprehension, her fear that saying the wrong thing could set me off.

"We're talking tomorrow, but actually, I meant to tell you—I had a meeting with Gonzo this morning."

She squealed and clapped her hands. "You wanted that for so long!"

I did. She was right. I thought of that much-posted quote: "Remember when you wanted what you currently have."

"Yeah, I have a choice, I guess." Bewildering to put it into words, but there it was: Goddess Effect or Gonzo. I couldn't do right by both.

"Well, assess all the options," she said, nodding to herself, as if I'd somehow know how to make the right decision. "Ultimately, a job is just a job. It's not who you are."

27

s I blow-dried my hair, I noticed that my legs were jiggling. Vibrating, actually. It was kind of like when you jiggle your knee under the table without meaning to, except I couldn't control it. Slow-twitch muscle fibers, I remembered. I'd read about them in *Effected*, how the method was meant to make your muscles shake and how the shake meant that you were doing it correctly, that you were transforming.

But wasn't the twitch supposed to stop?

My phone buzzed with a text.

Max: Hey, call me when you have a sec?

Bitch, don't kill my vibe, I thought, and then went to find that song.

I was about to plug in my flat iron when I had a thought: What if I just didn't? The Ranch's diffuser-equipped Dyson had given me waves not unlike what Riley had engineered into my hair before my first date with Jared, and while he still had a big red *X* over his face in my mental camera roll, my hair *had* looked fantastic that night. Also, I felt like dancing. The more time I spent on my hair, the less time I'd spend dancing.

Stacy said to come by her room; we could walk over to the marsh-mallow roast from there. I glided down the hall. I wondered if this was what it felt like to wear those sneakers with wheels.

By the time I reached her end of the hall, I was humming Calvin Harris's "Thinking About You" and waving my pointer fingers in little circles, as if I wanted two more rounds of daquiris.

"Yaaaas, oh my God, I want to dance, too," shrieked Stacy, flinging open the door. "Wait, I'm connected to the Bluetooth. Play something?" She handed me her phone. "I'll be ready in a sec."

I found the song on her phone, and the synth beat began pumping through surround sound speakers. Not only did Stacy have a room, she had a suite—of course she had a suite—with a dining area and a living room. Beyond the sectional sofa and chaise longue was a set of glass doors that led to a deck and a Japanese plunge pool. Steam rose from its surface. I took a photo. What would my caption be? Was *taking the plunge* too on the nose?

"Another!" Stacy called from the master bath. The song had stopped. She hollered her passcode; I tapped it in. I was maniacally adding songs to a new playlist I'd titled *OJAI VIBEZ* when she got a text. Her settings were such that the entirety of the message appeared on the home screen.

Colt: This type of charity just doesn't make sense

I bit the inside of my cheek. You shouldn't click, I told myself. It's a violation of privacy, friendship, probably other things. Maybe the law.

But what kind of person wouldn't click?

I told myself I wouldn't scroll up; I would just see whatever portion of their conversation naturally surfaced. But when I clicked, the message did that thing where it automatically jerks up a screen or two. Not my fault. Technology.

Stacy: How's Hualālai?

Colt: Be better if you were here

Stacy: Any other time, you know I would be 😢

Stacy: But I had to do this. For me, for Anita

Colt: So I pay for you AND your charity case to go to the Ranch and I get to go to Michael Dell's luau alone

Colt: Got it

Colt: I'm trying to explain this to Dell's caddy

Colt: Why did you pay for this girl again?

Stacy: BECAUSE AS AN ECONOMICALLY DISADVANTAGED PERSON OF COLOR SHE WOULD NEVER HAVE ACCESS TO A RETREAT LIKE THIS ON HER OWN

Colt: IS SHE economically disadvantaged? Didn't she have some fancy job in New York?

Stacy: She has credit card debt

Stacy: She doesn't own any Lulu

Stacy: That's disadvantaged

Stacy: How many times have we talked about this?

Stacy: We have SO much

Stacy: I need to give back in a way that proves I've made a difference

Stacy: Given everything I do, I've DONE, everything I've given up

Stacy: I would really appreciate it if you could support me on this one thing

The phone buzzed with a new message.

Colt: Dell's wife says you can be on the board of her Africa thing. Just do that???

***

A few minutes later, Stacy came out of the bedroom in fuzzy lavender sweatpants and a matching sweatshirt, pumping her fist in the air. "You are the best deejay, Ani," she shouted. "I swear, I never have this much fun sober."

I smiled in an aw-shucks kind of way. As "Eat Sleep Rave Repeat" pounded in time with my pulse, I had managed to screenshot the conversation, email it to myself from Stacy's phone, hard delete the email, hard delete the screenshots, and put her phone on the charger.

I didn't know what I was going to do with the screenshots, but I knew I wanted them. Proof, evidence, even if only for myself, that this had actually happened.

After reading the text messages, I decided I had a choice: get outraged, confront Stacy, storm out, stew. Or: act normal, process, figure out what to do later. Unsurprisingly, I embraced option two.

There was my fear of confrontation, of course. (Though, given Jared, Praveen, and Max, perhaps I was getting over that.) More than that, it seemed defeatist and dramatic to make a scene when I wasn't actually mad. If Stacy wanted to spend money on me, who was I to stop her? Frankly, Stacy now made a lot more sense than she had before. She had a massive case of privileged-white-person guilt. Not only was I her token brown friend, I was her token brown beneficiary.

Is a transactional relationship bad if both parties get something they want?

But there was the dishonesty part of it, the lie by omission. You can only be so close to someone who doesn't reveal themselves fully.

I assessed her anew, as she bopped her empty S'well above her head like it was an inflatable glow stick from the wedding, and wondered if she saw me as a grown-up version of one of those emaciated brown girls from the Save the Children commercials. The notion made me feel ill. I didn't want to be anybody's charity case. All those nudges to keep going with Gonzo, to not give up . . . why? So she could feel like she made a difference?

Colt was a dick, but he was also right. This type of charity did not make sense.

The fact that Stacy paid for me to come to the retreat also made Venus's comment about joining the team even more tenuous. The Goddess Effect had invested exactly nothing in me. What was I even doing here?

"It's strange," Stacy said, once we left her suite and started walking to the firepit. "Not only am I still not hungry, I also feel—I don't know how to describe this—super talkative? Like, I want to tell you so much. I want to tell *everyone* so much. Maybe it's Ojai, the energy vortex breaking down our walls."

"Yeah," I said. I had to bite my tongue to keep from asking her a list of questions that kept getting longer, like a CVS receipt. Some voice in my head told me to wait.

The firepits were in front of the great room where the trampoline class had taken place. A few women were already sitting in Adirondack chairs assembled around the biggest one; Venus was at the center. She wore a long-sleeved, low-cut black cashmere jumpsuit and a large jade pendant that reached below her bare sternum; a fringed, fuzzy gray throw was draped over her shoulders. She held a mug in her hands and was talking loudly as we approached.

"Look, you know my history," she said. "The stories I could tell you about my years on Wall Street." She chuckled to herself, as if remembering something. "I will. We'll get to me. But first, I want to hear more about all of you. Part of the work, we do in there." She cocked her head at the great room. "The other part happens out here, together. This is a safe space, a space where you can say anything, ask anything, open up about the stuff that your family and coworkers and lovers and therapists and non-Goddesses, in general, would judge you for."

Some heads nodded. Stacy and I had perched on the deep stone edge of one of the ancillary firepits, next to a tray of untouched, skewered, presumably vegan marshmallows. I was not in the moment. I was looking at Stacy out of the corner of my eye.

Enough time had elapsed that my initial laissez-faire attitude about being Stacy's charity project had grown edges and calcified into something more complex. Part of me was outraged. Part of me was confused. Part of me didn't want it to end.

If I was being honest, I wanted to spend more time in Stacy's world. To paraphrase the Bank of America ATM, I did, in fact, want to make another transaction. Several. But how long could we keep this up? The concept of a benefactor felt Dickensian, like bonnets and monocles. I pictured myself as Oliver Twist, all coal-smeared cheeks and puppy-dog eyes: "Please, Stacy, may I have some more?"

"Come on," Venus said, regarding us witheringly. "None of you have something you want to get off your chest?"

"Maybe if we do one of the prompts," Annalisa said, from behind her.

"Prompts are for pussies," Venus said. "On with it. Who's got a secret? Let it out." She slapped the arm of her Adirondack chair with her hand. "Let out the dark, gunky stuff that's clogging up your system, your neurotransmitters."

Was that how neurotransmitters worked? I wondered.

"Maybe if we have some mescal," Saffron said. She tilted a bottle over a row of ceramic mugs identical to the one Venus had and passed them around.

A brunette in one of the Adirondack chairs gingerly raised her hand. Her legs were tucked under her, and she wore a teddy bear coat so large it covered her knees.

Her words came out in a torrent. "We have a rule in our house about no processed sugar, and I feed my son Halo Top instead of regular ice cream and won't let him get McDonald's, even though he desperately wants it, but once a week, I go to McDonald's and get a McFlurry and eat it in the car and throw out the cup and the bag right away and get the car washed afterward, just in case, and my husband doesn't even know about this, he thinks I'm giving our son an eating disorder, but I just don't want him to get addicted to sugar, and oh my God, I feel so guilty, I can't believe I just admitted all that." She shrunk, improbably, further into her teddy bear coat.

"Wow, Nanette," Venus said, softly. "That's heavy. Hey." She walked over to Nanette and stroked her teddy bear–covered arm. "You're doing the right thing. With your son, anyway. Sugar's the new smoking, right? It might as well be meth."

"Meth's probably better for you, honestly," Ophelia said.

"Maybe we need to get to the root of the problem," Venus went on, "what's driving you to McDonald's, besides, obviously, your Range Rover." She chuckled lightly and gave Nanette's shoulders a squeeze. "We'll talk more in our one-on-one."

Venus drifted back to her chair and raised her mug. By this point, we all had one. "You all know the guttural cleanse. You could do it in your sleep. What we're doing right here, right now, is the mental version of that—the neuronic cleanse. The purge. And every time one of us takes the brave step of cleansing our neurotransmitters, of clearing space so that new thoughts, new ideas, new influences can come in, we raise our cruelty-free, biodynamic mescal and toast our fellow Goddess. Say it with me now—*purge*."

Stacy clanked her mug against mine as she shouted it. I said it tentatively, with a question mark at the end, the way I said "om" in yoga.

The first sip tasted like lighter fluid. After a few, I began to enjoy the burn. I sipped as Violet admitted to having an emotional affair with her middle school boyfriend, with whom she had recently reconnected on Facebook, as Marie revealed that she had filled her IVF syringes with saline solution without telling her wife, who desperately wanted a third kid. By the time Farrah admitted that she couldn't wait for her twin daughters to go to boarding school so that she could fully engage in her hobby of multiplayer online horror games without worrying that she was going to damage them for life, I had found my voice. With every toast, the chorus of voices grew louder. *"Purge, purge, purge."*

It was exactly the sort of exercise that would make Emilia salivate, and Sylvie admitting that she had staged photos of her daughter volunteering at an "Inglewood coding academy"—really, a Hollywood soundstage—would have made a mean *Daily Mail* headline. But profiting off the raw emotion pouring out around the firepits felt wrong. Extremely wrong. I recorded a few of Venus's toasts. That seemed like fair game. I didn't know what the story was, but my instincts told me that there was a story. It wasn't a bad idea to have footage, to have pieces to assemble when the missing link, whatever it was, revealed itself. *If* it revealed itself. If not, maybe this content would be worth something one day, when The Goddess Effect got the *Wild Wild Country* treatment or went public.

More mescal. More chants. I let myself get swept up in the energy of the purge, the heady aura of women admitting things to each other that they had probably not yet admitted to themselves, of being told it was okay, they were human, of being validated as normal by a group of people just as fucked up as them.

It took my mind off of what I'd learned about Stacy, though I did, at one point, imagine what would happen if I raised my hand and told the group that I'd just found out that my new best friend was perversely obsessed with people of color and was, essentially, paying for me to hang out with her. The look of horror on Stacy's face. The sheer embarrassment for us both. There would be no turning back. What would be the point? What would I do after that? Order an Uber?

Next to me, Stacy's hand shot up. "My turn," she said.

28

We were quiet, walking back from the firepits.

"Down for a dip?" Stacy asked, once we reached our floor. "The plunge pool should still be hot."

"Sure." I felt an urgency for us to get on the same page. Part of the reason my friendship with Pooja soured was because I never figured out how to confront her, how to stand up for myself. Be agreeable, I had thought, let it slide. I didn't want the same thing to happen with Stacy. What she admitted at the firepits bolstered the notion that her heart was in the right place, but she had no idea how to channel it in the real world.

Her purge wasn't as pointed as the others. "I feel like a bad person," she began, "like I'm part of the problem, not the solution." She then explained how she was trying to close the wealth gap and make up for her husband's "One percent excesses" by doing things like that Telfar bag stunt. She'd gone through with it. The superintendent of the Compton Unified School District had called her in and asked why she was trying to buy off young girls, "like I was a *sexual predator* or something," Stacy had said, hand over heart, aghast.

Perhaps the old adage is true—money changes you. The Stacy that studied social work and volunteered at an ashram would not have attempted to close the wealth gap with Telfar bags and Glossier samples.

But the current version of Stacy lived in an alternate reality in which money translated to goodwill and you could buy your way to fulfillment. Her charitable acts helped her as much as, if not more than, they helped others. She did them to feel like a good person; that much was clear. But if she recalibrated, she'd be a lot more effective and, probably, happier. She deserved to be happier.

While she was turned around at the minibar, opening a bottle of pinot noir, I stripped down and got in the pool. Under the moonlight, the surface of the water looked like mercury. A mist of steam rose up; a blanket of stars twinkled above.

I looked away as she got in. It was the polite thing to do.

"Why didn't you tell me?" I asked, once she'd handed me a glass of wine and submerged herself.

She frowned. "Tell you what?"

"That you paid for me to come here."

She gasped and lurched back, spilling wine on her collarbones. Dramatic, but better than a denial.

"I saw Colt's text when you gave me your phone to play music."

"Of course," she said, turning away and shaking her head. When she turned back, her eyes shone with tears. "I guess you don't want to be friends anymore."

"What? No—you're the best thing that's happened to me since I moved to LA." I meant to placate her. Only after I said the words did I realize they were true. "But I don't want to be your charity project. I don't want to be *anyone's* charity project. I'm just trying to understand why . . ." I trailed off as she dabbed at the corners of her eyes.

"I don't even know where to begin," she said. She talked about a pervasive sense of guilt that had turned her into a monster. "I'm, like, the dictionary definition of privilege. Call me Karen!" She knew that her one-off charity projects—the Telfar bag stunt, the unsolicited tips, me—were not the right way to go about "making a difference," but she didn't want to sit on boards and plan five-hundred-dollar-per-head events, and she felt compelled to somehow atone for all the luxuries that she and Colt enjoyed. "Like if I'm extra woke, I kind of balance him out," she said. This struck me as another sign that maybe they shouldn't be married, but it wasn't my place to point that out.

"When I saw you that day at Goddess Effect, you seemed so lost, so in search of guidance," she said. "I hope you don't mind me saying that."

It stung, but she wasn't wrong.

"So I thought, hey, here's a way for me to do good and maybe make a friend. I know this might sound crazy, but you really are my *best* friend, Anita." She talked about how the other women she knew were obsessed with fillers and lifts and their kids, and she'd probably be right there with them, had any of the embryos stuck. "You know how hard it is to make friends as an adult, especially when you're trying to break out of your circle?"

I felt for her. When I'd been in a rut, I'd done some pretty drastic things to get out.

Part of me wanted to ask if my being Indian had anything to do with it, but I kind of already knew the answer. What was I going to get out of hearing her say so?

I'd seen the antiracist books on her shelf. I'd encountered her breed of culture vulture, people whose genuine interest in ethnicities besides their own crossed over from intellectual curiosity to exotification.

The thing was, I was no better. I exotified her as the rich white older sister I never had. I put her on a pedestal, thought her black card and Gucci gym bag signified that she was worth knowing, that she had it all figured out. For the first time, in the hazy heat of the Japanese plunge pool, I saw Stacy as she was—just another woman with hang-ups and uncertainties trying to make her way in the world.

"Though, if I'm being honest," she was saying, "bringing you here was not selfless. I didn't want to go alone. Workout retreats are *awful* alone. You end up being that single loser trying to glom on to a table at mealtimes. You make retreat friends that you reveal all sorts of shit to, and you promise to keep in touch, but you never speak to each other again because they came on the retreat with their *actual* friends, and they never cared about you in the first place. It's like camp, but worse, because we're adults, and we should know better."

We laughed. The tension melted.

"It's like I've been trying to buy carbon offsets for my life." She sighed. "Which, I realize now, sounds ridiculous, but in my head . . ." She looked at me. "Do you ever wonder whether you're a good person?"

"All the time."

"And it doesn't eat away at you, not knowing?"

In the water, my shoulders shrugged. "How can anyone answer honestly? We're all biased." And often, we only asked that question to make ourselves feel better, to mentally tally all the evidence that demonstrated our goodness.

"Besides," I said, "how do you even define 'good'?"

She exhaled a big huff. "Well, that's the thing. 'Helping the less fortunate'—that's how I defined it in grad school." Stacy had wanted to start a nonprofit life-coaching service for people who normally wouldn't be able to afford that kind of counseling; career services for, say, a security guard who wanted to be a writer, "a place where they can get matched with a mentor who can offer advice, next steps, that kind of thing."

"That's a great idea," I said. "You should do it."

"With what credentials?"

"Credentials?" I scoffed. "Look at George Clooney. He started a tequila company and sold it for a billion dollars. What credentials did he have?"

"You have a point."

"And if it really matters, you could go back and finish your master's."

"I'm too far gone. I'd be like Elle Woods in *Legally Blonde*, except older and without the cute dog."

"Do you remember what happens in *Legally Blonde*? How Elle Woods basically shows all of Harvard that she's a boss?"

"Oh yeah," she said, quietly.

"Look," I said, raising my glass of wine, "we are friends. I'm not going to tell you that you were wrong to spend your money on me because"—I panned around the deck, taking in the wall of glass between us and the suite, the rising steam, the cedar, the night sky—"it's pretty sweet to be here, and I wouldn't be without you. But I don't want to owe you anything. And you should be putting your money into your brilliant business idea, not me. So this stops after this trip, yeah?"

"Fine," she said, raising her glass, "but I don't want to keep *you* from doing what you want while you're here. This is my treat, and this is the *Ranch*. How do you not want a 180-minute, four-hands, CBD lavender balm massage? I was shocked that you didn't sign up for any extras. *Shocked.* So it's only a deal if you promise to take advantage of my tab while you're on it."

"Twist my arm, why don't you," I said, clinking my glass against hers.

We drank our wine and talked about other stuff, relishing the sense of relief that comes after diving into the thing you've been perched on the edge of. Our toes were pruned by the time we finished the bottle, and Stacy waded over to the far edge of the pool to get out.

That's when I saw it clearly, lit by the unmitigated glow of the moon.

Her waist. Her teeny, tiny waist. Scooped out and snatched like Michaela's, the regular we'd noticed the other week.

"Stace," I said, treading lightly on this new ground we'd reached, "did you . . . get something done?"

"Oh, my nails? Pampered Hands on Melrose. They have the best cat eye shades—we should go sometime."

"No, I mean yeah, but—your waist. It's like Michaela's."

"Oh," she said, wrapping a towel tightly around her body and turning around to face me, in the pool. She looked guilty. "Is it that obvious? I'm not supposed to talk about it."

"Okay . . ." My alarm bells went from five to ten.

"But." She bit her lower lip. "You know what, it's *fine*. It's you—I can't not tell you!"

Well, then. I climbed out of the pool, grabbed a towel, and scooched next to her on the wicker sofa on the deck.

"Okay, so, I signed an NDA. 'Standard protocol,' they said, because it's a trial, or whatever, not FDA approved. It's this new procedure Venus is offering to regulars, totally comped. You're out of commission for, like, two days—remember when I said my period was, like, insane? It wasn't. I was just recovering from this thing. And then you're back at it. And the best part? You get to give back. Venus said it's kind of like Warby Parker—they're finalizing the details."

"What *is* it? Lipo? CoolSculpting?"

"Eclosion," Stacy said. "It's super new, it uses heat, it's, like, the opposite of cryotherapy. It does the work of a million bicycle crunches in a matter of minutes. I haven't had a waist this tiny since"—she bobbed her head back and forth—"probably ever. Probably since I was a baby. That's what the doctor said—it would make me feel like my baby best self. But this is it—I'm not going to turn into one of those plastic surgery wives, jetting off to Gstaad to have my face resurfaced, or whatever. And I only did it because of the give-back component. Well, that and the fact that it was comped. Another thing to not have to explain to Colt."

"The give-back component," I repeated. I had never heard of eclosion.

Stacy seemed the same as always, just with a tiny waist. If you didn't know her before, you'd just think, Wow, that woman is genetically blessed but possibly confined to wearing SKIMS and Fashion Nova unless she eats a Big Mac or eleven.

People made a big deal when Botox came out; now twenty-five-year-olds got preventative injections. Maybe this new procedure was like Botox. Everyone would be doing it soon.

But why was Venus arranging it? And for free? I thought back to the conversation I'd overheard in the back room—Venus and Ophelia grumbling about trials and covering Cheng's costs.

"Where did you get it done?" I asked.

"Oh gosh, I don't actually know. Is that terrible? They had a car take me there and back, because the anesthesia was gnarly. Everything was pink, I remember that: pink waiting room, pink caftans—caftans instead of hospital gowns, isn't that chic? Even the anesthesia was pink."

"Was the doctor's name Cheng?"

Stacy shook her head, blankly.

Huh. Not related? But how could the conversation I'd overheard and what Stacy was telling me not be related?

"Venus said that the trial participants—me, the other Goddesses who've done it, *you*, I'm sure, I can't imagine her not offering it to you—get to get in on the ground floor of something special," Stacy said, "something that's going to revolutionize wellness for all women, not just those of us who go to Goddess Effect. Honestly, Ani"—she placed her palm on my arm—"it's kind of the perfect story for Gonzo. It's got tech, it's got wellness. Maybe you should email that woman you met with. Just don't say you heard it from me, obviously."

29

I woke up starving. The agenda said that the catered breakfast on the Chumash Terrace would include carob-studded pea protein bites, grain-free parsnip oatmeal, and edible nasturtiums from a local farm that paid its undocumented workers a living wage.

There was an asterisked note below it: *Famished? Curb your cravings with a dāna or two.*

I picked up the handset on the nightstand.

"Room service? May I order a large pot of coffee and a chorizo egg scramble with a side of bacon, avocado, and an English muffin? Nothing else for now, thanks. Wait—do you have Cholula?"

It's what Stacy would've wanted, I figured. My version of a four-hands, 180-minute, CBD lavender balm massage. Plus, it was really Colt's money that I was spending, and Colt was a dick.

Stacy had signed up for a sunrise animal-essence reading ritual in which a licensed spiritual-discovery practitioner would use a series of mating calls to draw out Stacy's innate animal soul and educate her in ways that she could receive its help. "Wanna come?" she had asked the previous night, before I left her suite. "I'm sure they can do it for two. Wait, what if we're the same animal? I'm pretty sure I'm a lioness. I *was* weirdly drawn to the Gucci lioness crossbody."

I declined. It didn't seem like the type of thing that you could just tack an extra person onto, like reserving a table for two and showing up with three and asking your server to just bring an extra chair, you'll squeeze. We had agreed to meet at the Ranch's boutique at 11:00 a.m., before the noon workout. They were having a pop-up, Stacy had said, "the *best* way to find emerging designers. Did I tell you about the time I met that jewelry designer at the Four Seasons Punta Mita who had a whole line of earrings made out of found feathers and seashells?" She had. The earrings seemed wildly overpriced for what they were, but perhaps that's what you want when you go to a boutique at a luxury resort, a memento that signifies whimsy, a moment in time, and your ability to spend with abandon.

Handset back on the charger, I threw off the covers and reached for my laptop, in its usual place, keeping a spot warm for a potential life partner, should they ever choose to materialize.

Stacy's suggestion to pitch Gonzo a story about eclosion was uncanny to the degree that I wondered if maybe there was something to the notion of Ojai's electromagnetic vortex making things happen. But my research into eclosion—I googled it the night before, walking back to my room and for a while after, on my laptop—led me to believe that it was not, as Stacy thought, some kind of high-tech female empowerment vehicle. It was nothing. It didn't make sense.

I scrolled through the results again. Eclosion referred to the act of emerging from a pupal case, like when a caterpillar breaks out of a cocoon as a butterfly. I found no indication that it had anything to do with humans, let alone the shrinking of a human's waist. Was Stacy mistaken? Was it called something else? Or did Venus just make up some term? I thought, again, of latent periodic amnesia, how the sex-tape governor seemed to believe that if she kept saying it, it would turn into a real thing.

I had googled various permutations of eclosion, Cheng, and Calabasas, which led to pages of various professionals with Cheng in their name who lived or worked in Calabasas, one of whom collected butterflies. None of it seemed relevant. Still. They had to be connected.

I looked at my agenda for the day: two workouts, one at noon and one at 6:00 p.m., immediately after my one-on-one with Venus. For the first time since I'd encountered The Goddess Effect, I didn't want to do it, any of it. Something was off—more than that, *many* things were off, so many that, in my mind, The Goddess Effect now teetered at a precarious angle, half of it hanging off a cliff.

In the bright light of morning, alone and no longer under the influence of mescal, the purge struck me as . . . weird. Not good weird, like charcoal-activated ice cream. Cult-y, like Emilia had said. Why was Venus prodding us to share our deepest secrets, and why were so many of us willingly doing it?

Would I have purged, had I not been consumed with what I'd learned about Stacy? What would I have shared?

I pawed around the bed and found my phone. Another missed call and text from Max. Really, bro? Boy, bye.

I swiped through the eight hundred photos and videos I'd taken the day before. Some were beautiful, some were vibe-y, but the most compelling ones, without a doubt, were the videos of Venus around the firepits. The look in her eyes—hungry, borderline rabid. Ophelia by her side, alert, like a meerkat with better accessories.

Room service arrived; I lifted the silver dome and housed everything beneath it, along with half a bottle of Cholula. By the time I had finished and wriggled into a fuchsia Koio set, cursing myself for not having thought through the ramifications of high-waist compression leggings on an extremely full stomach, I had resolved to treat the upcoming workout as an assignment. Like I was a reporter. Which I could be, for Gonzo, if I could connect the dots between Venus, Cheng, Calabasas, and eclosion. The purge was part of the story, for sure, but my gut told me it was part of something bigger, something I couldn't quite see yet.

***

"Am I looking at Southern California's fiercest lioness?" I said, sidling up to Stacy. She was already in the boutique when I arrived, fingering a rack of silky caftans.

She turned and pouted. "She said I was a toucan. A *toucan*! Who takes a toucan seriously? I asked her three times if she was sure. Do you want to hear the sound I have to make to summon my inner toucan? You're gonna die."

Before I could answer, she squeezed her eyes shut and shrieked: *"CAW! CAW!"*

A woman rushed out from behind the register. "Is everything all right?" Her eyes darted from me to Stacy.

"Sorry," I said, clutching my stomach, trying to compose myself. "She just got out of her animal-essence reading ritual."

The woman nodded knowingly. Was she Indian? She had to be Indian. She had a slight accent. We had similar skin tones, and her hair was frizzy-wavy, like mine when I didn't blow-dry it. She was wearing what I would technically call a salwar kameez, except it was far cooler than all the salwars I'd known before—wide-legged pants, bell-sleeved top that hit at the top of the hips instead of the knees, graphic cheetah pattern. It was like one of those pajama sets that people had suddenly started wearing in public, but Indian.

"A woman came in here yesterday absolutely beside herself because she had been told her animal essence was a snake," cheetah-print salwar said, "but she ended up buying a pair of snakeskin Birkenstocks, so."

"Ooh," said Stacy. "Do you have any more of those?"

"You'd have to ask Carlotta, the manager of the boutique," cheetah-print salwar said, smiling genially. "She just stepped out for a coffee. I'm with the brand that's popping up at this space, SNS."

"So these caftans are yours?" Stacy asked.

"I picked up the silks in Bangalore when I was there last."

"Bangalore?" I interrupted. I usually hated Indian people who made a point of talking to you just because you were Indian, but the fact that there were not one but two South Indian women at the Ranch at the same time seemed like a rare event worthy of further examination, like a total solar eclipse. "That's where my mom is from."

"No way," said cheetah-print salwar. "Mine, too."

"What's your name?"

"Smita."

***

Was there something to this notion that the universe did, indeed, have your back? I wondered as Smita and I got to talking, while Stacy took to the fitting room with eleven caftans. Gabrielle Bernstein preached it. Riley, too. My mom—my mom and her sutras and her puja place and her uncanny ability to know what I needed, even after I put three thousand miles between us.

Yes, Smita was Rupa Auntie's niece, and yes, she had been working in a law office. "Accounting, paperwork, answering the phones—mundane stuff," she said. "I still temp from time to time. Helps pay the bills while I get SNS off the ground. By the way, sorry I never messaged you back—things have been nuts, getting ready for this pop-up." She leaned in closer and lowered her voice. "They told me to expect shopaholics like your friend, no offense. You'd take one look at that price tag and slap me in the face, but the Westerners who come here? If it's not at least two hundred fifty dollars, they can't be bothered. I paid three dollars for this fabric at Gandhi Bazaar." She lifted the hem of a light-gray leopard-print caftan with a fringe of tubular lime-green beads. "And seven dollars for labor. And that's *after* paying my workers five times what they'd make working for any fashion brand there. India is fucked up, you know?"

"Crazy," I said, dropping the price tag (three hundred dollars). "I can't believe my mom didn't tell me any of this. I thought she wanted us to meet so you could convince me to get a steady law job."

Smita hooted. "As soon as SNS is cash-flow positive, I never want to see another legal document unless it's a twenty-million-dollar acquisition offer from Sabyasachi and I'm signing my name on the dotted line." She mimed an extravagant signature, and I laughed.

It was a shame that my default setting was to be a bitch to my own. I'd grown up regarding other Indian girls as competition, thinking there was only room for one of us at the top, whatever that meant. But one brown woman's success did not mean that I had somehow failed. Smita was badass. Smita was who I wanted to be. Well, not exactly, but she radiated the sort of confidence and self-assuredness that I previously only associated with Venus and Stacy, both of whom, upon further examination, were not deserving of the pedestals I'd put them on. Stacy had issues. Normal issues: body image, marriage, life fulfillment. Venus . . . I did not quite know what was up with her, but she was no longer aspirational. If I ever had the look in my eye that she did during the purge, I'd go to a doctor.

"I think you've got Sabyasachi beat," I said, picking up the edge of a floor-length, cobalt-blue chiffon jacket. The back was printed with a black-and-white, Picassoesque face. A row of mother-of-pearl buttons ran up the front, and between each one was a tiny hot-pink pom-pom that reminded me of the lehengas I wore to kolattam practice when I was younger.

"I'm just glad the line's finally coming together," she said. "It's fulfilling, you know? To take charge of your own destiny, do what *you* want to do and see other people enjoy it."

Stacy emerged from the fitting room in a toucan-print caftan, arms out wide, like she was about to take flight.

"I have to, right?" she said. "It's a sign."

Black with a single toucan rendered in white but for its brilliant, multicolored beak, it looked like a beach coverup fit for Hailey Bieber or some other pretty young thing who surfaced on the *Daily Mail* every other day. Smita went over to show Stacy how to arrange the fringed tassels around her neck.

"Did you design what you're wearing, too?" I asked Smita, when she came back.

"Oh yeah, plenty more where this came from. I only brought the Western styles for this pop-up. You should come down to Irvine sometime, check out the whole collection. I just moved into a condo on the water with a sick rooftop. We can make margaritas and boti kebabs, have a nice chill by the pool."

It was the exact opposite of the time I'd envisioned having with Smita. I glanced at her hands—no engagement ring, no wedding band, presumably, no phantom husband with a selfie stick. Probably no steel cups, either, although what was the difference between steel cups and mason jars, when you thought about it?

"Maybe the weekend after next," she was saying. "It's my twenty-eighth birthday. I'm thinking about getting a few friends together."

Internally, I couldn't help but wince—younger than me, yet so comfortable in her own skin. But then, what was age? Weren't all the role models Gen Z now?

"I'd love that," I said.

"And I would love for you to wear this," she said, pulling the cobalt-blue chiffon jacket off its hanger. I protested. She insisted, picking up my arms and easing them into the billowing sleeves of the jacket. "It looks *so* good on you. And you brought me this," she said, cocking her head toward Stacy, who was piling two, three, now four caftans onto the register. "You're like my own personal Lakshmi."

I turned to the full-length mirror. I looked Indian in a way that I hadn't known was possible—modern, at ease, empowered. Was I standing taller, or was it just an illusion?

"You're too kind," I said, following her up to the register, rubbing the rich fabric between my thumb and forefinger. "By the way," I asked as she rang up Stacy, "what does SNS stand for?"

She smiled coyly. "Sorry Not Sari."

30

Venus was in the midst of a preclass soliloquy as we strode into the great room. "Nice of you to join us," she said. I rolled my eyes. Come on, Venus. This isn't freaking prison. We're allowed to be five minutes late.

We took the two remaining unclaimed mats, in the back. They were topped with five circular resistance bands in varying shades of purple. I carefully took off the SNS jacket, folded it, and placed it off to the side, on top of my track bag, which I had carried, in my hand, like a sack lunch. I refused to wear the track bag over the jacket. It would be like ordering yellowtail crudo and asking for ketchup on the side.

"We were just talking about dāna," Venus said. She elongated the first *a*, which struck me as vaguely Indian. I had neglected to google the gummy bears, what with the purge and eclosion. "What does everyone think?"

"What's in them?" I asked.

"I'm obsessed," said Nanette.

"*Love* their little kissy faces," said Trisha.

"What's in them?" I asked, again.

Venus turned to me, irritated: "It's proprietary." To the rest of the room: "What about your skin?"

"*Super* supple, like when I did a placenta mask," said Paloma.

Venus smiled smugly. "Let's get started."

The workout was called the Resistance, and Venus wove around the room, alternating between her usual, generic aphorisms—"Think of the band as the system that wants to keep you down, tell it to fuck off by *breaking* that band with your outer thighs, *push*"—and uncomfortably specific ones. "Your exes, your past loves, your past lives—show them how far you've come, how you're no longer that insecure little girl they used to know," while planted in front of Violet, who'd admitted to having an emotional affair with her middle school boyfriend. "We feel guilty when we deny our most authentic selves," in front of Stacy. "Guilt doesn't serve you. Guilt gets you down. Banish it. Get rid of it. Imagine it popping and fizzing when you push your heel against that band. Push *harder, higher*."

Interesting, I thought, as a bead of sweat rolled down my nose and fell on my mat with a satisfying *splat*. Ply us with mescal and the promise of female bonding, get us to admit our insecurities, then use what we said to inform motivational monologues that you bark at us while we're working out, while our adrenaline's pumping and our emotions are running high, when even the most ridiculous statements seem prophetic.

Very interesting. But was that all it took to get women to admit their insecurities? Artisanal alcohol and sister-wives vibes?

I focused more on listening than working out, which might explain why Venus drifted over to me during a set of donkey kicks and planted her lavender Alo-sheathed legs in my frame of vision.

"What are you desperate for? To be liked? To be loved? To be praised? Think about it, *really* think about it—and question whether you're desperate for the right thing. Maybe you should be desperate for The Goddess Effect, for this method, for this tribe."

Was she calling me desperate?

After repose, I lay on my back in a figure four, mind racing. Who was Venus, really? Since I'd last asked myself that question, she'd only gotten more confounding. She had said, the previous night at the firepits, that she would tell us stories about her time in finance, but she never did. She liked to allude to all this trauma she'd suffered but never elaborated on it. Trauma this, trauma that. Show me the trauma. Besides what she wrote in *Effected*, what did anyone know about her? Her social feeds regurgitated stills from fake Annie Leibovitz photo shoots. She had never done an interview with a reputable news outlet that would've dug into her past.

Left ankle resting on right knee, I reached for my phone and saw a notification.

One of the private commenters had accepted my follow request. I sprang upright.

It was the one who'd asked Venus if she was "on that Weinstein shit." She'd replied to my direct message, too: you working for them, or something?

Stacy's voice came from above: "Babe, I'm gonna shower real quick. These leggings are so thin, I look like I just peed myself. Meet you at lunch?"

Next on the agenda: sustainable sashimi lettuce wraps on the Topa Topa Terrace, and while I stanned ponzu sauce, I could not ignore the nagging sense that I had arrived at the precipice of something big, a huge story, the likes of which I had not told in a while, maybe ever. I had to see this through. I had to do the work. A job, a duty that I wanted to take on more to *know* what was going on than for notoriety or money—did Emilia even mention how much they'd pay? Was I so overwhelmed that I hadn't even asked?—stood before me. Purpose, spelled out in big, flashing lights.

There would be another time for sustainable sashimi, if it was so sustainable.

I hopped up to my feet. "You know, I think you were onto something last night," I said. "I'm gonna draft an email to Emilia. Don't worry," I said, giving Stacy's arm a reassuring squeeze, "I won't say anything." A different journalist might have used Stacy's violation of her nondisclosure agreement as the foundation of a whole piece, but she was my friend, and I was not a sociopath. I wasn't going to throw her under the bus.

I also wasn't about to draft an email to Emilia. Not yet. Not until I knew what I was working with. *Who* I was working with.

"Exciting," Stacy said. "Okay, work your magic. Text me when you're done."

31

I shrugged on the SNS jacket and hurried back to my room, enjoying the way the chiffon floated behind me like the cape of a superhero, or Beyoncé on an average Tuesday. I relished the sense of having done the *right* thing, even though I hadn't exactly done anything yet. (Well, I had said no to free sashimi. That had to count for something.)

My plan was to use Praveen's ABN credentials to run LexisNexis searches on Venus and Ophelia and draw out the Weinstein commenter through DMs or, dare I hope, a phone call. Maybe she knew the other commenters. Maybe there was so much more to this story than I could even anticipate.

Once I had a rough idea of the scope, I'd DM Emilia, negotiate a rate, push for maximum visibility. Yes, the desire to know was the greatest motivator, but if I was accruing and disseminating this knowledge, I might as well get paid for it.

Preoccupied by this plan, I didn't register that there was a guy leaning against my door until I was almost upon it, and then I jumped back.

No. It couldn't be. This didn't make sense. How? Why?

"What the fuck?" I blinked at Max. "What are you doing here?"

He deflated like a balloon. "I didn't know what else to do. I tried calling, texting, but you didn't respond." He looked like he hadn't slept. "I DM-ed you."

"I don't follow you."

"I know. I thought maybe—anyway, it's not important now. Can we talk?"

I rammed my hip against the keycard reader and let him follow me in. He had to apologize this bad? On the one hand, I was annoyed; on the other, I was flattered that anyone would Uber all the way up to Ojai for me. The trip had to have cost a hundred dollars, at least.

"All right, let's get this over with." I'd dropped my bag, perched on the bed, and crossed my arms. I figured he'd say his piece and then leave me in peace so I could get to work.

He paced and said nothing. His sweatshirt sleeves were pushed up, revealing arms more muscular than I remembered. Was he vaguely attractive, or had I just been surrounded by women for too long?

"Is it that hard?" I blurted out. "You came here to apologize, right?"

"What?" He looked up at me, confused. "No, I mean—you're talking about the other night in the kitchen?"

What else would I be talking about?

"Sorry, it's been crazy." He ran his hand through his hair and leaned against the desk, facing me. "Look, what I said came out wrong, and I'm sorry for that. But you must've heard the news."

"What news?"

"You haven't seen Twitter?"

"I hate Twitter."

He pulled his phone from his back pocket and showed me a *Deadline Hollywood* tweet from two hours before with rapidly escalating likes and shares: *Exclusive: Dane Ditch Targeting Minorities to "Muddy Up" Gonzo.* There was a link to an article.

My stomach dropped as the page loaded.

Deadline has exclusively obtained an audio recording of a meeting Dane Ditch held one week ago with senior Gonzo leadership, in which he issued an edict to "hire, or at least [expletive] entertain the idea of hiring, people who are not white because this [expletive] dweeb from the *New York Times* is threatening to expose me as a culturally insensitive overlord and also drop the bomb on our budget-friendly practice of waiting 180 days to pay freelancers. [Expletive] freelancers."

The article went on to quote Dane as saying:

"Look, we all know that what people want to see on TV, or mobile—whatever—is hot blonde chicks. Chicks like Emilia. Chicks who wear short skirts and low tops, or crop tops—obviously, we're down with those. Especially down with how Amber went topless to cover that women's march—you saw the graphs, you saw that spike. I hope it's branded on your brain the way it's branded on mine. What we do, what we *excel* at, is taking the formula developed by the late, great Roger Ailes and adapting it to Gen Z. Give them something to get outraged about. Give them something to share. Give them a reason to jerk off, which means once in a while we gotta have a dude, a trans, a LGBTQIA-LMNOP—whatever. But very few people find hot blonde women problematic. At least, the people that we care about. We know our manifesto. We live it, we bleed it. But for now, at least for a few months, we've gotta muddy it up. If they're Black, if they're brown, if they're yellow, bring 'em in. We don't even have to hire them. Just look like we're trying. Something to get this

wannabe Ronan Farrow off my back or at least make
his story look like fake news."

"Jesus," I said. Now the timing of Emilia's DM made sense.
"Cleanse" my ass.

"I'm not going to say I told you so," Max said, "but as a white guy
who's gotten turned down a lot lately, I may know a thing or two about
the hiring process."

I screwed up my face at him. "Did you ever wonder if maybe you're
just not the best person for the job?"

"Of course," he said. "But you can't take race out of the equation.
It's impossible. I'd rather face reality than pretend that we're all on an
equal playing field."

I bit the inside of my cheek. "You have a point," I said. I was
happy to trumpet my brownness when it worked in my favor. That was
the duality of being non-white in America. You embraced what made
you different when it benefitted you; you blended in when it didn't. If
brown skin was a trend, if my ass was a trend, if they could help me get
ahead, great. What person wouldn't use all the tools at their disposal?

Which brought me back to Max.

"What I don't get," I said, "is why you're out here hustling if your
family built Manhattan."

Max gave me a "Really?" look. "Do you know anything about my
family?"

"Your last name is"—I thought for a second—"Van. Is that Van as
in *Vanderbilt*? Are you a *Vanderbilt*, Max?"

"No, Anita, I'm not a Vanderbilt. I'm a Van der *Meek*, as in, the
son of Alexander van der Meek, whom you might have heard about
when the City of New York filed a one-hundred-million-dollar lawsuit
against him last year."

"Oh . . ." I trailed off. The *Post* had had a field day with that one.
Alexander, a descendent of Daan van der Meek, one of the first Dutch

immigrants to arrive in New York, had inherited a commercial real estate firm whose past successes included Madison Square Garden and the Time Warner Center. But Alexander lacked his great-grandfather's good business sense, and when he lost the bid on what would become Hudson Yards, he bought up high-rise buildings in low-income neighborhoods, hired slumlords to manage the apartments, got contractors to put up plywood walls in five-hundred-square-foot studios, and created units within units that were about as big as the average airplane bathroom. They were advertised on Airbnb for a hundred dollars a night. "He targeted Australian tourists who didn't know any better," one of his associates was quoted as saying.

"So you changed your last name," I said, dumbly.

"Made it official last month," Max said. "Wanted to get as far away from that legacy as possible. And in case you think there's a trust fund, my dad liquidated it to pay his lawyers."

"I'm sorry," I said, meaning it. "That's terrible." That applied to his situation and my own assumptions. I hadn't even bothered to question what Christina had said about Max; it was easy to cast him as a villain. In reality, he'd been nothing but helpful from day one, which made his sudden presence in Ojai even more significant.

"So wait, what are you doing here?"

He cupped his hands and breathed into them. "Something's up with Adil and The Goddess Effect."

32

Max knew that the "super secret, super lucrative" project Adil had conscripted him to involved the production of a supplement that helped you lose weight, be authentic, and look younger. He'd been hung up on the authenticity part of it—what ingredient could enable that? Adil said the ingredients were proprietary, and Max had to build a marketing deck without that info, so he was grasping at straws until the previous afternoon when Adil inadvertently revealed that Venus was involved.

You know when you mean to reply to one text message chain but actually send a message to another? Adil had done that, sending Max a string of messages that, presumably, were intended for someone else.

Adil: Couldn't you just advertise? Social, flyers, billboard?

Adil: Oh duh, Venus would see that. Right.

Adil: Maybe there's a way to individually target likely participants . . . maybe my guy can round up some bodies

It wasn't clear whether Adil knew he'd texted the wrong person. In any case, a few minutes later, Adil forwarded Max an email saying, Forget the marketing deck. Figure out where we can find women like this but who don't go to Goddess Effect . . . women who'll pay to be part of a special tribe of early adopters . . . who want a smaller waist . . . maybe hang out at the cryo clinic in Playa Vista, see who you meet??

"I hope he's giving you a huge chunk of equity for what he's putting you through," I said, glancing up from Max's phone. Humor as deflection, as ever. It was creepy that Adil seemed to know about eclosion and referred to women like prey. Creepier still that Venus was involved and that they were collaborating on a supplement. But why would Adil be conspiring against Venus—and so eager for me to feed him details about the retreat, as he implied the other night at dinner—if they were working together?

"Keep scrolling," Max said. He was pacing at the foot of the bed.

Some blank space, Adil's email signature, a "quote of the day," which made me wonder if Adil updated his signature every day, or if there was an app for that. Another swipe of my thumb, and I saw who sent the original email.

Ophelia.

The subject line: why we'll never fail

The body of the message:

FYI, sample of SOME of the intel we have should any of our clients ever abandon us . . .

There was a link to a Dropbox folder. I clicked. There were several thumbnail images, but my eyes flew to one: me, naked save for Riley's gold sequined tank top and a Target thong, kneeling next to Jared, a little play button over my chest. A video. The file name: "DesperateAni.mov."

"What the fuck?" I said. My wrist went limp; Max's phone fell. Thankfully, I was sitting on the bed, so it landed on eight-thousand-count Egyptian percale.

"I didn't watch it, just so you know." He'd stopped pacing and turned to face me. "I didn't watch any of them, besides—well, I randomly clicked on one to just understand what the hell was going on and, here, you might want to see." He tapped the screen a few times and gave the phone back to me.

It was a paparazzi-style shot of Stacy, in her kitchen, making out with Kris, her Thai butler. A plate of red chilis and another plate of unidentifiable ground meat languished on the marble island.

My first thought: some do like it hot. My second: well, that tracked. No wonder her "sessions" with Kris only happened when Colt was out of town.

There were screenshots of text messages between Sylvie and the photographer who shot her daughter "volunteering" at an "Inglewood coding academy." There was a video of another regular shopping at Ralphs. I couldn't resist pressing play on the video of me. It barely crossed the threshold for NC-17, but no way would I want it circulating online. The angle was awful.

Raven. Raven and her stupid phone, plugging it into the alarm clock dock like she was *so* responsible, she would *never* let her phone die during a threesome.

I had to hand it to her. It was a good cover. No one ever questioned why you needed to charge your phone.

It was unclear how Ophelia ended up with the video, but it was entirely possible that Raven and Ophelia knew each other from sound baths or reiki school or the store that sold peasant crop tops. It was entirely possible that Raven was, in fact, a plant from Ophelia, and that Jared—was Jared a plant, too? Was our night together a total sham?

I thought we'd had genuine chemistry, but in any case, none of that mattered now. What mattered was that Ophelia and Venus were collecting pieces of content that could be used to blackmail their regulars if we ever decided to leave, which was, of course, our right. It was a boutique fitness studio.

I handed Max's phone back and raked my hands through my hair. The file name bothered me more than the content. "Desperate Ani." That soliloquy that Venus had rained down on me.

"Adil has to go down for this," Max was saying. He went on about how Adil acted like this benevolent tech tycoon but treated the founders of the startups in which he invested like shit and only cared about his potential returns. "You wouldn't believe the way he talks about the Gig," Max said. "He'll send me emails at 3:00 a.m. being like, 'Where is the next Mark Zuckerberg? Where is the next Elon Musk? Why aren't they at the Gig? Why are the only people who want to live in this house that I built chicks and pansy-ass marketing bros like you?' As if he built it," Max scoffed. "All he did was hire the interior designer of Soho House. Delegate, that's what Adil does best. Delegates and gives keynotes." Most of those, according to Max, were excerpts from TED Talks given by other people: "He commissioned an algorithm that scans the most-watched ones on YouTube and randomly generates a new script every time. I keep waiting for him to get accused of plagiarism, but I guess no one pays attention to keynotes."

By this point, I was lying on the bed, legs splayed out in a diamond, chewing on a dāna, marveling at how the ceiling could remain so immovable while my world came crashing down.

"Can I ask you a question?" I asked Max.

"Of course."

"Do you think I'm desperate?"

Silence.

I shot up and glared at him. "Is that a yes?"

"No, it's just, you kind of glommed on to The Goddess Effect the minute you got to LA. Did you ever ask yourself why?"

Well, there was the three-month unlimited special, I wanted to point out. You had to milk those specials for all they were worth. But it was more than that, and I knew it. I wanted to belong somewhere and be good at something, and it was easier to work on perfecting my plank form than to work on other parts of myself.

I assumed that Stacy and the other regulars had figured out something that I had not, and that if I spent enough time around them, at their temple, bowing before their god, things would magically snap into place for me. As if, if I looked like Stacy, I'd have no problems. Pretty flawed logic.

"I guess I was kind of desperate." I sighed. "Desperate and misguided."

"At least you're self-aware enough to know that," Max said.

Pretty much nothing I'd encountered in Los Angeles was as it seemed. Maybe that was why people avoided this place, the world capital of smoke and mirrors. But Max was good. Stacy, though not what she initially appeared to be, was good. The rest of the women who went to The Goddess Effect were good, and they didn't deserve to be blackmailed if they wanted to switch up their workout routine. Jesus, Ophelia, get on ClassPass, offer a special, run an Instagram promotion. Enough with the dramatics.

I knew more, but still, not enough. Why would they resort to blackmail? How did eclosion factor in?

"Did you bring a computer?" I asked Max. He nodded. "Great. Wi-Fi's my last name and the room number. We've got some bitches to drag."

33

Max took Ophelia, I took Venus. LexisNexis didn't turn up much, but it did reveal Venus's given name, Valerie Turner, as well as a few misdemeanors—shoplifting, narcotics possession, all in Boise in the nineties. Nothing to make a fuss over.

More intriguing: neither Venus nor Valerie was on LinkedIn, which was strange, given that she'd previously worked in finance. I plumbed the depths of the internet for the institutions she'd mentioned in her book: the Idaho business college, the French finance institute, the Manhattan hedge fund where she had supposedly shoved a sweat-soaked term sheet in her boss's face.

Nothing. None of them existed. Well, there was a single web page dedicated to Russet Capital, but it was just a logo that you could save to Pinterest but couldn't click through. It was like the home page for Ashton Kutcher's fund, except Ashton Kutcher's fund had a Crunchbase profile and a lot of other evidence to show that it existed, like Ashton Kutcher going on *Shark Tank* and talking about it.

I ran a Google Image search for Venus. The second page of results included a photo of her and Ophelia at the previous fall's MindBodyWell conference at Pelican Hill, a resort in Newport Beach. Was that Adil in the background?

"Did Adil go to MindBodyWell last year?" I asked Max. He was at the desk; I was on the bed, hunched over my laptop, a picture postcard of posture fail.

"Gave the keynote," he said. "'Supplements: What to Expect When You're Expecting Recurring Revenue.'"

A Google Image search for Valerie Turner returned an IMDb profile dustier than a Discman. Pudgy nose, lip liner, green contacts, streaky highlights: the Contempo Casuals version of Venus. Credits included a 2003 Summer's Eve commercial and "bottle-service girl No. 4" in an episode of an *Entourage* spin-off that had lasted one season.

So she had been a struggling actress. So she had never worked in finance. Why did she feel the need to lie about it? Was a company not worthy if its founder didn't have some vendetta against the patriarchy?

"Anything on Ophelia?" I asked Max.

"There's this," he said, showing me his screen. It was a YouTube video of Contempo Casuals Venus and Ophelia—her hair black and bobbed like Uma Thurman's in *Pulp Fiction*—frolicking through a daisy field, feeling, if the voiceover was to be believed, "as fresh and clean as a summer's eve."

"Summer evenings are generally kind of humid," I said.

"Yeah, I never understood that branding, either."

"Okay, well," I said, sitting up and pulling back my shoulders, "what have we learned? Venus and Ophelia were struggling actresses who wanted to be wellness moguls. Join the club. I'd respect their hustle if it weren't for their intent to blackmail.

"And what about this supplement they're making with Adil?" I said, reaching for the canister of dāna. "And eclosion?"

There were two gummy bears left, and I banged the mouth of the container against my palm to get them unstuck from the side. They fell into my hand faceup, the kissy-face emoji winking at me from their synthetic, puffed-up bellies.

The kissy-face emoji. It struck me again: Why did the kissy-face emoji ring a bell? Because Stacy used it so often?

It wasn't just that.

"Wait a minute," I said, springing up to my knees and shaking the empty container at Max. "These gummies. These gummies are the supplement that Adil is making with Venus—they've got the same kissy face as Smack's weed nootropic vapes." The pale pink version of which I had annihilated that night at Retro.

"No way." Max whipped around in the rolling desk chair and eyed the gummy bears in my hand. "Shit. You're right. That's Smack's logo." He sat back and looked out at the view beyond the balcony door, seemingly putting something together.

For the first time, I took in his profile. Really took it in. Something about his jawline stirred me. I was reminded of the time that I prayed to God that I'd be partnered up with Brian Long, the uncontested eighth-grade heartthrob, for a science project—actually got on my knees on the shag carpet of my bedroom and prayed. Several times. It worked.

"They must've used Aggaracetam," Max said, turning back. "I can't think what else it could be." When Adil refused to tell him what was in the supplement, Max had done some research and discovered Aggaracetam, a new nootropic that could break down mental barriers, with some caveats. It was only available in gelatin form, and to work, it had to be combined with an amphetamine.

"Say that happened," I said. "What would be the effect?"

"You'd be liable to say anything," said Max. "You could admit deep, dark shit that you normally wouldn't want people to know."

"Fuck," I said.

"In clinical trials, they combined Aggaracetam with Adderall," Max said. "We'd have to lab test the gummies to know for sure, but knowing that Adil basically copies what other people do . . ."

The firepit confessions. The lack of appetite, the restlessness, the urge to dance. If it looks like a duck and walks like a duck . . .

"That explains those texts," Max said. He had gotten up and resumed pacing. His theory: Adil was planning to cut The Goddess Effect out of the equation and make dāna with whomever he intended to text when he accidentally sent those messages to Max, and he probably wanted dirt about the retreat because he hadn't been able to test dāna on his own group of guinea pigs yet. "Classic Adil," said Max. "Conniving piece of shit."

"We're still missing something," I murmured, staring at my computer screen. I was speed-reading the Wikipedia page for dāna. Indeed, it was a Sanskrit word, and it essentially meant to give in a ritual way, as with charity, to help others. I'd found nothing associated with gummy bear supplements that promoted magical (read: drug-fueled) thinking or youthful exuberance.

Out of the corner of my eye, I saw my phone and realized that I'd never messaged that commenter back. I mentally poured one out for the innocent I'd been when I had power walked back from the resistance band workout, surging with purpose. Part of me wanted to return to that prior version of myself or, better yet, the person I'd been when I'd first signed up for the heaven-sent special, when I thought The Goddess Effect was the answer to all my problems. How simple life would be if we didn't ask questions.

But you can't delete knowledge the way you delete bad selfies. I knew what I knew, and the only way forward was to seek answers to the remaining questions I had. "The truth will set you free"—a line I'd heard a lot but, as a compulsive liar, never really believed.

The commenter had asked if I was working for The Goddess Effect. No, I tapped out now, seems like they're up to no good and I'm trying to find out more. Within moments, my phone was buzzing. I didn't even know you could call someone through the app.

"Sorry, I'm driving," the commenter said. "And audio's probably safer."

"Of course," I said, putting her on speaker, motioning for Max to come closer, and explaining Max's reason for being there in the simplest terms possible.

"Honestly, I'm just glad someone's looking into this," the commenter said. "Those bitches are crazy."

Max and I exchanged a look. "Crazy how?" I asked.

"Crazy like they wanted me to remove my ribs."

My stomach dropped.

"You're the girl with the Jennifer Lopez for Kohl's leggings, right? With the glitter stripe down the side? I think we used to do 7:00 a.m. together. Until Venus pulled me into the back room and told me about this wack-ass procedure she wanted me to do. Only two days of downtime, and I'm like, how can that be safe?"

Her words buzzed around me. Rib removal. That plastic surgery freak who wanted the same waist-to-hip ratio as Barbie. That rumor about Marilyn Manson, back in the day.

"Doesn't that require intense plastic surgery?" I asked.

"Normally. But she kept hyping this new procedure, eclosion. Kept saying it was sustainable, all natural, super high tech—how can something be all natural *and* super high tech? Anyway, it's just bullshit Goddess Effect branding. Bitches think they're butterflies. The real name is thermotherapy."

Thermotherapy. I flashed back to Stacy's description: "It's, like, the opposite of cryotherapy."

"She's telling me, 'If you're scared, start with two! Stacy just did two, the lowest ones, the ones that are just, like, excess bone.' And I'm like, 'God gave me twelve pairs of ribs for a reason.' And then Venus starts in about helping other women and some global collagen shortage."

Collagen. Collagen made you look younger.

I reached for my computer and cupped my hand over my mouth. Quickly, I looked up how collagen was made. Usually from boiling bones: fish spines, cow bones, but really, any bones would do.

"I'm like, any procedure that liquifies your bones—that's gonna be a no for me. I'm non-GMO, you know?"

"Mm," I said, gulping. New tab. With one hand, I typed in "thermotherapy Cheng Calabasas" and pressed enter.

The top result: "Bebe's Baby Best Self."

The page that loaded was entirely pink.

Half scroll. "Bebe, a licensed surgeon, keeps it casual with her clients. They're pals, not patients. No need to call her Doctor when you're in her house!"

Bebe's last name was Cheng.

I bolted to the bathroom.

34

Max threw up, too, when I told him where the collagen in dāna came from.

"That's sick," he said, emerging from the bathroom with a hand towel. "That's cannibalism. Isn't that cannibalism?"

"I had twenty of them, Max!" I writhed on the bed. "Twenty little bears made of Stacy and God knows who else."

"'There are no laws against cannibalism,'" Max said, reading from his phone. "How can there be no laws against cannibalism?"

"I don't even eat foie gras," I moaned. "I've never had heart or lung or any of those organs that are supposedly delicious but freak me out. And now I'm eating *human collagen*?"

I tried to make myself feel better by rationalizing that the amount of human collagen I actually consumed probably amounted to a fingernail. Someone else's fingernail. Stacy's fingernail. The more I thought about it, the more I wanted to throw up again.

"We've gotta stop this," Max said, all resourcefulness and reason. "So, fine, cannibalism isn't illegal on its own—which, don't even get me started—but selling organs is a federal offense that can get you up to five years in prison and a fifty-thousand-dollar fine. There's gotta be a prosecutor who would jump at the chance to expand the legal interpretation of that, although, when you think about it, it's not much prison time or money—but then there's the Adderall. That's a huge factor. When you consider how many people went to jail for weed possession in the nineties . . ."

People who believed in liquifying ribs and turning them into gummy bears, what else might they be capable of? Murder, probably. Hiding the bodies. Turning the bodies into more collagen for more gummy bears.

I threw a pillow over my face. I wanted to rewind, to not have found this out, although, what then? Would I have done thermotherapy, too? Would I be "giving back" by literally giving a part of myself to a supplement? Would I be totally in the dark about how the giving back actually worked, or would I be fully in the know, working for The Goddess Effect, shilling these gummies, and trying to convince myself that this was all okay, people took all *sorts* of supplements, and who really knew what was in any of them? Weren't there so many worse things in the world to get upset about?

Were there, though? Could I live with the fact that I'd found out about this and done nothing? What was I made of, besides an infinitesimal amount of Stacy and a desire to be liked?

"Okay," I said, tossing the pillow off my face and sitting up straight. We had just over an hour before my one-on-one with Venus. "New plan, and you're gonna need to put on a bathrobe, because you got vomit on your sweatshirt."

***

Fine, Emilia said, via direct message, when I sent her my conditions: six thousand dollars paid up front, via Venmo, and a simultaneous rebroadcasting of my feed because I didn't want the video to live on GonzoDrip's platform.

Why six thousand dollars? That was about what my bank balance would be after an ABN paycheck cashed, if I'd been good the prior two weeks, and the two weeks before that. It was an amount that made me feel rich, monied, like I could pay my rent, get brunch at Jack's Wife Freda, and buy a Forever 21 jumpsuit without thinking twice. It didn't happen often.

I felt a pang of regret when Emilia instantly agreed. I should've asked for more. Clearly, Gonzo was reeling from the *Deadline* scoop. Clearly, this was my moment to cash in. Max had had a point, after all.

Turning it into a job bolstered my sense of purpose. Now I had a task at hand, money to make good on. For a moment, I blinked at the notification and thought about simply taking the money and not doing anything. How badass would *that* be? That would show Gonzo, that would be sticking it to the man, even though I'd be stealing less than what they probably charged for a thirty-second ad.

More than that, I wanted to follow through. I wanted to feel important. I wanted to take pride in something besides the number of burpees I could do in one minute. In my wildest dreams, I was a trending topic on Twitter and the subject of a think piece on every site that mattered.

For our scheme to work, I'd have to fully inhabit the role of Desperate Ani, the charity case they knew and exploited, eager to work for The Goddess Effect, exactly the type of devotee they'd welcome into their inner circle (hopefully, if I'd pegged them correctly, although we already knew that they liked free labor and doormats). Max would pose as a fellow Ranch guest I happened to meet.

"You're a consultant for hire based out of Montecito," I said, "the marketing guru behind Casper, WeWork . . . what's some other trendy company that they would know?"

"Peloton?"

"Perfect. You made Peloton a household name. You're here golfing with a potential client, and we got to talking by the serenity pool, and that's why you're in a bathrobe."

"What's my name?" Max asked.

"Benedict Williamson." Only people with names like that took business meetings in bathrobes.

At some point, Stacy texted, and I felt guilty for not texting her back. Stacy couldn't know that something was up, not yet. Not ever? Not until the whole world did?

I didn't know if she would share my outrage about what Venus and Ophelia were doing. She swore by The Goddess Effect. What would she do if it no longer existed? Pilates?

Sometimes people don't want you to burst their bubble. I thought, again, about that time in high school when I came home at 1:00 a.m., two hours after curfew, and my dad made me scrambled eggs and asked about my night in the way an adult would ask another adult. He'd laughed as I recounted the awful music at Matt Bateman's house party and the idiot who tried to skateboard down the living room banister. When I tentatively revealed that I'd had one rum and Coke, he'd said, "Just one? That's all? Thought you'd have more fun than that." I beamed. It felt like we'd reached the same plane.

As we loaded the dishwasher, he'd said, "You know, your mom is pretty upset. She'd be even more upset if she knew you drank. So let's just keep that under our hats, for now." He'd winked and ruffled my hair. I understood that you tell the whole truth to some people, others . . . It wasn't that they couldn't handle the truth, it was that they didn't want to. They liked their bubble. Sometimes it was best to let them linger in it for as long as you could.

I scheduled a golf cart pickup for part one; Max scheduled a Lyft for later. We had ten minutes to spare. I sat on the bed, kicking my feet against the expensive fabric that covered the expensive wood. Max sat in the desk chair, half facing me, half facing the wall, staring absently into space. I assessed him anew. What a guy. First my shower, now this. I'd begun to believe that decent men did not exist, but he was providing some pretty compelling evidence to the contrary.

"Why did you come here, really?" I asked. "I get wanting to take down Adil, but how did you know I would be game, too?"

He looked up at me with a sheepish smile and shrugged. "I didn't."

"What if I'd told you to fuck off?" I asked.

He shrugged again, got out of the chair, and sat down next to me, on the bed. Our fingertips brushed.

"Interesting," I said.

We sat like that for a minute. I'd stopped kicking my feet against the bed.

"Would you like me to fuck off now?" he asked, softly.

"No, I think you're—"

I was going to say, "fucking fine where you are," but then his mouth was on mine, and I was too into it to say anything at all.

35

The ringing of the landline stopped us.

"We can, uh, come back to this?" I stammered, blinking at Max. Had his eyes always been the sort of ever-changing hazel that one could get lost in? Had I simply never noticed?

He blushed a little and nodded. "I'd like that."

How cliché: my knight in shining armor had been under my nose, or more accurately, under my bedroom floor, the whole time. Well, who knew if he was my knight in shining armor? Max would have to convincingly play the role of marketing mastermind Benedict Williamson for our scheme to work, for us to not get kidnapped, tortured, and liquidated into collagen gummies. (I assumed these would be the consequences if Venus and Ophelia caught us. It was possible I had watched too much *CSI*.)

In any case, I was no longer a damsel in distress.

I squeezed Max's thigh and said, "It's go time," like that guy in *24*. Max grabbed the bags. I took one last, long look out the sliding glass balcony door, trying to commit the view to memory. Look with your eyes and not with your phone, I told myself.

I grabbed my phone and took eleven photos.

"Do you want one with you in it?" Max asked.

I ran through potential poses in my head: hand on hip, versus hand in hair, versus looking over my shoulder, versus turned around, facing the view, looking *back* over my shoulder, versus—

"Fuck it, we've gotta go," I said.

"Heading to Casa Chiara?" the driver asked, as we hurled ourselves into the golf cart. "Gorgeous villa. It's the gem of Ojai."

I had gathered as much from studying it online. Casa Chiara was a ten-thousand-square-foot, four-bedroom villa that sat on a grassy knoll above the rest of the Ojai Valley Ranch. It was technically part of the resort, but it had its own screening room, chef's kitchen, and a private pool and spa. Venus, Ophelia, Saffron, and Annalisa were staying there. It was off-limits to retreat attendees besides our individual one-on-ones, which, according to the agenda, would include a "cosmic health screening" and a singing-bowl ritual that Venus would conduct with a "sacred bowl procured during a transformational trip to Tibet during which she lived with and learned from a tribe of monks over the course of seven lunar cycles." Psh. I wondered if Venus could even point to Tibet on a map.

My phone buzzed with a text.

Stacy: Love and light for your one on one ✈️ 😊 Can't wait to catch up after!

I sent back three hearts. Guilt again. If she knew what I was about to do, would she still be my friend? My ally? All signs pointed to no. Whatever. I told myself that she would never see me as an equal, that I was not of her world, that Colt would've called ICE on me (erroneously) at some point.

I pictured us running into each other at Provisions, a year on, the strained greetings and awkward hug. I pictured us going to India together, in an alternate reality, her twirling in front of the Taj Mahal.

I told myself to stop. I had to do this. For myself, for Stacy, for untold numbers of women The Goddess Effect had preyed on or planned to prey on. I clicked my screen off and gave my phone to Max.

The lengths they must've gone to get that shot of Stacy, I thought, as we cruised past a blooming grove of jasmine. So what if she wanted to make out with her Thai butler? Colt probably had a harem of women between Hualālai and Holbox, the remote Mexican island where he was building his latest mansion. You'd think The Goddess Effect would be sex positive. But perhaps the sorts of businesses that resorted to blackmail to retain customers skipped the part that involved coming up with a mission statement, a code of ethics, etc.

As we pulled up to Casa Chiara, I saw Annalisa and Saffron on the front lawn, both in floaty, earth-tone Reformation maxi dresses, drawing circles in the air with bunches of smoldering palo santo. I had never seen either of them in a dress. They looked like cult children.

Annalisa beamed at me as the golf cart slowed, then saw Max, and her mouth turned down.

"It's only Goddesses, Ani, no males allowed," she said.

"Wait, you brought your bags?" Saffron observed.

"Oh, my bad," I said, playing dumb. "Since Venus said we're going to talk about me joining the team, I thought I might be bunking with you all tonight. Silly me, ha, ha!" I actually fake laughed like that. "But it's all good, I'll just bring them back with me." I got out of the cart.

"I can place them back in your room, if you'd like," said the driver.

"Nah, it's fine, I . . . have my period, and my tampons are all over the place." I shrugged. Max stifled a laugh.

The cart reversed. Nothing like period talk to drive a dude away.

"And this isn't just any male." I felt like I was talking about a horse or something. "This is Benedict Williamson, the marketing genius behind Casper, Peloton, other, you know, companies. We were just chatting by the pool, and with The Goddess Effect expanding, I thought Venus might like to meet him. Like, what are the odds?" I fake laughed again, and so did Max.

"Pleasure to make your acquaintance," he said in this weird British accent. Where did that come from? He picked up their hands and brought them to his lips, one at a time.

"If Venus is okay with it . . . ," Annalisa said, looking at Saffron.

"Let me ask," said Saffron, retrieving her phone from a pocket in her dress. "Venus? Yes, no, I know, no calls, only texts, but there's a man here with Anita—Benedict? He, like, founded Peloton? And Anita thinks that maybe you'd like to talk with him?"

"Not founder," I said, loudly. "Independent marketing consultant"—I turned to Max and gave him a look—"from *Montecito*."

Venus appeared at the arched entryway wearing a white bikini that I recognized from Emily Ratajkowski's Instagram feed. The bottom was a panty liner with strings that tied high on her hip bones; the top was triangles, also with strings.

"You worked for Peloton?" she asked Max.

"They called me the Lance Armstrong of recurring revenue," he replied, in his normal voice.

"Come on in," she said. "We're out by the pool."

"*Love* your jacket," Saffron cooed, fingering the edges of the chiffon SNS as we walked up to the front door. "Is that what your people wear, like, traditionally?"

"Not exactly," I said. Saffron walked by that "Harness Your Inner Lakshmi" quote every day and didn't know what a sari was? Maybe she didn't know who Lakshmi was. Possibly, she thought Venus invented Lakshmi. Poor Saffron.

The chef's kitchen was littered with bags of Doritos. More bags of Doritos than I'd ever seen, outside of a grocery store. Cool Ranch, Nacho Cheese, Nacho Cheesier, Sweet Chili, Salsa Verde, other flavors that I did not know existed. There were cardboard crates of Whispering Angel, some ripped open and spent, others full, waiting to be consumed. Max and I exchanged a look. In *Effected*, Venus called chips

"Walmart's heroin" and said that women who guzzled rosé needed to "take a hard look at what that buzz drowns out." What was this?

Annalisa turned around, as if reading my mind. "Venus would've had us clean up, but since you're going to be joining the team," she said. That she made it sound like a done deal was not lost on me. "Plus, we're stopping at Bebe's on the way back."

"Bebe's?" I repeated, playing dumb.

"Has Venus not told you?" She tittered and lifted her hand to her mouth. "I won't ruin the surprise."

We passed through the dining room into the backyard that framed the pool deck. Venus and Ophelia reclined, side by side, on blue-and-white-striped loungers. Ophelia was also wearing an Emily Ratajkowski direct-to-consumer bikini, same style as Venus's but royal blue. On the table between them was a bag of Nacho Cheesier Doritos, a magnum of Whispering Angel in an ice bucket, and a large ceramic singing bowl. They both held cigarettes; Ophelia ashed hers over the lip of the bowl.

As we stepped onto the deck, I saw that there was someone else.

An Asian woman in a carnation-pink Pucci caftan, also on a lounger, also with a cigarette.

Bebe Cheng.

We hadn't planned for this.

"Normally," Venus said, as we approached—she wore huge Celine sunglasses and gazed straight ahead at the aquamarine pool—"we'd stash all this before a one-on-one. But now that you're joining the team"—she tilted her head up and smiled wanly—"we can skip the bullshit."

"What about chips being Walmart's heroin?" I asked, all saccharine naivete.

"Oh, honey," said Venus, "that's for the plebes. We make the rules, so we get to break them."

"Not everyone has unfettered access to Bebe," Ophelia said, taking off her own Celine sunglasses and placing them on top of her head.

"This little roll"—she pinched what appeared to be a vital part of her midsection—"will be CoolSculpted off by Monday, gratis."

"Um, no," said Bebe. "At cost."

"You'd think it *would* be gratis, given all the new business we're bringing your way," Ophelia said, giving me a "Can you believe this bitch?" look.

I took in Bebe's Chanel sunglasses, voluminous caftan, and the Brink's truck's worth of Cartier Love bracelets (eight on each wrist). I figured that a surgeon who pioneered a procedure as revolutionary as thermotherapy would, I don't know, wear a white coat or something, but perhaps that was closed-minded of me.

Venus stood up. "Okay, well, before we do anything, you have to sign an NDA. You too . . . Benedict?" she asked, looking at Max.

Ophelia assessed him. "I've read a lot about Peloton. Never heard of you."

"I'm a stealth operator," he said, interlacing his hands behind his back. "I work behind the scenes, let the C-suite take the credit."

This appeased Venus to the degree that she snapped her fingers, and Annalisa and Saffron came running with papers for us to sign. Venus motioned for Max and me to follow her to a cabana on the far side of the pool deck. It was set up like a Vegas cabana—long, low couch, TV, refrigerator, portable sound bar—

The sound bar had an iPhone dock. Just like the alarm clock in Jared's bedroom.

If that wasn't a sign, then signs did not exist.

While Venus was turned around, yelling at Saffron and Annalisa to bring the wine and bring the Doritos and bring over two chairs—good God, was it that hard? There were two of them, it shouldn't take so long—I nudged Max and pointed out the sound bar.

"No shit," he said, processing. "That'll help."

"We'll need to get it in position, though," I said.

"Leave that to me."

We sat down in the chairs that Saffron and Annalisa brought; I took off the SNS jacket, stuffed it in my duffel, and adjusted the band of my sports bra to give my lungs a tiny bit more room to breathe. Breathing would be important.

Venus, Ophelia, and Bebe arranged themselves on the couch. The NDAs sat on the low table between us.

They looked pretty boilerplate, but Max and I had discerned that a nondisclosure agreement that involved an illegal medical procedure that was being used to produce an illegal supplement would be unenforceable. Besides, if things went down the way I hoped they would, enforcing an NDA would be the least of their worries. I scribbled a semblance of my name.

"Great," Venus said. "Now that that's out of the way—"

Max interrupted. "Would you mind if we put on some music?"

Venus glared at him.

"It helps my clients with the ideation process," he said smoothly, standing up to retrieve the sound bar, which was on a shelf behind Venus. "I actually have a special playlist."

"Whatever," Venus said, with a dismissive shudder. "Anita, Ophelia's moving into facilitator training."

Max put the sound bar on the table in front of us so that it faced Venus, Ophelia, and Bebe. He shoved my phone into the dock and put on Bob Moses.

"We'd like you to take over her job," Venus said. "It's $100K plus benefits."

She kept talking, but I had a hard time concentrating, because as soon as I heard "$100K plus benefits," a scene slid into my mind. Me, in my two-bedroom apartment on the top floor of a new-construction condo tower on Abbot Kinney, one of those steel and glass affairs. Me, sprawled out on my Restoration Hardware Cloud couch beneath a faux sheepskin throw. Me, retrieving my brand-new, latest-model iPhone from my smoked-glass coffee table, logging into Capital One. My payment was due, and I'd almost forgotten. Me, paying the full $15,748 balance—not only the amount due, but also the charges since my previous statement because I could. I had that kind of money now that I worked for The Goddess Effect. I had "fuck you, 24.99 percent APR" kind of money. I had a credit score of 797, a fifty-thousand-dollar limit, and little to no expenses. I got complimentary classes and free meals from Provisions because I'd finagled a sponsorship deal based on my rapidly expanding social media following. I was finalizing a new sponsorship deal with a startup that made leggings out of excess Amazon packaging.

"And that's just the front desk part of the job," Venus was saying. "You'd also be in charge of maintaining the client files. Ophelia's done a bang-up job of researching our regulars' social media feeds and figuring out what really bothers them. She's also gone on intel-gathering missions, which we're going to expect you to do, of course."

"Stacy and her Asian sensation, huh?" Ophelia said. She nudged Bebe. "Guess the rumors aren't true."

Through her Chanel sunglasses, I could see Bebe roll her eyes. "Duh," she said.

That brought me back to reality. I drew a big red X through my previous vision. Pretty sure new-construction condos weren't allowed on Abbot Kinney, anyway. And I'd be a terrible influencer. I sucked at posing and didn't own a Pomeranian.

"Sounds great," I said, smiling and nodding. "What else? That can't be it, right? With a salary like that?" I laughed a little to communicate disbelief.

Venus and Ophelia exchanged a look, and then looked at Bebe, who shrugged sarcastically and said, "Isn't this why you dragged me out here?"

"Well, if you're asking, Anita, there is one other thing," Venus said.

This was it. It felt like the moment. I couldn't know for sure, but my gut told me the time was right. Worst case: it'd be so boring, no one would watch.

From the side pocket of my leggings, I took out my lip balm. Max saw the sign. He reached over to the sound bar, ostensibly to change the song, but really to navigate to the app, go live, and put the sound bar back on the table, where it belonged.

The "one thing": Bebe had invented a wand that could do the work of thermotherapy outside the clinic. They suspected, anyway. They had yet to try it out. They needed a willing body.

"You don't even need anesthesia," said Ophelia. "It's no worse than a Brazilian, I mean, supposedly."

I played the part of a willing but super-curious body. I asked what thermotherapy was for. I asked why they needed collagen. I asked why they ventured into supplements, which led to a conversation, with Max, about how much they ought to charge, something they hadn't yet figured out because dāna was in its beta stage.

"What about three hundred twenty-five dollars for a one-month supply?" Venus posited. "Or three hundred fifty?"

"Note that Goop sells vitamins for ninety dollars a pack," said Ophelia, tapping the table with a French-manicured fingernail, "and those are *vitamins*, not like, a miracle supplement that makes you better at expressing your thoughts and increases your energy and curbs your appetite *and* turns back the clock, and, by the way, we're the only ones who have it. You can order Goop's ashwagandha on Amazon."

"Curbs your appetite, huh?" said Max. "Let me guess . . . Adderall?"

"Smart," said Ophelia, nodding at him. "Now I get why Peloton wanted you."

I asked if they were making the supplements themselves; Venus mentioned Smack and Adil. "But I don't know, I don't think he's the right long-term partner. He doesn't believe in The Goddess Effect." She took a sip of rosé, took off her sunglasses, and sat back. She seemed contemplative in a way that I'd never seen.

"Look, The Goddess Effect—and Bebe, of course—are the only ones with access to thermotherapy. All the collagen in the gummies? It's coming from us, from women that I've vetted, women whose collagen we'd *want*. Adil wants to open it up to every Tom, Dick, and Harry who wants to lose a rib or two. Not on my watch. We built this tribe, we determine who gets access."

"He literally said, 'What if The Goddess Effect goes belly up?'" Ophelia scoffed. "As if."

Bebe seemed intently focused on her wand, which she'd extracted from her Louis Vuitton tote. Understandable that she'd want to go rogue with Adil and bring thermotherapy to a wider audience. Understandable that she'd want to distance herself from Venus and Ophelia, who seemed about as easy to do business with as rabid squirrels.

"Right?" I said, echoing Ophelia's scorn. "I mean, no one would *ever* abandon The Goddess Effect."

"And if they did, well"—Ophelia cocked her head and gazed at me—"I'm not ashamed to admit that I even have intel on you, Ani. Raven and I do Kambo together. Jared sometimes comes, too. But I guess I don't need to tell you about Jared coming." She gave me a sly, sickening little smile.

"You really forge some bonds when that frog venom hits and you're throwing up into a bucket," she went on. "But anyway. We'll never need to use that bit of video I have of you. You're one of the good ones."

She got up and came behind me to rub my shoulders. Bebe got up to plug in her wand. It looked like the conical hair wand that Riley had used to engineer my waves, only it was pink, and probably eight thousand times stronger.

"Come," Venus said, patting the now-vacant expanse of couch next to her. "It's best if you lie down."

I got up as slowly as possible. In my head, on repeat: "The only way out is through."

"I guess I just don't get it," I said, innocently, taking my time as I arranged myself on the couch, faceup.

I hadn't rehearsed this part. I didn't know Bebe would be here. I didn't know how I was going to get out of this. I was not a gerbil. These days, they didn't even test lip gloss on gerbils. This wand was like an atomic bomb compared to lip gloss. Who knew what could happen if it hit my skin?

The irony of the song pulsing through the sound bar: "Tearing Me Up."

I glanced at Max; his eyes were wide with alarm.

"Why do we need to gather intel?" I asked, buying time, willing my heart to stop racing.

"You don't know how hard it is, Anita." Venus sighed. "You don't know how women jump from monthly special to monthly special, from Pure Barre to Soul to Barry's—fucking Barry's—to Equinox to the stupid new Pilates place down the block from them that has some grand opening discount."

"Even you asked for a discount, Anita," said Ophelia, coming around to brush a piece of hair off my forehead. "Even *you*."

"To succeed as a fitness startup without a streaming service, I mean, fuck, we're going to have to get into that one day, for sure, but for now," said Venus, "being strategic means building a fierce following."

From the backyard, Saffron called Venus's name.

"A community bonded together by more than sweat," Venus said, "incentivized by a greater purpose."

Annalisa had joined in Saffron's call. The urgency in their voices signaled that our time was up. The most viable option: bolt off the couch and run. Hope we'd timed the Lyft correctly. Pray to the God of rideshare that a Kia Soul was waiting on the road, at the bottom of the sloping lawn. But who ever outran anyone starting from a lying-down position? Even Usain Bolt would struggle. Surely, they would catch me. Surely, they would turn me into collagen. Surely, I'd soon be in a bottle that would retail for $499.99.

"We have to be strategic," Ophelia was saying. "We have to play to win. Do you have any idea how much funding Peloton has? Benedict, you must—"

An engine revved. An engine I'd recognize anywhere.

"What the fuck?" Venus said. "What do *you* want, Saffron? Can't you see that there's a Porsche Panamera driving up our lawn, destroying the grass? Jesus, are we going to have to *pay* for this? *Do something.*"

Bebe huffed and yanked her wand out of the socket. "So glad I canceled Nobu for this."

"She's *livestreaming*," Saffron said.

EPILOGUE
ONE YEAR LATER

The earth sank beneath the heel of my Hunter boot. Rain. The vines had gotten that much-needed rain. Fantastic. I mostly knew this, prior to stepping foot on the soil, since Lompoc was one of the locations programmed into my weather app, one that I checked every day, but it was satisfying to feel it for myself, to notice how the vines had leafed out, since I was here last, to know that this year's vintage would be worth the effort, barring environmental catastrophe, which you could never completely rule out. We'd *have* a vintage, at the very least. Better than nothing.

Block M, the area of the vineyard we had rented from Melville, amounted to about half an acre, but in the right conditions, this soil, a mix of clay and sand that benefited from the cool winds off the Pacific, could yield two tons of grapes. That worked out to 120 cases, or almost fifteen hundred bottles of minimal-intervention pinot noir. In short, a very decent showing for a very young brand, Solves for X. No great significance to the name other than that Christina and I thought it was funny. Not everything had to have a meaning.

The sun, low in the sky this late in the afternoon, hit one particularly gnarled vine just right. From my back pocket, I retrieved my phone and took seven pictures. The first was the best.

Just another day at the office (Gross, braggy.)

Plant it, and they will grow (What?)

Coming soon to a goblet near you (Maybe, but do you need to post this right now? Be in the moment. The moment is not in your phone.)

Old habits die hard. Christina was stronger. Christina had deleted her personal social media accounts. I, on the other hand, considered it a triumph when I managed to engage in pursuits that truly excited me without the filter of my phone, in front of my face, livestreaming or otherwise documenting the process for the general public or a future, theoretical version of myself that might one day look at all of this footage. The best way to experience something is without a phone in front of your face. It took me a while to figure that out. Progress, not perfection, as Saffron used to say.

Rumor had it she was in rehab. Pills. Poor Saffron.

The days after Ojai went by in a blur. There were the telephone interviews, the trips to CNN's Hollywood studio, the string of meetings that ended with promises to circle back and follow up. After the Panamera screeched to a halt, after Max ripped my phone out of the sound bar and tossed it to me, after he and I nearly knocked over the cabana, bounding over to the car and hurling ourselves into it, I pressed my phone against the passenger-side window and got one last look at Venus, hurtling down the sloping lawn, mouth open, arm up, magnum clutched, tit out. It wasn't wise to run in any bikini, let alone one you bought off Instagram. She looked wild and rabid. If she could have sunk her teeth into my shoulder, she'd have taken a bite.

Only after we sped around the bend, farther than Venus or an airborne bottle of Whispering Angel could possibly reach, did I glance down at my view count: 230,233 (one of whom was Stacy, who had the valet bring around her car the moment Venus asked me to be a test subject). Predictably, the story about a wellness mogul who plotted to blackmail her clients and encouraged them to dabble in illicit drugs, experimental surgery, and light cannibalism was breaking news. All over the *Daily Mail*.

Stacy helped me pick out my outfits for the TV appearances. Well, Stacy loaned me my outfits. Far from disowning me as a friend, my "radical act of courage" in "speaking truth to power" lit a fire under her and gave her the strength to divorce Colt. They'd had a prenup, but they'd been married long enough that her payout was nothing to sniff at. She'd bought two bungalows on the Venice canals, one of which functioned as a closet-slash-"ideation station" for her nonprofit life-coaching venture. She'd also gotten a part-time job at Provisions.

"It's really eye-opening, you know, to see the other side of the service industry," she said. "The other day, this woman goes, 'Why am I paying a health surcharge? Why am I responsible for *your* health?' As if she's unaware that there's a health care *crisis* going on our country. It's unbelievable, the things people choose not to know."

We were standing in her closet bungalow; she was smoothing the lapels of the Maison Margiela blazer she'd artfully draped over my shoulders. "If they don't hire you as a correspondent on the spot," she said, "there's something wrong with them."

"What if I don't want to be a correspondent?"

I was over it. Media. The churn, the chase. It sounds cliché, coming from a millennial who spent her formative years on AIM, but I wanted something to do with my hands. The six thousand dollars from Gonzo gave me time to figure out what exactly. That and Max's takeover of the Gig. Adil had been arrested on drug charges, and Max had ascended to the role of the Gig's CEO. Each of us signed agreements to contribute 10 percent of our monthly earnings to a collective fund to keep the lights on and the internet working. We relied on the honor system, which meant inevitable "human error," but when Jayson's virtual reality nightlife platform took off and the *Verge* wrote about how Jeff Bezos was clamoring to invest, it became clear that the Gig would be fine. More than fine. Miguel went back to buying name-brand Nespresso pods.

Five minutes after my first CNN appearance, Praveen FaceTimed me, dressed in a tuxedo, applauding and repeating "Bravo," like he was at the opera or commanding Alexa to turn on his favorite channel. He hired me as a consulting producer for ABN's primetime special on The Goddess Effect, which basically involved briefing the anchor and allowing ABN to license my livestream footage along with the video and photos I'd taken during the retreat. It felt strange and satisfying, this momentary reversal of power, but as ever, another, bigger story was just around the corner, and before long, the requests dwindled, and my inbox returned to its usual state of spam and newsletters I had never signed up for.

Venus and Ophelia were awaiting trial for an array of drug, fraud, and racketeering charges. Why they wouldn't plead guilty and take a lesser sentence was beyond me, but then, they had never been the type to admit that they'd been wrong. "What we did was no different than the new mother who makes a frittata out of her own placenta," Venus had said at a press conference organized by Michael Avenatti. She wore a low bun and a Theory suit, and at first glance, she looked like the former finance executive she had pretended to be, but a closer look revealed that she wasn't wearing anything under her suit jacket, unless a collection of rose quartz pendants counted as a shirt.

"We're just women helping women," said Ophelia. "What can be wrong with that?"

(Bebe had fled. The *Daily Mail* reported that Jho Low, the 1MDB mastermind and international fugitive, had taken her under his wing and airlifted her to whatever South Pacific island he now called home. They'd published a pixelated paparazzi shot, purportedly of the two of them on a beach. The pink blob could've been a Pucci caftan, but it also could've been many other things.)

There were a few Goddess Effect regulars who stood by Venus and Ophelia's side, who organized a poorly attended protest in front of the Venice studio, who made signs like GIVE US OUR GODDESS BACK and IT'S A WOMAN'S RIGHT TO CHOOSE. (To choose what? Cannibalism?) "I wanted to be tiny," Michaela told *Inside Edition*. "I don't need a bunch of men telling me what to do with my body."

A fair point. But a bunch of women telling you what to do with your body wasn't necessarily better. That was the wellness industry, in a nutshell: various entities looking to make a buck off your insecurities, revenue-generating companies with a vested interest in getting you to subscribe, try the treatment, get the special, charge it to the card on file, renew your subscription, come to the pop-up, attend the retreat, bring a friend, open a franchise, spread the gospel. All of which was fine, as long as you didn't seek some deep meaning in an inherently capitalist enterprise. In retrospect, it's embarrassing that it took so long for me to see The Goddess Effect for what it always was: a business.

I had wanted a tribe, a girl gang, a thing to which to belong, as if that association would magically make me a more secure person. Alas. But the nice thing about taking down your idols is that you realize that no one actually has it figured out. Everyone is a hot mess, even, perhaps especially, the people who seem to have it all together.

I was poking around the base of vine 213 when my phone lit up with a FaceTime from my mom. It was past midnight in India, where she was studying at an ashram in Rishikesh, in the foothills of the Himalayas, something she had always wanted to do but never gave herself the permission to pursue when my dad was alive.

"Mumbai flight, booked," she said. She wore a simple olive-green sari; behind her, on the nightstand, a single candle burned. "I took the itinerary you suggested, the one that gets in half an hour after yours. After so many days of prayer and simple food, it almost feels sinful." She giggled conspiratorially and lowered her voice, as if someone might overhear. "Our plan, the photo shoot, staying at the Taj."

"We have to do *something* to offset all your piety," I said. "Cocktails, sweets—ooh, can we get you to try weed?"

"We" was me and Smita. After her birthday party, she showed me her vision for SNS—the sketches, the samples, the master plan to create a global brand that was like Supreme meets Sabyasachi, equally fit for a skate park or a sangeet. I wanted in. I built out SNS's e-commerce site, social media accounts, and general marketing strategy. We outfitted Riley and her fellow instructors at the meditation studio; we sent samples to Mindy Kaling and Lilly Singh. We signed a profit-sharing agreement that gave me a 30 percent stake in the company; we were shooting our upcoming look book in Mumbai, in and around the Taj hotel by the Gateway to India. My mom would be one of the models.

Between Solves for X and SNS, I was able to pay down my credit card debt a hundred dollars each month. Most months. I still held out hope for a benevolent hacker. I ran on the beach. I occasionally hooked up with Max. There was something there, but I wasn't pushing to formalize it. People talk about how great your twenties are, but I only found my feet after thirty, and I had no intention of putting them up yet.

I had been to Pooja's mansion in Laguna (her prior insistence on not moving to the West Coast dissolved after the wedding or, more precisely, after Amit's parents presented them with the deed to a mansion just down the street from the Montage). She had, as planned, gotten pregnant during her honeymoon in the Maldives and now had a baby girl as well as a staff of nannies and night nurses. Maybe because we now led such different lives, maybe because I'd let go of my past grudges, or maybe because I'd finally accepted that Pooja was not a paragon of how a person (me) ought to be—for the first time in a long time, hanging out with her was fun. Gratifying. Fulfilling. Granted, we had lobster salads on her deck that overlooked the ocean while yet another member of her house staff continuously topped up our white wine. If you can't have fun like that, you can't have fun at all.

My mom and I said good night, and I saw that Christina had texted: our winemaker had arrived, and they were ready to pull barrel samples. **Meet us downstairs.** It was five o'clock somewhere, and somewhere was here.

As I made my way back across Block M, running my fingertips along the leaves of the vines, savoring the crumble of earth beneath my feet, my phone rang again: *Scam Likely*. I let it go to voice mail. I read the transcription once I got to the cellar door: . . . *calling to let you know about a new workout that you might be interested in, one that promises to strengthen you from the inside out. We're offering founding members—*

To delete now or delete later? I shoved my phone in my back pocket. Later. There was always later.

ACKNOWLEDGMENTS

In 2015, on a train from Los Angeles to San Diego, I wrote one thousand words (give or take) about a girl named Anita and a guy named Max, two strivers living in a house called the Gig. Were it not for the encouragement of many people, those words would not have turned into this book.

Thank you to my agent, Claire Friedman, who championed this manuscript from the moment it hit her inbox. Thank you to my editor, Carmen Johnson, who made these characters and this story the best versions of themselves (without the aid of motivational burpees or collagen supplements). Thank you to everyone at Little A and Amazon Publishing for your hard work in getting this book out into the world.

Thank you to my first readers for offering thorough, thoughtful critiques and a whole lot else: Amy Chozick, for life and career advice from Barry's Bootcamp to Runyon Canyon and beyond. Amrutha Jindal, for decades of heart-to-hearts, going-out tops, and mirror selfies. Ankur Dalal, for making me smarter, and making me laugh, from McGinn Elementary to modern times. Ashley Aull, for swooping in as a pragmatic cheerleader and coining the term *arch capitalism*.

Thank you to Colleen McKeegan for inviting me into a writing workshop of fiercely smart and wry women: Lina Patton, Avery Carpenter Forrey, Liz Riggs, and Brittany Kerfoot. The five of you compelled me to keep going when I was about to put this manuscript down. I can't thank you enough. Forever #unyoung.

Thank you to Arianna Margulis for endorsing an early version of this book and for being a shining example of how to be serious about your work but also have a lot of fun with it. Thank you to Kevin Kwan for your friendship, support, and real talk about writing life. Thank you to Andrea Bartz, Alexandra Kleeman, Amanda Montell, and the many authors I admire who read an advance copy of this book.

I've been privileged to work with some of the best reporters, editors, and producers in the business, and I wouldn't be the storyteller I am without their expertise. Thank you to Ramona Schindelheim, Jonann Brady, Eileen Murphy, Mark Mooney, Peter Travers, Susan Donaldson James, Andrew Nusca, Jon Fine, Lynda Richardson, Abby Ellin, Luchina Fisher, Jessi Hempel, Alexandra Jacobs, Dean Robinson, Charles Curkin, and Susan Morrison.

Thank you to the friends who've been a font of support, inspiration, and good times: Ameya Pendse, Stephanie Kwai, Jen Betts, Michelle Lam, Viktorija Hill, Nikita Mac, Alexander Ali, Aishwarya Ayer, Aditya Bhatia, Diana Myint, Laurel Touby, Anita Kulkarni, and Naomi Piercey. Thank you to Madhu Soma for telling me to "write that manuscript" years before I had anything to write.

Thank you to the Lal family. You welcomed me in the moment I walked through the door, and I am blessed to be part of your ranks. Thank you to the Sakleshpurs, the Subramanyams, the Marickars, and my extended family at home and abroad.

Speaking of home: the one I grew up in was filled with books, magazines, and newspapers—stacks upon stacks. I would not be a writer were it not for my mother, Padma, and father, Faruq Marikar, who I wish was here to read this. To my mother: thank you for supporting my every endeavor. I love you.

Finally, thank you to Nikhil Lal, my rock, my best friend, my love. What you said after I sent you those first thousand words was what I needed to hear to keep going, and your unwavering belief in this book made it real. Shots.

ABOUT THE AUTHOR

Sheila Yasmin Marikar's work has been published in the *New Yorker*, the *New York Times*, the *Economist*, *Fortune*, *Bloomberg Businessweek*, *Vogue*, and many other publications. Her *New York Times Magazine* profile of chef Gaggan Anand was selected for the 2021 edition of *Best American Food Writing*. Sheila began her career at ABC News. A native of New Jersey, she is a graduate of Cornell University, where she studied history. She lives in Los Angeles with her husband. For more information visit www.sheilamarikar.com. Follow her on social media @sheilaym.